Happy reading!
Donna McDonald

The Wrong Todd

BY

DONNA MCDONALD

EDITION NOTICE

This book is a work of fiction. Names, characters, places, and incidents either are the product of the author's imagination or are used fictitiously. Any resemblance to actual persons, living or dead, businesses, companies, events, or locales is coincidental.

This book contains content that may not be suitable for young readers 17 and under.

No part of this book may be reproduced, or stored in a retrieval system, or transmitted in any form or by any means, electronic, mechanical, photocopying, recording, or otherwise, without express written permission of the author/publisher.

Cover art by LFD Designs for Authors and Razzle Dazzle Designs
Edited by Mary Yakovets

ACKNOWLEDGMENTS

Thanks to my street team, Donna's Dreamers, for all their encouragement and support. I appreciate that you are helping me share my work with others. It's very nice to have you all to talk you when I'm writing through the hard spots. *Mahalo (thank you)*.

Thanks to Victoria S. who helped me with the final questions I had on the Hawaiian in the book. I used a fairly good website for the language references, but it was nice to have a real person. *Mahalo Nui Loa* with hugs.

Thanks to author friends J.M. Madden and Robyn Peterman for their love and continued support. I know you don't speak Hawaiian, but it seems appropriate for this book to say this in Koka's language: *Aloha Au Ia 'Oe (I love you)*.

DEDICATION

To my husband Bruce—you are every hero to me.

CHAPTER 1

Though she hadn't openly flirted with a good-looking man in a long time, Sabine smiled at the one smiling back at her. Then as casually as she could, she turned her attention back to her emergency phone call.

"So here's the deal. There's a cute guy sitting across from me just out of earshot. He smiles every time he catches me chair dancing to the canned music they're playing. Should I go over and say hello? Do women get to do that now?"

"*Depends, babe. How old is he?*"

Joe's excessively loud demand vibrated her eardrum and had her holding the phone away. She glared before pulling it back, but didn't press it against her head again. "Stop yelling, Joe. There's no crowd here."

Glancing at the guy again, Sabine saw him smile into his coffee. She hoped she was right about him not hearing her conversation. This could get embarrassing fast.

"It's hard to tell how old he is, but he's definitely not a kid. Judging by his clothes, he went to work today. But then what do I know? I haven't dated in over a decade. Maybe he's hanging out and hoping to pick up chicks," Sabine reported.

Her description elicited a snarky male chuckle. The phone ended up on her shoulder again as she listened to Joe's rumbling baritone as he lectured her.

"*Listen to me to me carefully, Sabine. If he's as young as the others you've been scoping out lately, they're hotties or babes to him, not chicks. Saying 'chicks' automatically means you're way too old to talk to him.*"

Sabine laughed at the critique. "Point noted . . . oh shoot. Never mind, Joe. Some teenage girl in a microscopic skirt just came in and sat down with him. My left leg is larger in circumference than her entire body. I'm hanging up now so I can cry in my coffee."

When full-out male laughter came through the line, Sabine laughed herself. The younger man she had been ogling slid a covert glance her way, even with his girlfriend present. Her smile back was wide. Maybe single life wasn't going to completely suck. At least she could legally lust now.

"Sabine, what I have been telling you? Skip the coffee shops and just go to a bar—an adult bar. Find a 'slightly' younger male who's had a few and let nature take its course. You obviously need to get that youth thing out of your system. Just remember not to take the kid's lack of attention too personally. The younger ones are all like that—gay or straight. The last cub I dated had the attention span of a gnat. Make him do the deed a second time if he doesn't get the job done on his first try."

Sabine laughed. "Wow. What great advice, Joe. Glad no one else can hear you giving it. You've been very helpful in educating me about navigating single life, but even I know the bar scene doesn't work very well for straight women my age."

"Then it's a good thing you don't look your age."

"Now that's why I keep you around. You're such a sweetie."

Sabine cooed the exaggerated endearment into the phone, smiling as she sipped the dregs of her cold drink. Despite all his teasing, she had to admit her gay best friend was way more grounded about men than she was. Even after two years of tortuous relationship limbo, her divorce had still rocked her self-confidence. Fortunately Joe hadn't let her wallow in her failure. Other than her two college-aged children, Joe Kendall was probably the best thing she had to show for the twenty years she'd been married to his brother.

"So are you going trolling for grown-up men later? If you want, I'll come watch and keep you out of trouble."

Sabine chuckled. "Thanks, but no thanks. When I go trolling at bars, I get hit on by old guys with open shirts and fourteen neck chains. They want a twenty-year old, but figure what the hell when they see my long blonde hair and big boobs."

"Sabine, it works that way for everyone at first. You can pass along the old guys to me. I prefer older men. Neck chains come off—right over the head. And yes, I've de-chained my fair share."

Sabine laughed at Joe's audacity, drawing her admirer's covert stare again. "Gross, Joe. Give me a thirty-year-old with lots of energy who can take direction. What's wrong with that? I just want to feel like my life isn't over, you know?"

"Yes dear, I absolutely know." There was a long-suffering sigh in her ear. *"Fine. Go back to trolling the coffee shop. Given how hard you work, your days off are way too precious to waste a minute."*

"Oh, I'm just getting started today. I'm moving on to canvassing bookstores this afternoon. Maybe I'll pick up a young single dad at story time after school," she said, drawing doodles on her sketchpad.

"God woman, you need serious help. Meet me at the Haunted Owl for happy hour if you're still unattached after five. We'll troll there together and I'll show you how it's done. I'll even try to look really gay this time so they don't think we're married."

Sabine giggled at his offer. "You would have been a much better life partner than your brother even without the sex—no offense."

"Offense? What offense? You know I refused to attend the wedding because I knew my brother didn't appreciate you enough. I tried to tell you that Martin was a player twenty years ago when I still had an open mind about women. Now that ship has sailed away from the harbor forever. Listen Sabine—don't stand me up tonight. I want to ask you a favor—one that will be fun for both of us."

"Oh God, I think a chill just ran up my spine," Sabine said.

"Chicken already? I thought you were Sabine Almighty, sassy image consultant?"

"Hold that dare. I'm one more coffee away from an espresso orgasm," Sabine said.

"Are you even listening to yourself? You need to do this, Sabine. You've almost forgotten what having real fun feels like."

"Alright already. I'll see you at the Haunted Owl." She hung up on Joe's laughter and tossed the phone in her purse.

On her way out the door, she couldn't resist winking at the good-looking guy. His answering guilty blush told her more than anything else that he was definitely too young for her.

***

The *Haunted Owl* was packed as usual for a Thursday evening. Patrons crowded the bar stools for drinks while their restaurant pagers glowed like fireflies in the low-lit room. Sabine lifted her soda and sipped.

"You have officially lost your mind, Joe. Saturday is Valentine's Day, and since I don't have a date, I'm going to treat myself to a spa. I'm not spending my first official love holiday as a single woman bidding on a new boyfriend for you. I love you, but no." Sabine grinned when Joe turned puppy dog eyes her way. "You can look as sad as you want, I'm still not doing it. A single woman has to draw a line somewhere."

"The auction is not Saturday, silly girl. The auction is Friday night. The *date* is Saturday. All you need to do is bid on my Todd for me. I'll keep the date for you. Come on—this is my chance to be his hero," Joe said, frowning into his coke.

"Weren't you the guy offering to show me how to troll bars this afternoon? Are you really that desperate for a hook-up with this one guy? The man's not even *out* yet, Joe. Why would you spend that much money for a date you could probably get in a hundred other ways?"

"I don't prey on straight men and Todd is not just another date. And he's *outed* himself to me—just not to all of Seattle. His company is making him do this charity bachelor auction. Winning bids will be in all the newspapers and they're taking pictures of the happy couples," Joe argued. "Come on, Sabine. It's a few hundred dollars. I'm good for the money back."

She laughed and shook her head. It was a bad idea—a very bad idea.

"I work for a high-profile PR agency. My refusal is about *all of Seattle* seeing me date shopping at a worse meat market than any bar. Who do you think bids on men at bachelor auctions, Joe? Women do. Women like me do—well not exactly like me. I have never done anything like that in my life. Hell, I've even avoided online dating sites so far."

"Yes, but just think how smashing you would look standing next to a Rundgren VP, Sabine. You could frame the newspaper clipping and put it in your office at work. Your boss would faint when she saw it."

"I could photoshop that same picture and save myself tons of humiliation," Sabine declared.

Joe nudged her arm on the bar with his elbow. "Come on. Where's your sense of adventure hiding? You've forgotten how to have fun."

Sabine laughed. "Fun? I didn't hear any fun for *me* in your suggestion."

Joe grinned. "Todd said he had a younger brother who is definitely straight. Once we start officially dating, I bet I could get you a date with him. See? You can legitimately feed that youth fetish thing you've got going on just by doing me this one *tiny* favor."

Sabine elbowed back. "Do you honestly think I'm desperate enough to trade an expensive date I'm not even going to go on myself for the possibility of one I might or might not get? Nothing you're offering is a sure thing. What if I get outbid and your mysterious Todd ends up with someone else? What if I buy him and he's straight after all? No. It's too risky."

Joe shrugged. "Life is full of risks. I know this is a strange concept to you because you aren't taking any at the moment. But I know you, Sabine. If you do this, you won't get outbid. Go as high as you need to, so long as it doesn't require me selling my car to pay you back afterwards."

"You don't even want to tell me his last name," Sabine said sternly.

"It's not that I don't want to. It's that I don't know it. He wouldn't tell me when we met and I don't blame him. Most men coming out are cautious about revealing their identity. He told me about the auction, thinking I'd never attend that kind of function. Maybe I even said as much—but you would have too, if you'd seen how nervous he was. The first step is always hard."

"If I don't know the man's name, then how am I going to know the right man to bid on?" Sabine demanded.

"With less than twenty bachelors involved, you might find a couple Davids, Mikes, or Johns—no pun intended. But it is highly doubtful there will be two men named *Todd*," Joe promised.

"First—why would you think a rational woman would agree to such a weak-ass plan? Because she wouldn't. Secondly—and more importantly—why on earth do you think you can talk me into this craziness?"

"Because while he didn't tell me his name, Todd did tell me he worked for Rundgren. He's a VP there—a VP in charge of *public relations*. This is a golden goose opportunity worth chasing. All I'm asking is for you to save my goose before you pitch your bid to him for work."

Sabine blinked as she sighed. Rundgren *was* the primo contract her boss had been trying to get for two years. Getting Rundgren as a client would definitely mean the promotion she'd been working toward for ages. The promotion would mean that she could easily replace everything Martin had taken away from her in the divorce. It was amazing how greed could make Joe's crazy favor look so tempting.

"Your brother took half my retirement savings and used the money to buy fake boobs bigger than mine for his flat-chested new wife. This Todd guy of yours better not cost me what's left."

"It's not going to cost all that much. Todd's charm is understated, so bidding will be manageable. He's a definite diamond in the rough kind of guy. I expect he will go for around six hundred—tops." Joe lifted his glass, smiling around it as he took a drink. "Think of bidding on Todd as buying yourself a contract with Rundgren. That might help you feel better about the initial investment of covering the bid. The fun will be priceless."

Sabine shook her head and closed her eyes. "Shit, Joe. I can't believe you've managed to talk me into getting on your crazy train for a ride."

"Sweetie, my crazy train is the most action you've seen in ages. You should be thanking me for giving you something productive to do with all that pent-up sexual frustration you're carting around," Joe said.

Sabine snorted. "Don't be blowing your paycheck on anything big this week. I will need my money back."

Joe just laughed as she nervously guzzled her second soda.

***

Koka glared at his show's producer and shook his head. "Are we really so desperate, Edwina? The ratings cannot be that bad."

Edwina Winston sighed as she laid her tablet device down on the polished marble counter of her client's amazing kitchen. "The ratings are down because you've cut back on personal appearances. People want to see you up close. The last appearance was over six months ago."

Koka ran a hand through thick black hair that badly needed a cut by his show's standards. He should have insisted on keeping it long from the beginning.

"It's not like I'm avoiding the real fans of the show. You know I have no choice about cutting back. I don't want to leave Pekala while she is so ill. My *kupunawahine* raised me."

Edwina nodded gravely. "I know, Koka. Your desire to stay in town so much is precisely why I booked you for Seattle's local bachelor auction. This televised event is local but it's a lot of bang for the station's marketing buck. The worst of it is one private date on Saturday and all you have to do is cook dinner for the woman. It won't harm your ethics and it will boost Todd Lake's reputation. You can use the set kitchen to make it even safer for you. I'll send in some network PR chaperones to take photos."

Koka snorted. "The whole thing is embarrassing. It looks like I can't get a normal date."

"Don't be juvenile," Edwina said, swiping the air with her hand. "All women want to date you. You're a walking Polynesian pinup poster with those muscles and all that tanned skin. We've had this discussion many times and I've seen you mobbed after appearances."

"No," Koka said firmly. "The women want to date *Todd Lake*—not me. But standing there and letting them buy me—I don't like the idea of it."

Edwina sighed and promised herself a sane job with only media-hungry clients in the future. She picked up her tablet and gave her most popular, yet resistant, celebrity a hard stare.

"You can argue all you want, but it's a done deal, Koka. The auction is tomorrow night. It starts at six-thirty and you're bachelor number five. The execs wanted you to go shirtless and wear just your network apron, but I told them no already. So wear a nice suit as a concession, will you? Maybe you could even shave and get a decent haircut before then. Try to at least give the impression you care a little bit. Just don't forget to pin the show logo to your suit jacket. And make sure the network cameras get a clear picture of it while you're standing on stage."

"I promise you that I will hate every moment of the pretense," he stated.

Edwina shrugged before she sighed. "Maybe you will, but you will also make a lot of money for a great charity. I'm sure you'll get a lot of bids. Hopefully, the surge in popularity will boost your ratings enough to keep your primetime slot. That's our real goal."

Koka nodded tightly. "Fine. I will be a good sport—this once. Please don't ask me to do this kind of event again."

"Give my best to your grandmother," Edwina said, knowing better than to make a promise she could never keep.

"I will tell her you said hello," Koka replied as he walked her to his front door.

When he returned to the modest kitchen he had extensively renovated four years ago, his grandmother was waiting for him. Pekala Whitman sat in her wheelchair as regally as any queen ever sat on a throne. His grandfather always said she had an 'old soul'. Koka had thought many times his grandfather was right. The woman who had stood in for his neglectful parents said exactly what she thought to him all the time. What wasn't uttered in regal commands demanding obedience was still advice often too wise to ignore.

"I'm sorry if my argument with Edwina disturbed you," Koka said regretfully. "Would you like me to fix you a cup of tea?"

"Yes, I'd like that very much," Pekala answered. "But I do not think what Edwina asks is so bad, Koka. Why does doing something silly for a good charity bother you so much?"

Koka shrugged as he filled the kettle. "The auction has nothing to do with my cooking and everything to do with me selling something that I do not wish to sell. I have enough problems with that as it is."

His grandmother's laughter made him smile, but Koka knew what she really thought before she even spoke. It was an old lecture—one he'd heard since he was a teenager.

"Yet like most men, you quite happily *give* it away when it suits you," Pekala declared.

"It is different when it is my choice," Koka declared in return. Then he frowned at the now boiling tea kettle. "And I can't even recall the last time I gave it to anyone. There are no good women in this town."

Pekala clicked her tongue in sympathy. "Where is your faith? Surely some of the women who would spend their hard-earned money for a charity are good. Perhaps the woman who pays for your company will be a nice person. Perhaps she will even be your *Ke Aloha*."

"That would be miraculous," Koka said stiffly, but then instantly regretted having taken too sharp a tone over her teasing. "I have some fish soup I could warm for you if you're hungry."

"No thank you. Just tea, *Ko`u Aloha*. Just tea tonight," she said. "I need to go pray to the goddess. I will ask her to send someone to whom you can give what you don't want to sell on Saturday."

He knew his grandmother meant well with her teasing. She meant to put him at ease. But thinking of an audience full of screaming women bidding on him, he rolled his eyes to the ceiling making sure his grandmother did not see.

CHAPTER 2

"I had to work late to handle an emergency for a client, but I'm here now. The auction is just getting started. Breathe, Joe. I'm sure I haven't missed him."

Sabine held her cell phone tightly to her heaving chest, blocking Joe from hearing just in case she needed to lie to him. "What bachelor are they on?" she asked, whispering the question to the woman filling out her paperwork.

"Number two I think," the woman replied equally quietly.

Sabine automatically took the auction-bidding fan that now had her identification printed in giant letters on it. Sighing to see Martin's name next to hers again, she ignored it and relayed the woman's answer into the phone. "Joe? They're just on bachelor number two. I'm sure I haven't missed your Todd yet."

"He's number five," the woman said, her tone perking up. "Wow, I wish I could bid on Todd. He's incredibly good-looking, even if he never smiles."

Sabine's eyebrows raised at the detailed praise of the man she came to buy. She winked at the woman as she spoke into the phone. "You're in luck, Joe. They just told me Todd's coming up soon. So relax and drive safely. If I win the bid before you get here, I'll call you."

Before Joe could protest Sabine ended their connection. Switching off the ringer, she dropped her cell phone into the bag she carried. "God, I really hate doing this," she grumbled.

The woman shook her and laughed. "If you win, I'll gladly take your date with Todd," she offered.

Sabine thought of how flustered Joe would get if she said yes and how badly she wanted revenge for the hell he'd put her through today. "Don't tempt me," she said, her sarcastic command making the woman laugh again. "My friend would deserve that and it's the best offer I've had all day. I traded going to the spa for this."

Leaving the still laughing woman, Sabine shouldered her favorite large purse and bravely headed into the bidding area. A restless, whispering crowd of aggressive women were actively bidding on some great-looking guy standing on stage. The poor guy looked almost ill to her, but the screaming women didn't even seem to notice. Or at least they didn't seem to care.

Looking around Sabine shook her head, unsure whether she should feel most sorry for the desperate women, the uncomfortable men, or herself for being stupid enough to do this for Joe. Regretting the decision, but determined to prove to Joe she wasn't a coward, she plopped down in a vacant chair near the back.

Counting seats to have something to do, Sabine came up with just a little over a hundred thirty potential competitors. Hopefully not all of them had auction fans, so maybe she could shave another twenty or so from that. Then she factored in Joe's comment about Todd being a diamond in the rough and thought maybe another fifty might not like him enough to bid. If her estimates were right, it meant the actual number of women bidding against her might be no more than sixty or seventy. Maybe she *could* do this—even if she hated every crazy second of it. She would just leave the moment she was done.

Sabine jumped in her seat when the woman next to her threw up her fan and screamed out a number. Her attention was snagged seconds later by the auctioneer yelling loud enough to be heard above the commotion.

"We have *four hundred fifty*. Do I hear *five hundred*? Do I hear *four seventy-five*? *Four fifty-five*? Going once. Going twice. Ladies, we have ourselves another winner tonight. The winning bid for bachelor number four is *four hundred fifty dollars*."

Sabine made a face at the winning bid, but was secretly glad the amount was so low. Seconds after the auctioneer's announcement, the woman's squeal of triumph was deafening. Sabine put her hands over her ears to protect them.

"Sorry. So sorry," the woman said in squealing apology.

Sabine heard the woman giggling non-stop as she stood up. It was all she could do not to belly laugh hard when the woman rushed to the back of the room on six-inch pointed-toe stiletto heels that any stripper would have envied.

"Oh good. One more bidder down," Sabine said under her breath. She watched the woman's tottering exit on her stiletto heels with genuine relief. Then she set her purse on the woman's vacated seat to save it for Joe in case he actually made it in time for Todd's appearance.

While she waited for the next auction to start, Sabine studied the black ballet flats peeking out of her nicest pair of black leggings. Paired with a sparkly gold metallic tunic that covered her hips, the outfit was a good look for her. And flats went well with such outfits, she assured herself. Maybe heels would make her legs look thinner. Was she going to have to learn to walk in those torture devices again if she actually started dating? She hadn't thought about the challenges of trying to impress a man outside of work. She hated the idea of nylons and heels almost as bad as she hated being single. Maybe she could find a guy who liked her in flats.

"Okay, ladies. I know you've all been waiting patiently for this one. Bachelor number five is Seattle's very own *Todd Lake*, *The Sexy Chef* himself. One of our sweetest deals tonight, Todd tells us *Seattle Live* is going to match whatever money is collected for the winning bid. And I hear Todd is planning to cook his date's favorite meal tomorrow night. So what do you think? Does dinner with *The Sexy Chef* sound good, ladies? Let's open the bid at five hundred dollars and see how many takers we have."

Sabine drew in a breath as nearly every fan in the place was raised. No one heard her shocked swearing over the squealing. "Well holy shit," she said, forgetting her role in the auction as she dealt with her surprise. Joe hadn't told her that the man was freaking famous, much less gorgeous. Was being a chef his diamond-in-the-rough's hobby?

She looked back at the stage at the tall stoic male who so far hadn't smiled once at the audience calling out flirty things to him. Being gay might explain his serious and brooding expression and his ability to ignore them all. To her, his scowl certainly seemed more natural for the intense face scanning the sea of squealing females.

And Todd Lake was way more good-looking than Joe had indicated. Somewhere between deciding for the hundredth time that all the best looking men were gay and realizing her fan was still lifeless in her lap, Sabine remembered to raise it to enter a bid.

"Wonderful! We now have a bid for *two thousand dollars*. Lady in the gold shirt—I saw your fan go up too. Do I hear *two thousand five hundred* from you?"

Before Sabine could recover from the shock of so much money already being on the block for good-looking think-I'm-gay Todd, a loud voice rang out from the back.

"Three thousand dollars—and he better be worth it."

Sabine pivoted in her seat to see an extremely tall woman standing at the back who was smiling evilly at the man on the stage. Sabine looked back at the stage and saw Todd Lake frown as he glared at the back of the room. Whoever the woman was, the man definitely did not like her—not at all. She studied him as the auctioneer was calling for more bids.

The last guy had looked ill as the bidding had neared a closing point. Chef Lake just looked really, really pissed. For some reason, Sabine suddenly felt very sorry for him. Her gut told her the woman at the back was up to no good.

"Three thousand five hundred," Sabine shouted loudly, turning to the back of the room and glaring at the woman for good measure.

"Four thousand," the woman shouted back, turning her evil smile toward Sabine. "What do you think you're going to get for that much cash, honey? I can tell you that it's only going to be dinner. The man doesn't put out. Trust me."

Sabine stood and felt all eyes turn on her. "Hey this auction is being televised. There's no need to be disrespectful. Mr. Lake is doing this for charity."

Sabine turned her attention to the stage. Her gaze sought and found his, while all female gazes were locked on her. There was a glint in his eyes and something else. A plea maybe. *Damn it, she was weak when it came to helping people.*

Turning once more, Sabine looked at the woman just as the auctioneer was counting down for her bid. Her final bid had to end it. There was no other way. She held up her fan. *"Six thousand dollars,"* Sabine said firmly, her voice barely carrying over the now madly cheering crowd.

"Are you are fucking crazy, lady?" the woman shouted.

Sabine shrugged and smiled at her competition. God, she loved being older.

"The bid is now at *six thousand dollars*. Do we have any others? . . . Going once . . . Going twice. Mr. Lake will be cooking dinner for . . . hold up your fan for me again, lady in the gold shirt. He'll be cooking for Ms. Sabine Kendall. Congratulations, Ms. Kendall. You have the winning bid for bachelor number five."

The applause that broke out was the most deafening yet. Sabine laughed at the sheer amount of happy female energy in the room now directed at her. Feeling righteous and heroic, she shouldered her large purse again and headed for the back of the room.

"You're an idiot for spending that kind of money on Todd Lake. He's so not worth it, lady. I was only going to make him pay for treating me like shit when we dated," the woman yelled as she passed.

"Maybe I am an idiot, but at least I'm the winning one this evening. And I think I just rescued a decent man from your evil bitchiness, which is the best thing I could have done at this meat show tonight. Do yourself a favor. Get help and stop hating the world," Sabine ordered, smiling in triumph as the woman gave her the finger.

She knew her smile would disappear the moment she signed over the remaining contents of her savings to some charity she had yet to identify, but what the hell? Rundgren was obviously supporting it too. That would look favorable for her. She would just split the difference of the money with Joe. It had been worth her half to put that bitchy woman in her place. She felt ten feet tall and thin at the moment. Those extra thirty pounds she was packing were wiped away in her triumphant female moment.

Behind her, she heard bachelor number six being brought forward. It made her cringe. Despite the momentary rush she'd gotten bidding on Joe's Todd, the whole auction business was still distasteful to her. Once again she shook her head at her stupidity for getting involved.

"Joe, you owe me."

CHAPTER 3

Sabine was sighing over her checkbook when an out-of-breath Joe finally ran in and skidded to a stop beside her.

"Did you win?" he demanded.

"Of course I won," Sabine declared. "And my now empty bank account can attest to that fact." She handed the check over to a giggling woman who congratulated her on her win.

"And just how much did you have to pay for his rescue?" Joe asked.

"Six thousand dollars, hotshot. There was some crazy woman bidding on your *diamond in the rough* that ran his price up to four thousand in like a minute. She was a real piece of work, let me tell you. It felt so good to outbid her though that I've decided to split the difference with you, so you only owe me three thousand. Plus I really enjoyed rescuing him. You were right about that. Saving your Todd was the most fun I've had in ages."

"Six thousand? *You paid six thousand dollars for Todd?*" Joe exclaimed.

Sabine laughed at his genuine disbelief. "Yes. Apparently, every woman in the place saw the same diamond quality in him that you did. Now come on. I've got to go get my picture taken with your stud. He's waiting for me in the winner's circle."

"I can't believe they got through nine bachelors so quickly," Joe commented as they walked.

"It was only five. Todd was bachelor number five—not number nine," Sabine corrected.

"No, Todd was going to be number nine. I got a text about ten minutes ago confirming his place in the auction line-up."

Sabine snorted. "Simply not possible, Joe. The auctioneer said *Todd Lake* and the room erupted in bid fans going up in the air. I bid on your Todd. Trust me."

"*Todd Lake?* Sabine . . . *oh my God. That's who you bid on and won? For six thousand?*" Joe bent from the waist as he laughed. When he straightened, he turned and started back toward the sign-up table. "I'm going to have to go bid on Todd myself. This is too funny. Wait until I tell him."

"Joe, what the hell are you talking about? Come back here. This is not the time for a joke. I spent the rest of my savings on your stupid favor."

Joe stopped laughing as he turned to look at Sabine's blank face again. "Sweetie, do you have any idea who you won tonight?"

"Yes. I won Todd Lake," Sabine said. "It has to be your Todd. There couldn't have been two Todds in the auction. You said so yourself."

Joe laughed. "What are the odds of two Todds? Sounds like a riddle, doesn't it? Now I wish I could stick around to meet *The Sexy Chef* in person, but I need to go save *my Todd*. Have fun with *yours*."

Sabine stomped her foot. It was childish. Plus it didn't help. "I already did save him. He's waiting on me to take a freaking picture with him, Joe. Now stop fooling around and come with me. I don't want to do this alone."

"Sabine, you bid on the wrong man. But don't worry, I'm sure you're going to have a wonderful time tomorrow on your expensive date. *Todd Lake* is a Polynesian chef and you love pineapple. I'm sure it will be fine. Oh, and I think he's a bit younger than you. See how great this has worked out? Win-win and you didn't have to hit a single bar."

Shocked at Joe's revelation—and assumption—Sabine remained frozen in place, staring after him. Todd Lake was a real chef? What the hell? She didn't watch cooking shows.

"Oh dear God—I bid on the wrong guy. Now what am I going to do?" she asked aloud as she watched Joe walking away.

"Sabine Kendall?"

A deep masculine voice followed by a sharp laugh had her spinning to face the speaker. Up close, Todd Lake was even larger and more impressive than he had looked on stage. His athletic cut suit fit his body perfectly. The shaggy black hair and day's growth of beard didn't do the suit any favors, but social defiance somehow suited those piercing chocolate eyes of his. He looked very real as he grinned at her shock.

Her sigh of resignation over what he must have heard was long and loud. Sabine ignored her face heating and sought for the composure she normally exhibited in uncomfortable situations. As a public relations specialist, she had handled some funky clients in her career, and certainly had her share of embarrassing moments. She just didn't usually cause them for herself.

"I'm so sorry. I didn't mean for you to hear all that, Mr. Lake. My error is not in any way your fault nor a judgment of your appeal. I'm sure you're worth every penny I paid—for the charity donation, I mean."

"So if I heard your friend correctly, you rescued me thinking I was someone else?" Koka asked.

"Well—yes. But it wasn't as bad as it sounded just now. I promised a friend that I'd rescue a guy he's interested in . . . no let's skip Joe's sorry story. It's too complicated to get into. Plus I'm still not convinced the other Todd even exists. Long story made short—apparently I bid on the wrong bachelor named *Todd*," Sabine said. "I hope you're not too offended."

Koka smiled—really smiled. The movement was so real and genuine for once that his face actually hurt. He put a hand up to rub the stiffness from his bristly jaw as he answered. "On the contrary, I am happy for the first time this evening—maybe this year. Thank you for bidding on me whatever the circumstances."

Sabine sighed in relief as she smiled back. She put out her hand. "That's very nice of you to be so understanding. I'm Sabine Blakeman by the way, not Kendall any longer. They took my name off my driver's license and checkbook. I just haven't changed it legally yet."

His hand engulfed hers and Sabine wondered how those large hands could possible manage in a kitchen. His fingers were long and the skin on his hands meticulously soft and clean. He was quite possibly the most beautiful man she had ever touched.

"They have a saying where I'm from, Ms. Blakeman. *Mahalo E Ke Akua No Keia La*," Koka said.

Sabine smiled. "That's certainly a beautiful mouthful. Is it Polynesian?"

"It's the Hawaiian way of saying *thank the goddess* such a pleasant woman won me," Koka explained.

When she belly laughed at his snarky compliment, the ruggedly handsome man towering over her smiled brilliantly at her. He tugged her hand gently until she just sort of naturally fell into step beside him.

"Well, at least the mean woman in the back didn't get you," she said.

"Never. Not even when we dated briefly. I think she may still be angry about my refusal," Koka said.

"*Oh,*" Sabine replied, the single word encompassing her total understanding. The woman had insinuated as much, but she didn't like to jump to conclusions. Then thinking about the sexually frustrated woman bidding four thousand dollars for another shot at him, Sabine snorted and felt triumphant all over again. "As good looking as you are, you can do a lot better than someone like her."

"My grandmother didn't like her either," Koka said, shrugging off his narrow escape. "So . . . shall we take the obligatory picture for the newspaper?"

Sabine sighed and nodded. She might as well have something to show for her zero bank balance. Why not get a picture taken with her six thousand dollar wrong Valentine?

"Sure. Why not? Otherwise tomorrow this is just going to seem like every other nightmare I've ever had and woken up from relieved to still be alive. I thought some of those women might murder me before I managed to write the check for your ransom."

Koka laughed and the sound coming from his chest surprised him. He couldn't remember the last time a woman had sparked humor in his soul. He took a closer look at her. "I am suddenly very glad you won me, Sabine Blakeman. Tomorrow I will make you the best dinner you have ever had. I heard your friend say that you like pineapple. Not one of my usual ingredients, but I'll see what I can do."

Sabine groaned at his sarcasm and felt a blush climbing her face again. "Again—I am so sorry. My friend Joe has an extremely big mouth. Make anything you want and I'll eat it. Promise. I'm not picky at all when it comes to food, but then I guess that shows, doesn't it? And for the record, I do like pineapple."

"You're very accommodating. It is a wonderful trait in a beautiful woman," Koka said, smiling again.

"Wow, if that's flirting Mr. Lake, you're really good at it. My accommodating nature is because I'm feeling a bit unbalanced. You're going to be my first actual *date* with a bachelor in twenty years," Sabine said, quote marking the dreaded "d" word in the air with bent fingers.

The photographer motioned them in front of a blue screen. They were asked to hold a large paper that had his bachelor number, the winning bid amount, and both their names.

21

DONNA MCDONALD

Sabine sighed. "You wouldn't happen to have a black marker in your pocket would you? I'd love to change my name on this paper."

Koka ignored her teasing question to ask what he really wanted to know. "Twenty years is a long time to not date. Are you freshly divorced?" Koka asked.

"More like irrevocably divorced. My ex has already re-married," Sabine said.

Koka smiled at the news. "Well, I'll try to make the evening memorable enough for your first real date in twenty years."

"Oh, I think that's guaranteed by our odd circumstances," Sabine said. "Where do you want to meet tomorrow?"

Having decided to accept Edwina's suggestion, Koka had been going take the winner to the *Seattle Live* stage kitchen, which he considered neutral territory. He was even going to let the network people come by and chaperone in case it turned awkward. His plan had been to let fame be the woman's payment for her contribution to the auction. Now he wanted something more. He wanted time to get to know Sabine Blakeman.

"You seem like a trustworthy person. If you don't mind, I'd like you to come to my house. My grandmother's health is not good. I don't like to be away from her for any longer than I have to," he said.

Sabine nodded. "Sure. I don't mind that at all. She's welcome to join us for dinner."

"After spending all that money on me, I find it interesting that you are willing to share my attention with other people," Koka said, frowning at her open expression. Would the woman really not mind sharing his company? And why did that idea bother him? She was being nice.

"Why would I mind if your grandmother ate with us? It would be rude to exclude your family. Besides, the dinner is a charity event. It's not like tomorrow is a real date."

"True—but what if it was? I'm just curious. Would you still feel the same?" Koka demanded.

Sabine frowned. "Well, it's not a real date, so that's a rhetorical question not in need of a definitive answer. Right?"

Koka laughed at her sharp response. His pride was stung a little, thinking Sabine Blakeman didn't want to be alone with him. What a strange response to a woman who was only being kind.

His gaze traveled over her blonde hair and lush womanly figure covered in sparkling gold. Her sheer comfort with herself made her more alluring than any woman he'd seen screaming

22

his name tonight. Evidently, his grandmother's prayers to the goddess had been answered in his rescuer.

"Since you told me your real name, I suppose it is only fair that I should tell you mine. I will ask you to please not reveal it to the world. My real name is Koka Whitman. Todd Lake is my TV show name," he whispered.

Sabine smiled up at him as the photographer made lens adjustments. "*Koka?* That's a very different kind of name."

Koka waited, grinned, and then let it drop. "Yes. It's Hawaiian for *Todd.*"

Her spontaneous rolling belly laugh had him smiling down into her open face again. The camera snapped and for once he didn't care. All he cared about was making the woman beside him belly laugh again until her eyes danced.

"You made that up just now because you heard Joe say that I bid on the wrong person," Sabine declared. "Just because I'm a natural blonde doesn't mean I'm gullible and stupid—unless you count letting a friend talk me into this stupid auction—wait, I didn't mean that the way it sounded. I'm not unhappy to have won you."

Koka laughed hard as Sabine bit her lip and stared a little fearfully at him. He was both charmed and offended by her honesty. The camera snapped again. Remarkably, he still didn't care. He had even forgotten to count. Now he would have to guess at how many photos had been taken.

"Could we please try for one normal picture?" the photographer asked.

Sabine felt a blush climbing her face again as she looked forward at the camera. "Oh God—I'm really sorry. Of course, let me. . . *oh* . . ." She stumbled a little when Koka's arm came around her and pulled her closer to him behind the paper they held between them. Good thing she'd worn the flats and not stupid stripper shoes like so many of the bidders had been wearing.

"That's a pretty strong grip you have there—*Koka Whitman,*" she whispered.

Koka chuckled, delighted with her mock outrage over his touch. He liked the idea that he could make her nervous. "Smile at the camera Sabine—and stop making me laugh."

"I wasn't doing it on purpose. You started it with your fake Todd story." But she did as he ordered, vastly relieved when the photographer finally said he got one he was happy with for the paper.

"We want copies of all the pictures you took," Koka said firmly, staring at the photographer. "It was part of my participation agreement. I believe there were four prior to your good shot. I will be looking for that many at least."

"Certainly, Mr. Lake," the photographer answered. "There's only one acceptable shot, but I'll send the others along to your producer as well."

Koka nodded. "Please do that. Thank you." He looked down at Sabine Blakeman. "Can I have your phone number? I will need to call you with details for our—date."

"My phone number? Oh . . . sure," Sabine said.

She dug into her purse for a business card and a pen. Seeing no surface to write on, she picked up one of Koka Whitman's large hands and put her card in it. She raised and lowered his arm until her vision focused. No way was she digging for her reading glasses. Flipping the card over to the back, she wrote her cell number on it. All the while, he laughed at her.

"Am I really that funny to you?" Sabine asked.

"The word I would use is *charming*," Koka said.

Sabine snorted as she capped her pen. Her heart fluttered as she watched him tuck the card into some hidden pocket in his jacket. When his eyes crinkled at the corners, she just had to know the cause. "Do you mind telling me how old you are?"

"Thirty-seven last year," Koka said. "And you?"

Sabine shrugged. "Forty-three last year."

"Why does age matter to you?" Koka asked.

"I've been teasing Joe about dating a younger man. Now that's going to be something else I can check off my post divorce to-do list," she said.

Koka snorted. She was an easy woman to read. "How old was the woman your ex married?"

"Okay. You got me. My husband married a woman half my age, but I'm not trying to get even. Men half my age remind me of my children. I joke about it, but I couldn't go there."

Koka smiled again, but actually he wanted to laugh. Sabine was very at ease making fun of herself. "I have a daughter who is nineteen. She started college this year—University of California at Berkley. She's majoring in music."

"I have a college sophomore *and* a freshman. Both are at University of Washington. One has been talking about Berkley, but that's a bit out of my college budget. Neither have chosen majors yet. I'm just happy they're both in school and getting decent grades. Hopefully they'll find their calling as they find themselves."

They stood looking at each other in shared understanding until a flash went off nearby. It was not the professional photographer.

Koka released a long breath. "Sorry, Sabine. It happens to me all the time. We'll be on social media later."

"It's okay. I'm a PR person. Most of the time those random pictures are a good thing for your popularity, but I can see how it could get old after a while. Is that why you rebelled today and didn't bother to shave?"

Koka rubbed his jaw as he grinned over her criticism. "You consider this a sign of rebelling?"

"Yes. Assuming you're not one of those men who are just lazy about hygiene. I somehow don't see that being the case with a TV personality," Sabine declared, smiling to soften her statement. "Not that an unshaven man in a well-fitted suit doesn't have his own rugged appeal. You raised every bidding fan when you walked out on the stage. I'm sure you didn't miss that."

Liking her directness, Koka laughed and shrugged. "Will you expect me to shave for our date tomorrow?"

Sabine giggled at the question. The man had such a funny way about him. For a moment, she almost wished tomorrow could be a real date. But given the broad base of females this man has access to, those thoughts would lead only to deep disappointment.

"Expectations haven't worked out well for me lately, Mr. Whitman. I think I'll just take whatever presentation you're offering and be grateful."

"Now it's my turn to ask. Are you flirting with me?" Koka grinned at her head ducking.

Sabine sighed as she made herself meet his gaze. "Why? Am I doing a terrible job of it? I admit I'm really rusty."

Koka shook his head as he turned. "No, I can't remember the last time I looked forward to a woman's company. I'll call you tomorrow, Sabine."

"Okay. Sure. Oh hey—that answers your other question. Your phone call is one thing I will be expecting tomorrow," she teased.

Sabine watched Koka walk away laughing, heading in the direction of the back door. She smiled and sighed softly as she turned back toward the front of building. Joe and a man she figured was his actual diamond in the rough were standing nearby and grinning at her.

Sighing again, but this time in resignation, she lifted her chin and braced herself. "Don't start on me," she ordered, as Joe threw his arms around her and hugged.

"I'm so proud of you, Sabine. It's all I can do not to start dancing in joy. You were flirting with *The Sexy Chef* and he was

25

flirting back. I can't wait until I see Martin again, just so I can tell him you've officially moved on."

"Stop teasing me," Sabine said firmly, her palm smacking Joe's chest. She turned her attention politely to his companion. "Hello. You must be *the right Todd*."

When he grinned, Sabine grinned back and decided he had a nice smile.

"Not sure how to answer that. I guess I must be the right one if you consider Todd Lake the wrong one. It's a pleasure to meet you, Ms. Kendall. I'm Todd Masterson."

"It's Blakeman—Sabine Blakeman. It's my pleasure to meet you, Todd Masterson. Joe says we're in the same line of business."

"Actually, Joe says you would very much like to do business with my company," Todd said, laughing when Sabine Blakeman blushed. "How charming. A PR person who isn't jaded."

"Joe talks way too much. And it's been a day for blushing at everything that's said. I paid six thousand dollars for the wrong man. I think I'll probably be doing more blushing tomorrow when he fixes me my six thousand dollar pineapple dinner," Sabine said.

"And I imagine speculation will be rampant about my orientation preference when I go out with Joe tomorrow," Todd said. "I may be blushing the whole evening as well."

Sabine chuckled. "Well, at least you have the satisfaction of knowing I would have paid a lot more money for you than Joe ever would have. He told me I had to stop at six hundred."

To her delight, Todd laughed while Joe flushed and swore she was lying. At least the right Todd had a keen sense of humor. Maybe the man was worth all the trouble he had indirectly caused her.

"Joe, I need a drink and you're buying because, thanks to you, I'm broke," Sabine said. "Todd, are you interested in joining us? When I'm out with Joe people tend to think we're a married couple. The question of your orientation should be moot if you want to chance it."

"Only if you make mine a double. Joe bought me for three hundred dollars. Knowing you paid thousands for the wrong Todd, my ego is now totally deflated."

"*Three hundred?*" Sabine repeated, glaring at the snickering man next to her. "Joe—I'm seriously going to hurt you."

"No you won't. I was eavesdropping and heard what Todd Lake said to you. I will bet you half the money you spent on him that *The Sexy Chef* asks you out for a real date tomorrow. The man was into you," Joe said.

Sabine laughed. "Deal—and I'm not even worried that I don't have any money left to pay you in case you win. The man was being polite and friendly, Joe. He was fun and a lot more real than what everyone probably thinks."

She saw Joe and Todd exchanging a look over her statement. "What was that look for? I'm telling you Mr. Lake was just playing nice for the cameras. I bet he can't go anywhere without being tagged. My ignorance was just a refreshing change for him."

"And she already cares about how he's perceived by the media," Joe said. He shook his head and sighed dramatically as Todd laughed. "My brother never deserved this woman. She's great at her job too. Unlike some public relations agents, her clients get to maintain their dignity."

Sabine's face flamed again at Joe's praise in front of a potential client who now knew too many intimate details about her life. But there was no retracting what had been said.

"Well, at least I'm spending Valentine's Day Eve with two handsome men instead of being alone," she said sweetly.

When the right Todd smiled at her statement, Sabine saw exactly what Joe had seen. Todd Masterson was interesting and very nice, which was sometimes better than being extremely good-looking. A mind that sharp would probably be fun to challenge too.

"Todd—I wish I had bid on you," Sabine declared.

"Tell you what, Sabine Blakeman. Rundgren supports many charities. If you get *The Sexy Chef* to cater a meal for one of them, I could probably get you a contract for some of our work," Todd said.

Sabine belly laughed at his offer. "Oh sure. I'll just ask *The Sexy Chef* tomorrow, right after the grilled pineapple entrée that Joe made sure I would get."

She listened to Todd laughing while she glared at Joe's shrug of indifference. But she also felt envious of her friend's extraordinary luck in finding good men.

CHAPTER 4

"Sabine, thanks for coming in on a Saturday—and on Valentine's Day no less. Why didn't you tell me you were going to the bachelor auction last night? I would have gone with you. Now I'm messing up your date time for a client panic attack that's probably unwarranted," Blanche declared.

Sabine eyed her first line supervisor. The woman was barely better in regards to men than the vindictive one she'd bid against to win Koka. "The client's panic attack was justified. Besides, the auction last night was no big deal. I only went as a favor to a friend."

"Some favor. I would love to do one of those if it meant winning a date with the uber sexy Todd Lake," Blanche said, laughing at her own joke. "So the big date is tonight—right?"

"I wouldn't call it a date exactly. Chef Lake is fixing me dinner. Then tomorrow morning we'll have individual interviews about how it went. I'll make sure I mention the company and our excellent work record. You should pick up a copy of the special edition tomorrow afternoon," Sabine suggested, hoping to derail further queries about Koka.

Blanche nodded and waved her hand. "Of course you'll make us look wonderful. But what's more important is that you butter up Mr. Lake so he'll cater something for us sometime. Imagine the press coverage. He's *Seattle Live's* hottest moneymaker. People—and by that you know I mean *women*—flock to any appearance *The Sexy Chef* makes anywhere. You will have found yourself a PR gold mine if the man likes you."

Sabine frowned. "I'm having dinner with him, not trying to recruit his services. He's a really nice man, Blanche."

"Didn't your ex recently remarry? Honey, your ego must need stroking in the worst way. Why else would you have bid so

28

high for him? Trust me. You're recruiting his services alright and not just his cooking ones," Blanche declared.

"No. It's not like that at all," Sabine protested, shaking her head.

Blanche laughed as she walked to the door. "Really? Did you buy a new dress to wear to dinner? Better pair some heels with it if you did. I heard that Todd Lake is like six foot four or something. With shoulders that wide, the man should have been a pro ball player."

Sabine frowned. Did she need a new dress for her date today? Koka hadn't called yet and it was only hours until their "date" was supposed to happen. There was no time for shopping even if she had wanted to go buy something new. Besides, she'd been at work all day.

"I don't need a new dress, Blanche. It's not that kind of date. This is just something we're both doing for charity," Sabine declared, raising her head.

But Blanche had already disappeared and she was left wondering if she should have taken the dinner with him more seriously.

***

The ride from her house to Koka's had only increased her clothes guilt. *Seattle Live* had sent a limo. The Seahawks were attending a Supersonics game for charity, but she had cruised through heavy traffic listening to a smooth jazz concert while sipping champagne. Forty-five minutes later, reality caught up again and she was glad for her flat shoes. When she climbed out at the modest, but well-kept house nestled in a prominent gated community she was way too tipsy to walk on high heels.

Thanking the driver who informed her he'd return later, she walked slowly down the pristine sidewalk, her bag slung tightly over one shoulder and clutched under her arm. But at the door, Sabine looked down at her black ballet flats and groaned before she rang the bell.

"I should have at least worn the red shoes. He's going to think I only own one pair."

She told herself it was all that champagne on an empty stomach that brought on full-blown fashion guilt. Wishing now she'd worn a dress, or at least a skirt, she sighed over her light-weight blue tunic fluttering softly over another pair of black leggings that she hoped like hell made her look thinner than she actually was.

When there was no answer, she rang the doorbell again and ordered herself to stop being so silly. If Koka Whitman—aka

Todd Lake—was expecting a dress, well too bad. Rebellion was one of the true joys of being an older woman. So what if comfort had won out over the need to impress him? She ruthlessly pushed away all lingering feminine regret and tapped the toe of one of her flats.

After a few more moments of her nervously waiting, the door finally opened. Sabine was greeted by a wide, muscled-filled blue t-shirt with a white food-splattered apron struggling to cover some of it. Her gaze lingered on Koka's impressive chest longer than was polite and her face heated as she raised her guilty gaze to his.

"*E komo mai,*" Koka said, telling himself not to stare at Sabine's soft, open-mouth expression. The woman's lips with her chewed off lipstick practically begged for a kiss. Perhaps his instant physical reaction should have surprised, instead of pleasing him.

Normally, he had to know a woman far better to have such interest. He was sorely tempted to deepen her blush by asking if she liked what she saw as she continued to stare. But in the end, he chose to be polite. His grandmother would be very angry if he insulted a guest.

"Welcome to my home, Sabine Blakeman."

Sabine nodded mutely as the Polynesian God of Muscled Perfection ushered her through the front door of his home. Soft music was playing in a distant room and it was remarkably similar to what had been playing in the limo.

Wonderful scents filled the air, reminding her of how hungry she was. She put a hand over her suddenly rumbling stomach, blushing hard when Koka laughed at the noise. His refusal to politely ignore her physical distress instantly deflated his god-like status and snapped her back to reality.

She shrugged and tried to look as unrepentant as possible. "Sorry. I missed lunch and the champagne in the limo made things worse."

"To assuage that basic animal need will be my pleasure. Come to my kitchen and let me feed you," he said, holding out his hand for her to take.

Not sure whether to be offended or charmed, Sabine opted for the latter and let Koka lead her by the hand through his house. In the kitchen, a frail older woman in a wheelchair smiled in welcome. Her chair was parked by a small table near a wide doorway leading to another wing of the house. Somehow Sabine couldn't see Koka sitting at that tiny table. The seats were much too delicate for someone his size.

When she smiled back at the woman, Koka's hand tightened on hers momentarily as if he might keep her from going over to say hello. Reaching out without thinking about it, she patted his chest through the apron, until his grip eased. "It's all right. Go back to your cooking. I can introduce myself."

She patted a second time until Koka finally released her. She felt him watching warily as she walked over to greet the woman still smiling at her.

"Hello," Sabine said, holding out a hand. "I'm Sabine Blakeman—the woman who won the bid at the bachelor auction."

"*Aloha*, Sabine Blakeman. I am Pekala Whitman—Koka's grandmother."

"Hello, Pekala Whitman. It is a pleasure to meet you. You must be very proud of your famous grandson," Sabine said.

"I am indeed. Koka has done all this for me instead of opening the restaurant he has been saving for since he went to cooking school," Pekala said.

Sabine looked at Koka who was now head down in his cooking, but she knew from his eavesdropping yesterday that his ears were sharp. Knowing the man was listening to every word said, she still slid into the tiny chair nearest the wheelchair. She positioned her body until she was eye level with Koka's grandmother.

"Koka is young enough and talented enough to open a restaurant any time he wants. I have clients in my work who are local celebrities like him. TV fame is often fleeting. I think it's very wise of Koka to ride the wave of his popularity while he can."

"You talk very sweetly of him. Do you admire my grandson?" Pekala asked.

Sabine nodded. "Yes, of course. A man who honors his commitments to his family is very admirable. Your grandson is also following his passion. I personally think that is the secret to a happy life. His talent will take him wherever he wants to go in his career field."

Pekala chuckled as she looked across the room. "Now I see why you shaved before she got here."

Sabine's eyebrows rose. "He shaved? Oh my God, I didn't even notice. My stomach was growling and I was mesmerized by the food on his apron."

Pekala laughed roughly, the effort hurting her chest, but making her soul sing with joy for her grandson. "*Ko Aloha Makamae E Ipo*. It has been a long time since I laughed. And an even longer time since a woman so thoroughly ignored my Koka's pretty face."

"You're embarrassing our guest, *Kupunawahine*. You would be angry if I was the one doing that."

Sabine grinned at his comment. Koka's musical masculine voice, while full of gentle chastisement, also carried a hint of true embarrassment.

"If anyone is embarrassed, it's not me," Sabine denied. She grinned at the man in the kitchen whose doubtful gaze held hers briefly as she spoke. "I am sorry I didn't notice your face, Koka. Thank you for shaving for me. I do appreciate it."

Her stomach chose that moment to growl loudly again. Mother Nature was not helping her pathetic attempts at flirting. When Pekala laughed a second time, Sabine sighed and rubbed her stomach. "Well, now everyone knows I'm an honest woman at least."

"You need to hurry and feed her, Koka. Your *Ke Aloha* is starving while you amuse yourself listening to her polite conversation with me."

"Oh, I'm not really in a hurry to eat," Sabine began, only to be made a liar by yet another loud growling rumble. It echoed louder in the room than whatever Koka had sizzling over a fire. "My God, I just can't catch a dignified break tonight."

Shrugging away her fading need to impress the man instead of the cook, Sabine grinned and shook her head while Pekala covered her smiling mouth with a shaking hand.

"Please tell your stomach that I am hurrying," Koka ordered, pausing to look over and grin at her red face.

Sabine groaned and dipped her head. "Okay I lied. I have never been so embarrassed in my entire life."

Pekala smiled. "Koka, your Sabine brings life and energy to this dreary, rainy town. Her nature is full of the sunshine you miss so much."

"Sunshine? Are you talking about me?" Sabine asked, laughing at the poetic description of her embarrassment.

Pekala nodded. "Yes, *ku`uipo*. I am speaking of you."

"Thank you then. Those are wonderful compliments. Please continue to laugh at my growling stomach all you wish," Sabine said, smiling as the woman nodded.

She watched as Pekala pressed a button on a remote hung on the arm of the wheelchair.

"I would, but laughing has made me tired. And yet very happy, too. *Mahalo E Ke Akua No Keia La.* Thank you for the gift of your visit. *Aloha*, Sabine Blakeman. Please come back again."

A woman in a nurse's uniform discreetly appeared in the wide doorway. Sabine returned her soft smile as she guided the wheelchair back through it.

"*Aloha*, Pekala Whitman," Sabine said, hoping it was the right thing to say.

CHAPTER 5

After Koka's grandmother disappeared from the kitchen, Sabine stood. She left her purse on the small table and went to the large kitchen island across from where Koka was still cooking.

"Is it okay if I sit here at the counter?"

"Yes, but I could bring your food to the table if you preferred," he said.

Sabine shook her head and climbed up on one of the low back stools. "No thanks. I'd rather watch you cook, if that's truly okay."

Koka nodded and placed a small glass in front of her. "Of course. Pineapple juice cocktail for a starter—it's my own recipe."

Sabine laughed. "Pineapple. Of course—pineapple. Too bad Pekala got tired. She'd probably find this funny too. I'm going to hurt my friend Joe first chance I get."

"I did not fix this because of him or his teasing. Now stop fussing and drink," Koka ordered, tapping the counter with his finger.

Snorting at his order, Sabine lifted the tiny glass and sipped. The heat of whatever liquor was in it settled in her stomach like a small fire while the flavor of the fruit burst against her tongue. She lifted the glass again. "Oh wow. This is really good."

"It is called a *Sunshine Shooter*," Koka said. "I named it just now in your honor."

Sabine laughed at his comments. Was he for real? Or was he being sarcastic? It was hard to tell, but she decided to give him the benefit of her doubt until she was sure.

"Now I know why all those bid fans raised so high in the air when you appeared on the stage. I may have been the only woman there who didn't take one look at you and instantly know you were one of those guys with a master's degree in charming women."

Koka ignored her jab at his bossiness and pointed at the rest of her drink. "Finish it all. It will set your palate for the rest of the food."

Rolling her eyes at his second dramatic order, Sabine tilted the tiny glass and swallowed the rest of the contents down. Then she snorted when Koka put a full martini glass of what looked like more of the concoction in front of her. "I'm going to fall off this stool if I drink any more liquor on an empty stomach. Got some pretzels I can munch on to soak up the alcohol?"

"Don't make me come around there and punish you for your smart mouth," Koka warned.

Reaching behind him, he lifted two small plates and set them in front of her. "This is your first course—welcome bread with a typical Polynesian salad."

"Aren't you eating with me?" Sabine asked, blinking at the beautiful presentation.

Koka smiled. "Eventually. I eat enough of first courses while I am preparing food. We'll have the main entrée together. Thank you for asking. Now please eat what I have prepared. The next course is already waiting."

Sabine speared a mandarin orange and something green beneath it. Her tongue wept for joy with the first bite. Groaning in appreciation, she dug in and devoured the offering, not bothering to praise it until the last bite had disappeared.

"That was wonderful," she declared finally.

Koka instantly swept the empty dishes away and replaced them with another plate.

"You're having two entrees for your meal. The first is Furikake salmon over pad Thai noodles. Just a little. I wanted to offer you a variety of food since I wasn't sure what you liked. I would rather die than send you home hungry."

"I'm much too easy for that to happen. I love food—pretty much all food," Sabine teased, smiling at his concern. She lifted a fork and dug in. It was just as good as the salad. "I can see why you want to do a restaurant. You'll make a fortune. This is wonderful—and spicy too. Do I taste some sort of chili?"

Koka tilted his head. "Very good. Yes—red chili. It's tricky to get the right amount. Too much and it burns the palate for the rest of the dinner."

"No worries here. The amount is just right," Sabine said, cleaning the contents of the plate in her enthusiasm.

She watched Koka remove the now empty dish and deposit it into a sink with the others. He stepped to the stove, lit a burner, and splashed something from a tall slender bottle into it as it started to sizzle.

"I make my own dressings, oil blends, and seasonings. They are Polynesian, but more modern than what Pekala would have used in her cooking. I worked many years to perfect them, but it was important. Otherwise, I would be like every other chef from the islands."

"I can't imagine you being typical at anything. Do I smell ginger? And . . ." Sabine sniffed the air, ". . . something sweeter?"

Koka snorted and grinned at her. "Surely, you recognize your favorite ingredient."

Sabine laughed and rolled her eyes. "Pineapple—of course."

Koka's back was turned to her as he plated a portion of the entrée for both of them. Her gaze dropped to his backside, encased in jeans that flattered his athletically fit form. It made her grin when she thought of all those women bidding on him and yet here she sat in the man's own kitchen staring at his butt.

"I feel your eyes on me," Koka said. "Are you staring at my ass? I thought you sat at the counter to watch my cooking."

Sabine laughed at his nerve and wondered what he'd say if she said yes and admitted she had been staring at his ass. She'd probably get a lecture. For some reason, Koka found open desire from women offensive. If only the bidding crowd had known to play it cool for this interesting man.

"Good thing your grandmother retired for the evening. Now she won't have to hear this discussion. That's a very rude assumption for a first date, Koka Whitman."

"Rude? I don't know about that. But yes, it is an assumption. I would still like to know if it is true," he demanded.

Sabine shook her head and lied. "No of course it's not true. For your information, I was just wondering how you managed to get your apron tied behind you in such a perfect bow. The tails are completely even, like you have OCD or something. That's amazing considering how big your hands are. I can't even get a bow shaped into two normal size loops when I'm watching what I'm doing. You are a man of many talents, my friend."

"On the surface that sounds very much like joking, but I prefer to believe you are flirting with me again. It is a poor attempt, but a man can be generous when he likes a woman enough," Koka declared.

He lifted the apron over his head and hung it on a nearby upper cabinet knob, checking out the length of the tails. So what if they were the same length? It was a habit. How many times had he tied apron strings? Hundreds? Thousands?

Ignoring Sabine's smirk as she sipped the milder fruit juice cocktail he had made for her, Koka walked around the counter carrying two plates of steaming food. He liked it when Sabine leaned back as he slid one in front of her. He was tempted to brush his wrist against her breast to see if it was as soft as it looked, but that really would have been rude, and he didn't want her to leave angry with him.

"Be careful—the plate is hot. This is pan-seared pork with pineapple-kiwi salsa over a mixed bean salad. Normally, this preparation is a creative next day use of leftover pork chops. Enjoy it, but please stop eating when you start to get full. I want you to leave a little room for dessert," he ordered.

Sabine sighed in pleasure as she picked up her fork. "I'm going to have to start watching your show. No professor could possibly be more charismatic. Your musical voice is as enticing as your cooking, Koka. Thank you for my personal cooking demonstration tonight."

Koka nodded. He could hear the sincerity in her voice. Maybe his ass accusation had been out of line. "Thank you. Now eat before it gets cold."

Sabine smiled at his bossy command and sliced a piece of pork off before speaking again. "So tell me the truth, Chef Lake. Are you always so austere about your cooking or is it that you're just deeply unhappy with the way your career is going? Because anyone with your looks, your voice, and your cooking talent ought to be one of the happiest human beings walking around on the planet."

Pausing to let him respond, Sabine popped the bite of pork she had cut into her mouth and groaned in pleasure again. She swallowed and sighed.

"If all leftovers were this good, I'd be the size of my house. I've had enough trouble keeping my weight down since I turned forty. I do not need the possibility of delicious leftovers haunting my refrigerator."

Koka looked sideways. "You hide your body so well that a man can have no opinion on the matter of your weight."

Sabine laughed. She wished that were as true as he made it seem. "Who says I want another man to have an opinion? I just escaped that fate. I'm not even officially dating yet."

Koka laughed. "So when you do start dating, are you going to wear something that shows your figure and lets a man have a look at the possibility of you?"

Tired of his baiting, Sabine stared at him as she slowly licked the glaze from her fork, exaggerating the slowness when he started to squirm in his seat. "I don't know. Maybe. Do you think it's important how I look?"

Koka sighed at the sight of her pink tongue sliding up and down over the tines. The woman was sneakier than she looked. "Nice trick, Sabine. I admit I am now thoroughly distracted from being curious about the rest of you. Your tongue holds my full attention, much like my ass held yours."

Sabine laughed loudly at his extreme honesty. "Okay. The fork licking wasn't really fair of me—or good first date etiquette either. I was just teasing you so you'd stop talking about my clothes. I'm a little sensitive about my aging body."

"I don't care about first date etiquette. It's been a long time since I was attracted to a woman. As soon as I can walk comfortably, I'll make us dessert. How is that for honesty? Get comfortable, Sabine Blakeman. This could take a while," Koka said.

Sabine snorted. "Now who's the one flirting?"

"Maybe I am. If I give you a spoon with dessert, are you going to lick it clean too?"

"Depends on how good your dessert is. I have high standards," Sabine said softly, leaning on the counter as she studied his profile. "I'm also good at my job and I predict that one day the restaurant you eventually open is going to be enormously successful. But I also predict that years after that happens, you will look back on this time with your grandmother as one of the most important things you ever did in your life. It will be far more important than having your TV cooking show do well or opening even the most astounding restaurant. I wish I could wave a wand tonight and help you be happier in your current choices until time changes things for you."

Koka slid from his seat and landed as close as he could to Sabine's still-seated body. Grinning when she leaned back, he lifted a hand and put it against her cheek. "*Mahalo*, Sabine Blakeman. Thank you for your kindness today and yesterday. One day perhaps I can return the favor and be equally as kind to you."

Sabine swallowed hard at the sudden racing of her heart. Koka smelled like spicy aftershave overlaid with limes and pineapple. Had this exceptionally attractive man really gotten aroused by her teasing? It was going to take a long while before she'd ever find the nerve to explore such a prospect—like years probably. She sighed over how much her dating cowardice was going to limit her life. It was a real effort to rein her longing in and smile at him like she didn't have a care in the world.

"How about you make me dessert and we'll call it even on the favors? I'm having the best first date ever and that's not even an exaggeration. Joe is going to be incredibly jealous. That achievement alone is worth every cent I donated on your behalf."

Dropping his hand from her cheek at her resumed teasing, Koka walked around to the stove again. "How does fried rum bananas sound?" he asked.

"It sounds as delicious as the rest of the dinner. I'm gaining weight just thinking about it," Sabine said.

Koka stopped his preparations and came back to lean over the counter as far as he could to get close to her. "I think you're beautiful with your golden hair and smiling eyes. But it is your kind heart that draws me most. The rest of your body has me curious because that is the nature of every man. I want to ask you a question before the rich dessert puts you into a food coma and clouds your mind."

"If it's anything legal, the answer is probably going to be yes. And that's not the fried rum bananas talking yet," Sabine joked.

"Be serious for a moment," Koka ordered. "Will you go out with me again? On a real date? This is a serious request."

Sabine groaned. "No . . . don't ask me that. You're going to bankrupt me."

"*Bankrupt you?* That's hopefully another joke, but I'll gladly give you back the money you spent on my behalf yesterday if you would say yes. What do you say to that level of honesty?" Koka demanded.

Sabine leaned back in her chair, way back. "Didn't you see that room full of beautiful, screaming women? I'm sure one or two of them would be way more suitable for you. The ink is barely dry on my divorce decree and. . .well. . .I have a lot to work out in my mind before I can date anyone."

"Until yesterday I have been saying all women I meet are like the one at the back of the room who bid so fiercely against you. Those women don't really want me, Sabine. They want to be fixed, to be made alive, to become something more because of being seen with *The Sexy Chef*, with *Todd Lake*. True compassion is absent from them. I'm tired of women like that. But you are not like that. I can read your heart and I'm rarely wrong," Koka said, pointing his spatula at her.

He was disappointed at Sabine's nervous gaze darting around as it avoided his. Unable to think of anything else to say that might persuade her to go out with him, Koka turned and started preparing their dessert. The task at least kept him from going back and trying to physically convince her. Pride was pushing him to either ignore Sabine or seduce her. There seemed to be no polite middle ground in his feelings.

Sabine stared at Koka's strong back as he cooked, her gaze not even dropping to his appealing backside this time. Instead, all she could see was the invisible weight his too public life had put between his shoulder blades. It was an unfortunate by-product of her job to notice such things, one she could see now was going to cost her a hell of a potential romance with the man across the counter. Koka Whitman was part jaded and part innocent. But his vulnerability was something she wasn't ready to violate for the sake of an amazing date or even ending her long streak of celibacy.

A date with the sexy, fun, and talented man was more appealing than pretty much anything that had happened to her in a decade. But it wouldn't be fair for her to work out her dating issues at Koka's expense. For all the female attention he drew, he didn't understand that all women were a bit like the woman at the back of the auction room—even her. A woman's sexuality was just as rampant as any man's. Men who looked like him quickly discovered that not all women managed to keep their beast side in check.

She was vulnerable too, but worse she was needy. Martin had shredded her sexual identity when he had re-married before she had even had a chance to take a deep breath. Even counting the last two years of separate bedrooms in her favor, there were a hundred other little demons she still had to wrestle about getting naked with a new man. Clothing might even be one of those demons if Koka was right about all men wanting a look at what she was hiding. Tonight her soft, aging body had morphed from a matter of acceptance into yet another big obstacle to moving forward with her romantic life.

"I'm more flattered than I could ever say that you would ask me out. But I don't know if I'm ready for a real date yet," Sabine said softly. "When I am ready, I could let you know—in case you might still want to date me then."

Koka plated the still sizzling bananas and drizzled more coconut rum over them. "Well, at least it's not a complete rejection," he groused.

"Oh come on—you can't be that heartbroken. Be honest here. Does a woman ever say no to you? If so, I imagine it doesn't happen often," Sabine said quietly.

"No, it doesn't happen often. But lately I haven't even felt like asking. You're the first in almost a year who has even interested me."

Sabine nodded in sympathy. "Then I'm even more flattered."

He grabbed two spoons and headed around the bar to her. When he got back to his seat, he scooped up a bite as he sat. "Open your mouth," he ordered.

Sabine snorted again. "I bet you like to be in control all the time, don't you? See—things would never work between us. I like to be in control as well."

"Sabine, stop talking and open your mouth for me," Koka said more firmly, envying the spoon he held for getting to go where he wanted to.

She stared at the spoon for long moments trying to decide. When she finally did open her mouth, a bite of heaven slipped inside. Flavors of the rum, the banana, and spices she didn't recognize slid along her tongue. She swallowed and sighed. "Okay. That's pretty amazing. My high standards are more than met."

"I know. And I made it for kissing," Koka declared, staring at spot on her lip that she unconsciously licked clean. "The flavors lubricate the palette and it has spices that neutralize dinner smells and tastes."

Sabine felt her eyebrows rise, but smiled at his innocent look. "I swear to God—that is the best line to ask for a kiss that I have ever heard."

Swearing under his breath at her relentless teasing, Koka scooped up another bite for her and fed her again. Then he scooped one for himself using the same spoon. He dared her to say a word about it.

She pondered the decadence of having Koka feed her and the intimacy of sharing the dish with him. Even if it was just some practiced seduction or clever intention to charm her, his serious frown would have kept her from believing it completely. On the next scoop, she placed her hand over his.

"That's enough of that for me. I think I'm ready for my real dessert now," she said, holding his quizzical gaze. "Let's test your kissing theory."

Fearing the offer might be retracted if he didn't accept it quickly, he leaned forward and pressed his lips gently, but firmly to hers. Banana, coconut, and Sabine hit his taste buds. It was a heady combination. He pulled away reluctantly. "I cannot trust myself for more than one kiss. You are completely delicious."

41

"So are you," Sabine whispered, her mouth still amazed at the lingering tingle.

Koka sighed, frustrated to have to let her go home. Pekala's prayers had been answered in a way that surprised even him. "The limousine that brought you is no doubt waiting impatiently. I was supposed to send you home thirty minutes ago. Pekala delayed the schedule."

Sabine nodded and slid from her chair. "Pekala was a wonderful delay and I'm very glad I got to meet her."

She walked on shaky legs to the small table where her purse had landed earlier. That simple little kiss had rocked her harder than she realized. On her way back, Sabine paused by the seat where Koka still sat unmoving. Evidently, he wasn't going to walk her to the door.

Maybe he couldn't do so yet.

The thought that she had caused him more masculine discomfort after their kiss went to her head faster than his pineapple cocktail. She looked at Koka and wanted to find out more than she wanted to take her next breath. She ached for the chance she was too afraid to take, but thanks to him she now believed she would one day have a sex life after Martin.

"Thank you for one of the best evenings of my entire life. I truly will never forget the pleasure of it—*all of it*," Sabine emphasized softly.

"On the islands, we say *Mahalo* to give thanks," Koka said, his gaze asking her to act on what was in hers.

Sabine nodded and smiled, the effort forced. "*Mahalo* then. Good night, Koka Whitman. Thank you for a wonderful dinner."

"Happy Valentine's Day, Sabine," Koka said.

"Seriously the best one for me that I can ever remember having," Sabine replied.

Then she walked to the door as quickly as she could to make her escape.

CHAPTER 6

Joe held up the special edition Sunday afternoon paper and looked at Sabine over the edge of it as he grunted.

"Your very expensive Todd Lake told all of Seattle that you were the most enchanting woman he'd met in years. All you said about him was that he was a great chef. Sabine, you're in public relations for pity's sake. Couldn't you have thought of something more eloquent to say about a date with one of Seattle's premier bachelors?"

"Todd Lake is a great chef," Sabine said firmly. She wasn't explaining herself no matter how hard Joe glared. It was bad enough that she was struggling with the guilt Joe was causing. First she hadn't even bothered to wear a dress to dinner when Koka's show had sent a limo for her. Now she was having morning after guilt for not kissing him back like she had wanted to.

Normally, she was a woman who made plans and took actions. Indecision was a torture to her nature. She knew it wasn't logical to be on the fence about a relationship that didn't have great odds of working out. They had flirted, but that meant nothing these days. He was a sweet man, but so far out of her playing league she couldn't stay in the same park as him.

Frustrated with her depressing thoughts, Sabine glared over her coffee at Joe. "Since when are you such a poet? What did you and your Todd say about each other the day after his first public outing on a man date?"

Ignoring her glare, Joe went back to reading the interviews. "Our situation is different. My Todd is still cautious about coming out all the way. In our interviews, we each sort of joked about the dinner being nothing overly important. I said he was a good sport for putting up with a flaming gay like me for the evening."

"Well there. Doesn't that just sum it all up? We both said what was necessary to protect our dates from excessive media hype and negative speculation."

Sabine dropped her gaze from Joe and turned her attention back to her lackluster meal. The reason she had called Joe to come over was because she couldn't stop thinking about Koka's banana and rum flavored kiss. It had haunted her all night. And Joe was not making things better with his nagging questions.

"I will never believe it was nothing more than a simple meal. I saw the way the man looked at you. Whatever *The Sexy Chef* might have fixed for dinner, tasting you was high up on his menu plans," Joe said bluntly. "And you haven't said if it happened or not. Want me to guess?"

Sabine ignored the uncomfortably accurate comment and went back to eating her dry chicken. "Last evening is a blur now. I had most of a bottle of champagne in the limo, some killer pineapple shooter concoction he invented, and then a third glass of something I couldn't identify with the two entrees he cooked. I was in coma after all that. Limo transport is the only reason I made it home in one piece."

"I'm not buying any I-was-too-tipsy excuse either," Joe said, folding the paper. "It's okay if you don't want to tell me what really happened. You have a right to protect your privacy even from someone who has known you for a couple decades."

Sabine sighed. "How do you do that? How do you make me feel guilty for no good reason? Okay look Joe—I know I promised you three thousand on a second bet, but I'll be damned if I spend one more cent on your hare-brained ideas where any man named Todd is involved."

Joe slapped the table in triumph. "*I knew it.* I knew I was right. He asked you out."

Sabine nodded. "Yes, he did ask me—but I said no."

When Joe looked deeply disappointed, Sabine wanted to laugh.

"Come on. It was not the kind of evening a newly divorced woman should take too seriously. I'm not ready to date a normal guy yet, much less one that looks as good as Todd Lake does. Martin already did enough damage to my ego. I'm not ready to risk letting another guy have a go at it. Besides . . . I would only be an additional complication in the man's already complicated enough life."

Joe shook his head. "Pulling the freshly divorced card doesn't work with me either, Sabine. I know you and Martin were over long before you two divorced. Don't you know how lucky you are to find someone actually worth dating?"

"I didn't say Todd Lake wasn't worth dating. Don't put words into my mouth," Sabine ordered.

To make a point, she filled said orifice with another bite of tasteless food while she watched Joe throw up his hands. She loved Joe, but he was definitely a drama queen when he didn't get his way.

"Sabine, you got your very own valentine delivered neatly into your hands and you threw the damn card away before you even read what it said. That was a very dumb move, woman. You need to take flowers to where Todd Lake works and apologize for your cowardice."

"Give it up, Joe. He was the wrong valentine, or at the very least, not one meant to be mine for more than one dinner. In a week, he will have forgotten all about me. I'm just one tiny fish in the vast sea of his adoring female fans."

"No. I don't buy that at all. I saw the way he looked at you Friday night. Unless you were super bitchy to him over his pineapple concoctions, his heart is breaking right now because of your refusal. The man was interested—like sincerely interested. Do you know how rare that is?"

"Shut up, Joe."

"No, I won't shut up, and don't give me that disbelieving look. I swear, talking to you is like talking to a wall sometimes. If Martin wasn't my brother, I'd go kick his ass for making you feel like you're not attractive. Because you are, even if you are older and curvier than that bony plastic doll Martin married. Hell, even my Todd said you were hot. He made me think he was going to turn out to be bi the way he went on and on about you."

Sabine hid her face in her hand. "Joe, can we *please* drop this discussion? When I start dating again, it's going to be some normal guy. Todd Lake is going to end up with one of those soccer mom workout queen types. The man's muscles have muscles. The only working muscle I have is my brain."

"Oh, I bet you have a few others he would find appealing. I bet he has some you'd like as well. That's the full benefit of actively dating, sweetheart."

Sabine pointed her empty fork at her torturer. "I will get laid in my own time and in my own way. I'm not using that sweet man for casual sex no matter how gorgeous he is. I like him, but he's just not right for me. Now *please* . . . let's change the subject. Finish your dinner before it gets even more inedible. Last night may have just ruined me for cooking my own food."

45

"I'm hoping it's ruined you for a lot more than that," Joe said, picking up his fork. "Want to bet he comes up with a way to be in your life?"

Sabine laughed at Joe's endless optimism. "Valentine's Day is over, Joe. You can drop the romantic stuff now."

"Fine. I'll skip the romance. But I bet dating sexy Todd Lake is going to look like a much better prospect when you see the double-D assets my new sister-in-law got compliments of your retirement."

Sabine snorted and glared. "Why are we friends?"

Joe made a smoochy motion with his lips and kissed the air. "Because as a man who fell in love with you at first sight, I immediately saw the signs when Todd Lake did the same thing."

"This is the sad story of my love life. My husband left me for a skinny woman and a gay man loves me madly," Sabine said. She rested her fork on her plate and gave up trying to eat. "And this has got to be the worst meal I've ever cooked for another human being. Don't eat it, Joe. I'll give you money to buy takeout on your way home."

Joe looked at his food and back at her. "You're just having withdrawals. Plus, I'm a way better friend than that. Now go open a can of pineapple for dessert. After I eat this, I'll sing Blue Hawaii while you dance the hula."

Sabine thought of what Koka might say if he ever heard Joe being flippant about his homeland and culture. He would probably make some incredibly nasty insult in his native language and say it meant something benign like "thank you for smiling". But she would know the truth by that little huff of exasperation Koka would make when Joe looked merely pleased at the poetic sounding Hawaiian words.

"Are you thinking about Elvis before or after the banana sandwiches?" Joe asked.

Shaking her head at his teasing, all Sabine could do was laugh at them both.

***

At her request, her day nurse, Denise, opened the newspaper and began to read. Suddenly, she laughed. Pekala searched the younger woman's face trying to decide if she wanted to know what had been said or not.

"My old eyes make it too hard to read. What does it say?" Pekala finally demanded.

"Your grandson called the woman *enchanting*," Denise said, emphasizing the old-fashioned word.

"That's beautiful. Why is that funny?" Pekala asked, wrinkling her wrinkles in her confusion.

Denise laughed again. "The woman said he was a great chef."

Pekala chuckled at Sabine's understatement. "No wonder he's off lifting weights instead of cooking us dinner. She said nothing to give him any hope."

"How long will he stay mad over this?" Denise asked. Her personal infatuation with her good-looking employer had died swiftly with the first sample of his sullen moods. The man never smiled—not really. He was kind to Pekala, but that was the only evidence of warmth.

Pekala shrugged. "Who knows? Koka is very much like my husband who only smiled over one thing. I did my best as his wife to make sure he smiled often."

***

Koka pushed the bar and the weights up until his arms trembled. Then he let the bar drop down with a loud clang into the bench brackets where it struck metal against metal. Normally, the sound made him cheerful because it meant the workout had ended. A professional trainer had started his program, but he continued it because he enjoyed the results.

Until today.

Now he was sweaty, tired, and still frustrated beyond what a sane man could handle without going mad. Sabine Blakeman was all he could think about—including her incessant teasing and that soft, hot mouth of hers connected to his. She had licked his kiss from her lips after, and he had been afraid to move for fear of what he would do.

The woman had intrigued him from the moment she had stood up in the auction and yelled at Felicity—or Hayden—or whatever that woman's name had been that he'd dated as a favor to Edwina. Neither she nor her name had lingered in his mind for a second whereas the soft, round blonde with a warped sense of humor continued to star in the endless fantasies playing through his mind non-stop.

He should have really kissed her. He should have devoured her while he had the chance because her disgust would have been better than the torment of not knowing what the rest of her was like. The lightning bolt of lust that had struck him was worse than what he'd felt for his first love—the mother of his child—the woman who had slept with a seventeen-year-old when she was in love with another man. He thought nothing would ever compare to the torture of watching his first and only

47

love marry someone other than him, but he'd survived it finally. There had been other women since that first one—temporary women. Certainly, he was not an easy man and most women hadn't lingered long.

But he'd thought he'd understood a lot of things about love and life and himself until he'd talked to Sabine. The woman had told the newspaper he was nothing more than a great chef. Well, he was a lot more than a chef. And at thirty-seven he should have a more grounded sense of himself. So why didn't he?

Losing his parents as a teenager had hurt. Losing the mother of his child had hurt too, but at least he'd gotten to keep his daughter—mostly. Now she had gone to college and his life was more empty. But if he lost Pekala too . . . No. He would not let himself dwell on that loss. Pekala was ready to go. She had told him as much. "Just send my body home to the islands after" had been her only command to him.

But what kind of life would he have without her support? Of what real value was a TV show that bored him in a dreary city where sunshine was rare? It paid well, but fame was not what he wanted for his life. Gaining more fame was not worthy of being his dream. He wanted to see pleasure on the faces of those he fed. That was the purest joy. Only kissing the soft-mouthed Sabine had held near as much satisfaction for him.

"When was the last time I felt like I had to have a woman or die?" He asked the question aloud hoping his mind would provide a quick answer. But he honestly couldn't remember wanting a woman this badly since the first one he had wanted half his life ago. Sabine's kiss had made the longing even stronger than when she had stood to bid for him. Had he really fallen in love so quickly?

"*Ka Honi Mai Me Ke Aloha*," Koka whispered, thinking once more of his mouth on hers.

As he went to shower, he prayed fervently to the goddess for another chance.

48

CHAPTER 7

Koka ran a hand over his face. He could not remember feeling so desperate since he was younger than Halia. *What was the matter with the woman?* Sabine was ignoring his phone calls and had removed voice mail from her phone so he couldn't even leave her messages.

He hadn't lowered himself enough yet to actually chase her down at her place of business, but he wasn't far from doing that.

First though, he had an idea that would let her see him again in a public situation where she might feel safer. And it would provide him another chance to convince her to go out with him.

"Edwina, I want you to invite Sabine Blakeman to be a guest on the show," Koka said flatly.

Edwina stared at the most difficult talent she managed in complete disbelief. "You want me to ask the auction woman to come on your show and do a guest spot? Do you know what she does for a living?"

"Yes. I had Sabine thoroughly investigated. As you know, the last stalker made me cautious. I investigate anyone now that makes me nervous, even in a good way," Koka said.

Edwina blinked in shock. "You had the woman investigated? Well I sure didn't see that coming. Sabine Blakeman's online profile at the PR company she works for says she's an image consultant. That means she helps people improve their public persona. Inviting her on the show is like giving her company thousands of dollars worth of free advertising. I don't know if the execs will go for it."

"Ask anyway," Koka ordered. "She's ignoring my phone messages and I want to see her again. Be discrete though. Sabine will be less likely to rebel against this if she thinks this is your idea."

Edwina snickered at the high school approach Koka was taking in pursuit of the woman, but fortunately caught the full laugh before it escaped. "Not to be crude, but I just have to ask this. Why are you chasing a chubby, older blonde when attractive women fall at your feet wherever you walk?"

Koka frowned at Edwina's description of Sabine. "Chubby? I don't think she's chubby at all. But Sabine's physical attractiveness is not the only reason I'm interested. I like her, Edwina. Sabine may be my *Ke Aloha*. I am only asking you to help our fate along."

Edwina studied her most finicky talent while he stared serenely back at her. The man's expression gave nothing away. Surely Koka had to know how strange his request was, at least the part she understood. He knew damn well she didn't speak Hawaiian.

"The woman couldn't have been that good," she said finally.

Koka sighed heavily. "Do not harass me over the first real favor I have asked of you. Just do this, Edwina. You said we needed to start inviting guests on the show. You invite Sabine and I'll do one with the woman that wrote that book you love."

Her eyebrows shot up in the air. "I stand corrected. Evidently, she was that good. Okay, you have a deal."

"But Edwina—no Sabine, no author either," Koka warned.

"Oh, I got that was part of the deal," Edwina said sharply. "No worries. I'm just as good at my job as you are at yours, Chef Lake."

"I am counting on it," Koka declared. "It's my last resort before I go to her work."

Edwina shook her head. "Is the woman really worth all this trouble?"

"Her ex-husband married someone much younger right after they divorced. From what I learned, there were several younger women before that one. Sabine sees herself through his eyes still. It makes my sincere interest in her seem unbelievable. However, she knows I would reject that reasoning which is why she is avoiding me. She knows I would make sure she puts her past away."

"I can't believe you seriously got all that from one dinner with her. You never fail to surprise the hell out of me," Edwina declared. "Now *I* want to talk to Sabine just to see what kind of woman snagged the heart of *The Sexy Chef*."

"You know I hate that moniker," Koka said.

"And yet you wear it so damn well," Edwina declared, grinning at his glare. "I'll get back to you after I've spoken with Sabine."

50

"Thank you. This means a lot to me," Koka said, breathing a sigh of relief as he walked to Edwina's office door. At least he had done something productive today about resolving his problem with Sabine. He would have to content himself with that until she showed up.

***

"No, Blanche," Sabine said. "This involves my personal life, not my business one. The man asked me out. I said no because I wanted to say no. End of story. The rest is no one's business but mine."

She ignored Blanche's look of disbelief and went back to her paperwork.

"Maybe you didn't hear what I said. Todd Lake's producer called Anthony. They want you on his show to promote their matching contribution to the charity *Seattle Live* supported. What the hell happened on your date, Sabine? The man is chasing you full out. And why in the hell are you running away so hard?"

"Nothing happened on our so-called date. Chef Lake fixed me dinner and sent me home in the limo *Seattle Live* paid for. That's all," Sabine said, not raising her gaze.

Blanche snorted. "*Bullshit*—but that's beside the point. Anthony told them you'd do it without checking first. It never occurred to him that you'd turn down an opportunity to be on *Seattle Live*. If you refuse to do the show, Anthony's going to shit bricks and be extremely embarrassed. He said they even offered to pay for your appearance if you wanted money."

"Great. Tell them I want six thousand dollars," Sabine joked, not really serious. She just was tired of talking to Blanche about her evening with Koka.

"Fine. I'll get Anthony to call them back and give them your price," Blanche declared.

"Stop—don't you dare." Sabine huffed out a breath and swore as she tossed down the pen she'd been using. "Damn it, Blanche. I wore my blue tunic, black leggings, and flats. I did not wear a dress or stripper heels or even talk all that nice to him. The man fixed me dinner—that's all that happened. I swear."

"If that's really all that happened, then going on his show should cause you no problems at all. Right? I'll just tell Anthony you're happy to do it," Blanche declared, crossing her arms.

Sabine found herself locked in a stare down with her immediate boss, but in the end, she was the one that looked away first. "I can't believe Anthony would expect me to do this. I'm not going to date the man just because Anthony wants a social connection to Todd Lake. There will be no favors asked as

51

a result of this. He's a good person. I won't tolerate him being used because of his connection to me."

"Listen to you. Who said anything about exchanging favors? Anthony didn't call *Seattle Live*. They called *us*—about *you*. Chef Lake is the one asking. I can't believe you're not fainting with joy that *The Sexy Chef* is crushing on you. Was he like crass or gross? Did he ask you to play naughty games?"

"Stop it, Blanche," Sabine said. She couldn't listen to another insinuation. "He was the perfect gentleman and the perfect host. The food was wonderful. It was an incredible evening. I'm just not ready to date. I told him that."

"Then what—for the love of God—is your problem with going on his show?" Blanche demanded. "You'll both be on a set full of professional people filming. You're not even going to be alone with him."

Sabine leaned back in her chair and groaned. "You don't understand how complicated this is. When I went to that damn auction, I bid on the wrong man. Todd Lake was not who I went to win, but I made a mistake. So I ended up with the wrong Todd and we both made the best of the situation. Maybe if Chef Lake had come along a year or two from now, things might be different. Who knows? But at the moment, I'm not ready to date one of Seattle's premiere bachelors. That's my final decision on the matter."

"Woman, you need to get some serious therapy. Do you know how hard it is to find someone really worth dating in this town? If you don't get it now, you will in a year or two of bar trolling and online dating services. I'm telling Anthony that you're excited about doing the show. You can thank me later for lying for you. In the meantime, you need to find a way to manufacture some positive emotion for it even if you don't feel any for the man every other red-blooded, normal woman is drooling over."

Sabine glared. "Are you saying I have no choice but to do the damn show?"

Blanche glared back. "I'm saying none of us do, Sabine. And if you ever want to make partner in this firm, you better put on your big girl panties and buy a dress that makes you look thin on TV. You just became a high-profile spokeswoman for the company. Maybe if you're really lucky, something will knock some sense into your head and you'll say yes to anything Todd Lake offers you. Honey, men like him don't come sniffing around very often."

Too upset to discuss the matter any longer, Sabine got up and stomped out of her own office, leaving Blanche following behind shaking her head.

***

"Go away. I don't want to talk to you either. If I hear the name *Todd* tonight, I may just scream."

Joe laughed as he patted Sabine's back. "You're going to need something a lot stronger than diet soda to take the edge off that kind of mad. I'd recommend sex to burn it off, but I guess that's out of the question since you keep turning down dates."

Sabine snorted. "He actually tricked me. His producer called my CEO to ask me to be a guest on his show. Anthony said yes and Blanche ordered me to do it. Apparently, I have no say in the matter. Why should my career be jeopardized by my refusal to date?"

"What are you complaining about? It's not like it's a real date. It's a TV show," Joe said, fighting not to grin at *The Sexy Chef's* cleverness. "So technically you're still holding out on him. I don't know why you would want to, but hey, I'm willing to validate your insanity for a little while longer."

Sabine stared into her drink, frowning as she pondered what she had to do. "I am under orders to buy a dress that makes me look thirty pounds thinner—for the good of the company's image. I'll have to wear two layers of spandex just to go down one size."

"Blanche didn't use the F word did, she?" Joe demanded.

Sabine shook her head. "No. But it was *heavily* implied."

"Ha. Ha. Was that whining you just did supposed to be a weight joke?"

Sabine pushed the cola aside enough to lay her forehead on the table. "He asked me why I hid my body from men. Did I tell you that?"

Joe's eyebrows rose. "And what did you tell him?"

"Nothing. I said nothing. I shut up and licked my fork while he watched and drooled," Sabine reported.

Joe's loud laughter had all eyes turning to their table. "You must really like him to tease him that way."

"I do really like him," Sabine admitted. "But can you imagine what would happen if we dated? Every newspaper and magazine would be posting all the fat photos they can find of me. All the scorned women that he's ignored would be laughing their asses off that someone with a body like his would be interested in someone so average and normal like me. I do this

53

publicity thing for a living, Joe. I know what kind of press a TV celebrity who looks like him generates."

"Wait . . . I'm confused. I thought this was about your insecurities, not your Todd's popularity with his female viewers," Joe said. "Because I can tell you honestly that real men don't care about a few extra pounds on a woman—or man in my case. And sweetie, that's all you have. What they care about is a willing, hot body. Talented fork licking would be considered a huge bonus."

"Oh, shut up. You're gay. How would you know what a heterosexual man likes?" Sabine demanded.

"I have three mega heterosexual brothers. Besides—fork licking is a non-gender specific talent appreciated by all. I'm sure you know that at your age. If you don't, you have permission to kill my younger brother for being so totally worthless in bed. I'm sure Mom wouldn't miss him at all because she's still mad at him for cheating on you."

"Martin wasn't totally worthless. If he had been, I would never have stayed with him so long. He was plenty talented in bed. He just wasn't faithful. But he—like most men—liked his women to look better than he did. Every time he cheated on me, he blamed it on my lack of caring about what I looked like."

"Well what else was he supposed to say to the perfect woman and mother of his children? He's afraid of getting old and dying. You know that's Martin's problem. He hyperventilates every time he sees a new wrinkle on his own face, much less yours. Why are we rehashing this?" Joe demanded.

"Because I ignored his petty excuses about cheating, but now I'm the one panicking over how I look. There's not enough time to fix myself to go on any TV show. I let Martin's behavior depress me, and the next thing I knew, I was forty and round. I validated his complaints by making them my reality. Hell, I was sleeping alone anyway. What did I care what I looked like?"

"Sabine, how many of your friends have solid relationships despite carrying around a little extra weight?"

"Several I suppose," Sabine admitted.

"Then only you can decide how important it is for you to look a certain way, and whether or not it's going to stop you from finding happiness," Joe said. "You look great. Most people think you're in your thirties and those mythical pounds you see in the mirror aren't even noticeable. You're just afraid Martin might be right. Let Todd Lake prove him wrong.

"Next time Blanche tells me I need therapy, I'm going to give her your phone number," Sabine said.

Joe shrugged. "When you forget to judge yourself—or forget to do that stupid comparison thing—you are so damn charming that every guy wants a piece of you. Chef Lake tapped that best side with less effort than any man I've ever seen cross your path. That's pretty rare."

Sabine swore softly as she realized she was about to fall in line with plans she really wanted no part of. Maybe she should just call Koka back and get the "real date" he wanted over with. Maybe she should ask him to come scratch her current itch so they could both get some relief from their non-dating.

"I guess tomorrow I'm shopping for industrial strength spandex and a fitted black dress," Sabine said, thinking how uncomfortable all that would be.

"You're thinking about it all wrong. Don't downplay the negative. Instead, highlight the positive. Get your hair curled and fluffed, and buy a fitted red dress with a full skirt. Show as much breast and leg as possible without being obscene. It is just a cooking show after all."

Sabine rolled her eyes. "I'll look like an outdated fifties housewife trying to fit into the sixties."

Joe grinned. "Yes. But you'll also look like a skinny Marilyn Monroe. How's that for a perspective?"

Sabine leaned over and laid her head on Joe's shoulder as he laughed. "I love you. I truly love you."

"I know, baby. I know. But you need to give your Todd a chance to replace me. My love life is doing a lot better than yours. I won't always be available to mop up after your pity parties. It's time for you to get cheerfully laid."

"Okay," Sabine said, sitting upright again. "Red dress. Fitted top. Show some boob. I can do this."

"Just be prepared for a stronger reaction than you got to the fork licking," Joe warned.

Sabine closed her eyes and thought once again of banana rum flavored kisses.

CHAPTER 8

"She's here," Edwina informed her nervous chef, marveling at the way Koka's face lit up as his gaze searched the set. "Well, not *here—here* yet. They're touching up her makeup, but she looks great. All that fluffy hair makes you focus on her face more than the rest of her. She'll do well on camera. So you like blondes, eh?"

Koka shook his head. "Not necessarily. I just like Sabine."

"Right," Edwina said, hiding her grin in her hand. *Like* was an understatement. "Okay. Let's get prepped. We'll start filming when your Sabine arrives. The audience is being seated now."

"Audience? We have a live audience today?" Koka asked, inwardly cursing. He didn't like the pressure of retakes being done in front of a crowd. Today, he also didn't like the idea of them watching him with Sabine.

"Yes. We figured we'd pan to their faces now and again to get an assessment of their interest in a guest's interaction with you," Edwina explained.

There was little more he could say against it since people were already taking their seats, so Koka nodded and went back to laying out what he would need on the shelves below his counter.

***

Wearing what had to be half a tube of red lipstick, Sabine trailed slowly down the *Seattle Live* corridor behind the assistant they had sent to collect her. She put a nervous hand on her stomach and breathed out in relief as she felt the waist of her dress still snugly holding her in. It boosted her confidence greatly to feel her body so well restrained inside the fabric.

Taking Joe's advice, she had bought a dress that was red and full. The dip in the front was more cleavage revealing than her normal clothing, but she had decided a 'what the hell' attitude would serve her best. She at least looked sexy and hot from the waist up. She just hoped one chocolate-eyed male agreed.

"Just walk around the curtain, Ms. Blakeman. Try to ignore the audience. They tend to react to anything new, but they'll settle down in no time once you become part of the set. Most say they forget about them as the show progresses."

"Thank you—and thanks for the advice," Sabine said, smiling goodbye at the intern as she proceeded forward.

But as she stepped out into the open set, everyone was suddenly invisible to her except for the man in a blue button-up shirt wearing an apron with *Kiss The Sexy Chef* emblazoned across his wide chest. With sleeves rolled to his elbows, Koka looked ready for kitchen duty. When he turned around and bent to retrieve something from a lower cabinet, his khaki slacks molded way too excellently to his extraordinary rear. Excitement zapped most of her remaining brain cells. A fine sheen of sweat suddenly challenged the mineral powder they had brushed on every inch of her exposed skin just minutes ago.

Her sigh over her feminine reaction must have alerted him to her presence because Koka's head snapped up as he turned and looked for her. Then when he saw her, the man who obviously didn't care what anyone thought just stopped and stared. His assessing gaze raked every inch while her face turned the same color as her dress. How in the world did he have the ability to affect her with just a look? If she hadn't felt her job credibility was on the line, she might have pretended to be sick and fled from the intentions in his gaze.

Out of the corner of her eye, Sabine could see that many of the workers on the set had stopped their tasks as well. But they weren't looking at her. Oh no. They were looking at Koka staring at her while he remained frozen in place. Mentally pulling up big girl panties that she wished she could reach under her skirt and adjust for real, Sabine walked forward until she stood just on the other side of what appeared to be a long counter with a sink built into it. Clearing her throat, she put on her brave face and spoke.

"Hello, Chef Lake. Good to see you again."

Koka nodded at Sabine's lukewarm greeting, unsure whether or not he still had the power of speech after staring at her so long. He cleared his throat like she had, just to be sure. "Nice dress—really nice dress. It suits you."

Ignoring the reaction of her body to his compliment, Sabine searched for professionalism. "So where do you want me?"

Koka's gaze went down to Sabine's red heels and back up again. "We better save that answer for later or this show is never going to get taped."

"*I meant for the show*," Sabine hissed. "Will you please stop staring at me? Everyone is looking at us."

"I'm trying to do just that, but it's nearly impossible. Now I understand why you were hiding yourself, *Ku`u Lei*." He grinned at the flash of annoyance in her gaze. "Come around the counter. You'll be standing in the kitchen area with me during the show. They taped an X on the floor where you'll be most of the time."

"Can I sit until we get started?" she asked. She walked slowly around the counter until she could smell his unique aftershave again. Her stomach fluttered and her pulse jumped at his nearness. He brushed against her arm as he pulled a stool over to her marked spot.

"Here you go. If you want to take those pretty shoes off, I don't mind," he said, pointing to her feet. "I'm wishing I could do it for you. I would like that very much in fact. They make you look very sexy."

"*Stop doing that. You're embarrassing me*," Sabine hissed. "I'm a woman over forty. My face is not supposed to be red all the time."

"That's a matter of opinion. I happen to think that's a good thing," Koka said, staring down at the part in her hair when she looked away. "No one can hear us. Your body mic is not turned on yet. Are you truly embarrassed by my feelings for you?"

Sabine snorted. "There are a hundred strangers staring at us right now, wondering what the hell we're whispering about. Actually, I'm more worried about what they're thinking."

Koka grinned. "I'm sure some are wise enough to figure it out. I am trying to behave, Sabine. I'm only saying a fraction of what I'm thinking."

"Try harder. You're making me nervous. If I screw up, my boss and her boss are going to fire me," Sabine declared.

"*Anthony?* I don't think so. I found him to be a very accommodating man. That's a good trait in people you do business with," Koka said.

"Yes, well—that's what you said you admired in women too," Sabine said sharply. When Koka laughed, she felt stares on her again. "See? They're all looking at us."

"They're probably growing more and more curious about how long it's going to take me to act on my attraction to you. I feel like I'm broadcasting it with my eyes, but I do not think I mind. For the first time in a long time, I am happy to be openly connected to a woman."

Uncaring of anyone's judgment, Sabine reached out and smacked his arm as hard as she could to get him to stop staring. Her hand stung from the impact of slapping muscles that felt like rocks. Instead of yelping in pain, the smug bastard gave her a grin instead.

"Where's a good ball bat when you need one?" she grumbled.

"You don't need to be angry to touch me, Sabine. You have my permission to touch me all you want," he said. "And I seriously can't wait for my turn to touch you back. I suggest we discuss it as soon as the show is over. I missed you even more than I realized. I really wish you'd taken my calls."

Sabine's mouth dropped open in surprise at his suggestion of touching her, which went beyond dating and straight to the possibility of fulfilling the fantasies she had been having about him. Her brain suggested a smartass response, but only a tiny squeak actually escaped her throat.

A woman's voice nearby interrupted the inner debate she was having about how best to kill him.

"Hello, Sabine. I'm Edwina Winston. We spoke on the phone," Edwina said, her mouth twitching at the glare the woman gave a grinning Koka.

"Nice to meet you. Sorry if I made you uncomfortable just now. Chef Lake was being rude. His particular brand of smartassness seems to bring out the worst in me," Sabine said, returning the woman's smile. "I promise to ignore him better once the cameras start rolling."

"Don't spare him any punishment on my behalf," Edwina said firmly. "Koka gets treated like a prima donna by enough people. It's fun for me to see him get chastised for his bad behavior."

"I am ready to begin, Edwina. You can go back to producing now," Koka declared.

Sabine snorted at his bossiness. "Who died and make you the big *Kahuna*? I'm a guest. She's the producer. She's just doing her job."

Koka lifted his eyebrow. "Do you defend everyone?"

"No. I almost never defend anyone because it always gets me in trouble. Case in point," Sabine declared, sweeping a hand to include the whole set of his show. "I felt sorry for you at the auction and ended up with the wrong Todd. Now you've blackmailed my boss to get me here. Don't even try to deny that's what you did."

"Why would I deny it when it is true?" Koka asked with a shrug.

"If you two want to defuse the sexual tension between you before the cameras start, you can use my office. You still have twenty minutes," Edwina said.

"There's no tension of any kind between Chef Lake and me. Everything is just peachy," Sabine said, her voice quiet and firm.

Beside her, Koka chuckled at her protests.

"Stop laughing or I'll tell Pekala on you," Sabine ordered.

Edwina laughed at the well-placed threat. Pekala's opinion was the only opinion Koka really cared about. Apparently one date *was* all it had taken.

"Honey, let me tell you about this man. If you keep that chastising stuff up, he might do you right here on the counter if he takes a mind to. *The Sexy Chef* is starting to look determined and everyone around here knows what that means. He's used to getting his way."

"Well, he's in for disappointment with me. And there's nothing like that going on between us. You have nothing to worry about," Sabine insisted.

"Well that makes one of us, but it's not me he's giving the look," Edwina said with a wink, shaking her finger at a still grinning Koka before she walked away.

"We're changing the subject. What are you cooking on the show today?" Sabine asked, desperate to find a normal footing.

"We are making grilled pineapple and pork chops in memory of our dinner together," Koka said. "Please don't lick the fork when I feed you. Between that and the dress, I do not think I can control my animal nature enough to behave. A man can only be so good and then he snaps."

"If you try to feed me on camera, I swear I will bite you," Sabine warned.

Koka froze again as a clear picture of her biting him appeared in his mind, though it probably varied greatly from how Sabine was visualizing her threat.

"After the show," he said hoarsely. "Everything I want must wait until after the show."

Sabine smacked his arm again, standing to pace as she shook her stinging hand.

***

When Edwina yelled that the show was a wrap, Sabine took off at a fast clip to escape.

She had suffered seventy thousand boob grazes from his arms reaching across her in the small kitchen set. The intoxicating smell of Koka sweating aftershave under the hot lights had been a constant torture. Now she was all done. There was no more fight left in her arsenal of denial. Every molecule she possessed was vibrating and turned on and ready to pounce on him if she ever got the chance.

The moment the cameras started, Koka had launched into teacher mode. He had talked smoothly non-stop while moving effortlessly through his preparations. Of course the show's magic was that he'd cooked the final food in advance, so really he was just going through the preparation motions for the audience. For her part, Sabine had answered every question he'd asked her. She had also let him feed her from a fork. It had made her so hot for him that the stupid red lipstick threatened to melt off.

After two hours, her entire body ached with a longing worse than any she could remember ever having for a man. But the torture hadn't stopped with the physical. Oh no. She was mentally confused too.

Why in the hell was Koka so stoic and depressed all the time if he could command a show and an audience with such simple grace? The man had a voice like music, a panty-dropper smile when he bothered to use it, and enough charisma on camera to run for a damn political office.

She couldn't figure him out.

Not that she wanted to figure him out.

But damn. Who was he really?

Sabine dashed into the first women's restroom she came to in the corridor. It turned out to be a tiny one-room version. Sighing in disgust at her reflection in the short mirror, she pulled a handful of tissue from the paper roll to remove the remaining seventeen layers of goop from her mouth. When she was done, her lips were still stained red but at least they felt liberated. Grossed out by the red gloss covered wad in her hand, she tossed it in the trash with a sagging sigh of relief.

Her hand was on the door to leave when an anxious Koka pushed it open and sent her staggering backwards on her stupidly tall heels that she'd worn to impress him. Her arms flailed around trying to help her balance. She ended up grabbing the sink to keep from falling into the toilet.

"Whoa . . . don't fall," Koka said softly. He closed the door quietly behind him as he crowded his enormous bulk into a room that was barely large enough for her.

DONNA MCDONALD

"What the hell are you doing? Did anyone see you come in here?" Sabine yelled.

Koka looked at Sabine in relief because he'd thought she'd run away before he could talk to her. He put out his fingertips to touch her now naked mouth. "*Mahalo nui loa.* I'm so glad you removed the lipstick. It was beautiful, but I do not need such adornments to want this."

Then he stepped into the woman he craved and did what he'd been dying to do since he first saw her two and half long hours ago. He slid his hands around her waist and pulled her to him while he bent and closed his mouth over hers. The fact that it was still slightly open in shock was a happy accident that he silently thanked the goddess for. He nibbled across her plump lower lip and whispered love words while she moaned in his arms. "*E Ku'u Aloha.* I am going to teach you to speak Hawaiian. It is the language of my heart and all my best words must be said in it."

When he let her mouth be free for a few moments, Sabine giggled at what he had said and hid her face in the center of his shirt. "I don't care if you become the next Iron Chef and make national TV. You can't just barge into a woman's bathroom and attack me. It's not fair, Koka."

"What does fair have to do with this? Seeing you in that dress stole my sanity. The kiss was what we both have needed for hours—or at least it was what I needed. I'm sorry if you didn't want it as much as I did."

"*Humility?* You're actually trying to play the humble card? I bet you don't have a humble bone in your entire muscled body," Sabine said. "What the hell am I supposed to do with you?"

Her joking insult netted a result Sabine hadn't anticipated. Koka wrapped a firm hand in her hair and held her head while he kissed her hard and deeply. It robbed her of breath as well as the ability to tease him further. When he turned her loose, she wobbled back on her heels again. In response, he slid hands up her waist until they held the sides of her breasts. He stroked and she thought she might pass out from the pleasure.

"Please date me," he said. "I am dying without you in my life, Sabine."

"*You don't even know who I am,*" Sabine exclaimed, shaking her head even as she leaned into his teasing thumbs.

His answer was yet another mind-blanking kiss, but the hands dropping to her outer thighs jarred her back to reality. He kept her mouth pinned to his as he flipped up her skirt. Then he ran his large, talented hands under it until he cupped her backside like he already owned it. Knowing Koka, he probably

THE WRONG TODD

thought he did. Another urge to giggle rose up but she bravely fought it back. The man was so full of himself that he would undoubtedly see her humor as encouragement.

"Your hands gripping me desperately is not just dating, Koka. That's sex. I like sex and I like you. I'm not going to stand here while you squeeze my butt and pretend I don't like it. I'm just still not sure this is a good idea."

She lost her breath again when Koka bent her backwards as his hands squeezed and lifted her to rub against an erection as hard as his biceps.

"What is dating if not an exploration of a connection? I need you, Sabine. This is a truth. But I want your company too. That is even more important in ways I can't explain well. I haven't laughed since the last time you made me do so," Koka said.

Sabine rubbed herself against him, so close to the edge of madness that little stars danced behind her eyes. It had been years since she'd had a lust-induced orgasm. "You chasing me into the bathroom is going to make me infamous. Don't ask me to trade my reputation and my career for sex with you."

"Do you think this madness is all just you? My brain shut down the moment you rubbed against me and I still know nothing. Was that your way of saying yes to a date?" Koka asked hoarsely. He groaned loudly as he pulled her soft, ready-to-yield body flush against his throbbing, anxious one.

"If you're going to keep chasing me into bathrooms, something has to give. Will Pekala be okay if you come to my house for dinner?" Sabine asked instead of answering directly.

She was trying really hard not to move. Dry humping *The Sexy Chef* in a bathroom was not going to be the story she recalled about her first post-divorce sexual encounter. No matter how hard or amazing or clever his hands were, even a horny divorced woman had to exercise some restraint.

Koka nodded. "Yes. I think my grandmother will be happy that I will not be sulking any longer. I have avoided my kitchen because it was filled with too many happy memories of you."

Sabine groaned at his admission and wrapped her arms around his massive shoulders, sliding her hands up into his freshly cut hair. "Stop. I'm seduced already. My panties are ready to drop. You can quit flirting now."

Her confession had him tightening his grip on her. He put his face in her hair, close to one ear. "Wear the dress for me tonight. Please. I want to enjoy it in private."

Sabine sighed and wondered if he seduced all his women with his pleading commands.

63

"Okay. I'll wear the dress," she said, inwardly shaking her head at her weak-kneed agreement.

Koka made himself ease away from her as he nodded. His tension was both increased and appeased by Sabine's invitation to come to her house. "Why don't you squeeze around me and leave? I need a few moments."

Sabine nodded at the unrepentant, and very masculine, look on his face. "I don't cook like you, so you may regret saying yes."

"Never," Koka said firmly. "Now go while your panties are still in place."

Sabine snorted at his intimate comment, but didn't argue as she traded places with him in the small room. She whispered a soft good-bye before she cracked the door enough to walk out of it.

It took all her willpower to ignore the people in the hallway gaping open-mouthed at her wobbly exit.

CHAPTER 9

Male laughter was just plain annoying sometimes and tonight was definitely one of those. She had better things to do than deal with it.

"Joe, you have to leave right now. He'll be here any minute."

"Don't you own a better apron than that? *Never Trust A Skinny Chef* is not sending the right message when your weight makes you so self-conscious," Joe said, grinning at Sabine's glare. "And I can't leave yet. I owe you for saving my excellent—most excellent Todd. What kind of friend would I be to abandon you in your time of need?"

"Go away, Joe. I'm too busy to verbally play with you," Sabine ordered. She tasted the sauce simmering around her chicken before adding a little more wine.

"Well okay, but I thought you might want me here to diffuse things when Martin shows up to collect his weights from the garage." Joe shrugged. He grinned at the wide-eyed stare he got in response to his statement. "Oh—I see you finally heard me that time. I've been trying to tell you for the last thirty minutes that Martin is coming by to check out your story."

"*Jooooooe—damn it. Nooooo*," Sabine exclaimed, stomping both her bare feet as she danced back and forth in irritation. "Martin can't come tonight. I told him that earlier. Why would he come anyway?"

Joe snorted. "Yeah . . . well . . . you shouldn't have confessed that a date was the reason he couldn't come by this evening. Good thing I happened to be at Martin's house when he called you. The shocked look on his face when he heard what you were doing was kind of alarming actually. My brother will be bringing his possessive ass by here tonight. Trust me."

"*Damn. Damn. Double Damn*," Sabine chanted.

"Yeah, baby. I hear you. You are having some run of bad luck lately," Joe agreed, rubbing her back lightly.

Sabine rolled her eyes just as the doorbell rang. "*Oh shit.*"

"Maybe you need to think of something more eloquent to say outside of swearing this evening. Your Todd didn't seem like the swearing type to me. He seemed like he used language very sparingly and with great import to the meaning of things."

"Thank you, Mr. *Not-Helpful*," Sabine hissed loudly. She untied the apron from her waist and whipped it over her head.

She brushed back her newly fluffed hair with her fingers and smoothed the front of her dress as she left the kitchen. She was at the door when she realized she had no shoes on. Too late to go dashing to her bedroom for the cute heels again. She had kept Koka waiting too long already. Her bare feet couldn't be helped.

Sabine opened the door with a smiling flourish, which faded as she stared up into the most beautiful, freshly shaven masculine face she had ever laid eyes on. "Hi," she said breathlessly, feeling like a dizzy teenager when Koka smiled down at her.

At first sight of her flushing face and welcoming eyes, Koka held out the flowers he brought. "*Aloha,*" he said, the greeting emerging roughly.

"*Aloha,*" Sabine said back, accepting the massive bouquet that filled her arms. "Thank you. I'm not sure I have a vase big enough for all these."

Koka smiled and waited.

"Oh . . . *sorry.* Come in. Please," Sabine said.

Koka walked across the threshold and sniffed. "I smell something wonderful. Chicken Marsala?"

"Hopefully," she replied, not surprised Koka had so accurately identified dinner. "It's been a while since I fixed it for anyone, but I think it will be okay."

Koka smiled and nodded in support. "Can I see your kitchen?"

"Sure. Of course," Sabine said graciously, swallowing hard. "It's not anywhere near as nice as yours, but I fed a family out of it for years."

He stopped mid-stride. "Sabine—why are you so nervous? I'm not going to judge your kitchen. And I'm very happy to see where you live."

Sabine snickered. "Maybe the state of my kitchen is the least of what concerns me this evening."

He lifted her chin with a finger and leaned down to brush her lips gently. "You look stunning in that dress, but relax for now. I promise to warn you before I attack next time. I am in control—at least for the moment."

Sabine swallowed again and nodded. "Well good, that makes one of us at least," she teased, spinning Edwina's warning to fit her current situation.

Koka laughed softly and then heard a noise. "You have other guests?"

Sabine sighed and nodded again, resigned to playing nice even if it killed her. "Yes, but not on purpose," she said firmly. "Come on. I'll officially introduce you to Joe."

They walked into her kitchen and found her friend staring wistfully into her bubbling skillet. Sabine walked to the stove and smacked Joe on the arm. "Quit staring. You're not staying for dinner. I'm having a real date tonight whether anyone likes it or not."

Joe laughed and turned to the sexy stranger standing quietly in Sabine's kitchen. His eyes widened at the freshly shaved, incredibly well-dressed man staring longingly at Sabine's ass as she leaned over the stove. His affection for the superb male was instantaneous. He walked over and extended his hand. "Hi. I'm Joe. Nice to meet you, Mr. Lake."

Koka pulled his gaze from Sabine to offer his hand to the male who looked very much at home in her kitchen. "You're the friend who went to bid on the right Todd. How is that working out for you?"

"So far—so good," Joe reported. "As to whether or not he's the right Todd, I think that depends on who we're talking about. I'm starting to think there might just be two right ones."

"Call me Koka. That's my island name. I prefer friends to use it," Koka said, returning Joe's firm handshake. Then his gaze went back to Sabine's frown over the sizzling pan. "Do you have an apron I could borrow? Maybe I could help with dinner. Please—I would really like to cook with you."

Sabine turned and looked up into his imploring gaze. Should she let him have control here too? She chewed her lip and then the doorbell rang again. *Shit*—Martin.

"Joe, go out the utility room into the garage and let Martin in to get his weights," Sabine ordered, her tone defying any argument.

As Joe grinned and left, Sabine went to her pantry shelf and sifted through a pile of aprons. She wasn't about to give him one of Martin's stupid barbecue ones. Those were going to a charity first chance she got. Sighing, she pulled down the least feminine one she owned and took it to him. It had been a gag gift from her children. Not bothering to even look at it, Koka threw it over his head and deftly fastened the ties behind his back.

"Turn around and let me see," Sabine ordered.

Smiling at her demand, Koka obeyed and did as she asked, holding his hands in the air as he turned. Her snort had him chuckling.

"Unbelievable. Seriously, how do you do that? They're both perfectly even." Glancing up at his laughing eyes, Sabine could tell he was not going to dignify her fascination with a response.

She walked back to her own apron and picked it up just as Martin burst through the utility room doorway into the kitchen. Glaring, the apron ended up in a fisted hand on her hip.

"Martin, the weights are in the garage, not in the kitchen," Sabine said sternly, glaring at her former husband who was staring at Koka in complete shock. Behind him, Joe was laughing uncontrollably. "This is no time for laughing, Joe."

Joe pointed at Koka's chest. "Why did you pick that apron for him, sweetie?"

Confused about Joe's comment, Koka looked down, read his apron, and laughed hard. "*Food Porn Star*—I like it. I need to get one of these for the show. I get tired of wearing *Kiss The Sexy Chef.*"

Sabine felt almost faint when a laughing Koka turned a radiantly white smile in her direction. It was a killer combination paired with the wicked intentions blazing from his eyes.

"You look like a completely different man when you smile like that. You should do it more often. And for your information, I thought that apron was more appropriate than the one that said *Cookie Goddess*. But as much you love drama, maybe *Kitchen Diva* would have been a better choice for you."

"If you stay in my life forever, I will laugh and smile until my last breath," Koka promised, ignoring the other two men for a moment. He held Sabine's startled gaze, pleased that he'd silenced her teasing again with his honesty. Finally though, he had to look at them. It was only polite. He walked to where Joe and his near twin were standing and put out a hand.

"Hello. I'm Todd Lake," Koka said, unwilling to give his real name to the man he suspected was Sabine's ex.

"*You're* Sabine's date?" the man asked, his tone one of shock.

Koka raised an eyebrow. "Yes. Why?"

Sabine watched Martin shake his head in disbelief—*the bastard.* He couldn't believe someone like Koka found her attractive when he no longer did. Well, screw him. She was having enough trouble believing Koka herself. She didn't need more doubts.

"That's enough of being nosy, Martin. I don't go to your house and harass your wife. Now get your weights and leave. Joe will help you," Sabine said. "And I'm pretty sure that's the last of your belongings. So don't come back anymore unless I invite you."

When Martin blinked in surprise at her firm order, Sabine saw Joe grab his stunned brother's arm and steer him back to the garage. She turned to Koka and sighed again. "Sorry about that. My ex is just being nosy. He didn't really come by to get his weights. He just wanted to see if you were real. I told him I had a date but I guess he didn't believe me."

Koka nodded and untied his apron. "I can see you are distressed about his presence. I think I will help with the weights so that his departure will happen more quickly."

"You really don't have to do that. In fact, I'd rather you not get involved at all. Joe will see Martin behaves," Sabine said softly.

He tipped her chin up again with one finger. "I'm already involved. And I want your ex to know it. Do you have a problem with that?"

Sabine sighed and bit her lip. Finally, she shook her head faintly.

Koka tapped underneath her chin to keep her aware of him. "Can I go help if I promise not to beat my chest like an ape and scream at him?"

"That was a joke, right?" Sabine asked.

Koka chuckled and leaned down to drop a kiss on her mouth. Too tempted to be a complete gentleman, he ended up nipping the lip she had bitten, wishing he could do more.

"Mostly I was joking," he said quietly. "But I want to carry his weights and see his understanding of the metaphor I mean it to be. I am sure it will cause him surprise again that he has truly lost the most beautiful woman he will ever know. This is his day for seeing the truth."

The breath she had been holding escaped slowly. When she was empty of it, she nodded. "Fine. Go beat your chest a little, but make it fast. I hate to eat dry chicken."

When Koka grinned and headed out the door, Sabine shook her head. "I truly have lost my mind."

Less than three minutes later, Joe and Koka strolled back into the kitchen laughing and talking. She looked at Koka's hands in horror and pointed to another door. "Bathroom is down the hall and on the right. There's degreaser under the sink. You should have let Martin lift the ones from the garage floor, you big dummy. Get that grease off before it stains. I don't need Edwina tracking me down for ruining your hands."

Koka laughed as he headed in the direction of her pointing hand.

Sabine turned when he left to see Joe staring after him. "Stop drooling. He's completely straight. Trust me."

Joe turned his gaze to Sabine. "No, that's not it. Martin and I picked up two forty-five pound weights each. Koka picked up the rest of the pile all at once and carried them to the trunk of Martin's car. He was very polite and gracious about it the whole time. Martin was poleaxed with shock, but I think I was too. Did you have any idea the man was that strong?"

Sabine bit her lip and stared back at her entrée that was nearing the end of its edibility.

"Yes. I'm somewhat acquainted with Koka's muscles," she admitted, unwilling to admit to Joe that her hands had memorized his biceps.

Joe reached over and kissed her cheek. "Okay then. Since my heroic deed is now done, I'm leaving. Have a good date. I like him, Sabine."

"Yes," she said softly. "I like him too. That's my problem."

CHAPTER 10

In the process of making dessert, Sabine was spooning store-bought whipped topping onto glazed pears when Koka's arms slipped around her from behind. Her hand froze mid-dollop as both his hands slid from her waist up to her breasts and back.

"I love this dress on you," he whispered.

"Dessert is ready," Sabine whispered back, the words sticking in her throat.

"I hope so," Koka said. He turned her around and lifted her to her toes as he bent to her mouth for a mind-numbing kiss. Her groan had him gripping her tighter than he had intended.

"Sorry," he said hoarsely. "I promised you a warning. I forgot."

Beyond his unapologetic gaze, Sabine saw the spoon of whipped topping was still in the hand she had rested on his shoulder. Holding his stare, she brought the spoon to her mouth and licked it clean while he watched with hungry eyes.

"Bad Koka. Very bad for not keeping your promise," she said. "I'm not sure you deserve dessert."

Laughter almost choked him on its way out, but his hands were busy finding their way under the full skirt. "*Nou No Ka `I'ini.*"

"Ha—I know what that means and I don't even speak Hawaiian," Sabine declared, standing on her toes so he wouldn't have to bend down so far.

With her skirt finally out of the way, Koka pressed himself against the heat of the woman he found under it. Her soft body was the most erotic thing he could remember lusting for in his entire life. "I desire you, Sabine Blakeman. That's what I said."

Sabine heard the words, but Koka's voice seemed very far away. What he was doing with his hands as he molded her lower half to his was seriously distracting. He was just so sure in his actions, so insistent in expressing what he felt in any moment.

"I desire you too," Sabine parroted back. After the words were out, she realized she would have said most anything to prolong her drowning in the sensual ocean Koka was creating around her.

Her confession made him moan. "Do you want to have dessert first? Or after?" It killed him to ask and offer any choice at all, but Sabine had gone to so much trouble to cook for him.

"I want it right now," Sabine said, reaching up to link an arm around his neck. It was quite a stretch, but well worth it when Koka let her pull his head down. Her mouth sought his and found it hot and waiting for her. When she finally let him go, she swept a hand down his neck and over one massive shoulder. "I have high standards for dessert though."

"Sabine—consider yourself warned," Koka declared, his voice low.

To her shock, he scooped her substantial form up in his arms and started down the hall with her. She had never been carried before and the experience was startling.

"Which room?" he demanded.

"The big one," she squeaked, hanging onto him as best she could.

Yet being carried was nothing compared to landing on her mattress with a rock solid male heavily on top of her. His mouth devoured hers while his hands divested her of everything under her dress and went exploring. Finding the answer he was looking for, he groaned and cupped her possessively.

Unwilling to passively accept her fate, Sabine unbuckled and unzipped until she could work her hands down inside his clothes to a backside that felt like molded bronze under her fingers. There was nowhere soft on the man. "I can't get pregnant and there hasn't been anyone since I divorced. I just wanted you to know."

Koka's answer to her—if you could call it that—was to hold her thighs in his hands while he wiggled his pants off his legs. For a big man, he had some amazing moves. Right after she heard his pants hit the carpet, his hands ran up the inside of her thighs as he separated them.

"In case you have any doubts left about anything at all, I want this and the answer is yes," Sabine said.

"'O Ku'u Aloha No 'Oe," Koka whispered, beginning the journey inside her.

Sabine let her body sink into the mattress and give under the pressure of him sliding into her. "Your language is so beautiful," she whispered.

"I have wanted to do this with you since you stood up at the auction. Will you let me love you now?" Koka asked, the words strangled as he completed their joining. Her head nod against the pillow was accompanied by rapid panting. He went a little crazy. "*Na'u `oe.*"

Whatever Koka whispered to her in his native language acted like a trigger. Sabine groaned and arched her body, amazed to feel such a sense of rightness with a man she had known for such a short amount of time. "I have no words nearly as poetic as yours, but I want you too. This is even better than your rum fried bananas. Can we do this a little faster?"

"Not yet. It is too much and yet not enough," Koka declared, rolling them over until she sat astride him.

While a groaning Sabine unbuttoned his shirt, he reached behind her and unzipped the beautiful red dress until the zipper stopped at her waist. There was no way to free her from it completely. He wasn't even sure he wanted to yet.

Lying back on the pillow, he used his hands to ease the dress off Sabine's shoulders. When it fell away from the front of her, he was delighted at the sheer red lace bra under it.

"Beautiful," he said, feeling her quiver in happiness.

Bound in lace cups, his large hands covered only part of her breasts. Loose—she would spill around his fingers, lush and soft. When she moved, he shivered beneath her rocking weight, suddenly fearing that Sabine's pleasure would be lost in his prolonged sensual exploration.

"*Koka,*" Sabine said hoarsely, feeling the first orgasm in two years hitting her hard. A muffled scream erupted when she found herself buried again under a plunging male body that seemed bent on maximizing her pleasure as he plunged slowly with each shiver.

"Beautiful Sabine," Koka whispered. His body shuddered as it found perfect sanctuary in the groaning woman beneath him. Heart thudding after he'd spent the last of his energy, he tried to spare her his full weight without separating himself from the quiet joy of her sated body.

Finally, he eased away to lie beside her. He closed his eyes so his mind could take a picture of her sexy blonde hair splayed across the pillow. Once committed to his memories, Koka realized how much danger he was in. If he looked too long in Sabine's softly, satisfied eyes, he was going to tell her the depth of his feelings no matter how much instinct warned him against the action. When he gave in and opened his eyes to stare at Sabine once more, her red lace covered breasts above a sex-crumpled dress sent blood rushing through him. Koka rashly decided was going make Sabine wear it every year on their anniversary.

He quivered under her exploring hand as Sabine caught him watching her and rose above him. She leaned over to stare into his face.

"*That,*" Sabine declared, "*was the best dessert ever.*"

Koka laughed at her teasing and reached out his hand to brush back her hair. "That was not our real dessert," he teased. To his delight, Sabine giggled.

"It wasn't?" she asked.

Koka shook his head and fought his twitching mouth. "No. That was an experiment that went very well. When it becomes our real dessert, you will know. Such perfection will make you feel like singing."

Sabine sighed and laid her head on his solid chest, rock hard muscles smooth under her cheek. "I'm humming now. That's pretty close to singing."

She raised her head to get another look at Koka's relaxed face. It made her feel pretty proud of herself. "Can I ask why your name is Whitman? Or is that bad pillow talk?"

Koka stroked Sabine's hair as he gazed into her expressive face. Her sweet curiosity about his family was one of the things he liked best about her.

"Pekala married someone from the mainland. His name was Whitman. They had two sons, both of whom followed the goddess and accepted Pekala's genes for the face they presented to the world. My father and his brother both married island women, but the mainland name carried on. Some believed the job I took in Seattle was due to my dead grandfather's influence. Really, it was because I needed enough money to take care of Pekala and save for my restaurant at the same time."

Sabine sighed over his story. "Do you miss your homeland?"

"The islands are part of me—so yes. However, Pekala says she is content here. And my daughter is mainland-minded. Pekala says Halia has my grandfather's true mainland spirit. I think she is right. Halia does not plan to live on the islands. For now, I like being on the mainland and nearer to her."

"Halia is your daughter?" Sabine asked.

Koka nodded. "Yes. She looks Hawaiian and favors her mother. She is turning out to be a good person. That makes me feel successful as a parent, since I was still a child myself when she was born."

"I know what you mean about that making you feel successful. My children are turning out to be good people too. I feel very blessed until they buy me a *Food Porn Star* apron. Then I start to wonder where I've gone wrong," Sabine said.

Koka smiled at her teasing. She just couldn't seem to help herself. "Would you like to have your other dessert now?"

Sabine giggled. "Are you talking about cold, soggy glazed pears with melted whipped topping? Or something hot and fresh from the cook's talented hands?"

Koka chuckled at her innuendo and harder as she ran a hand over his twitching interest. "You are a demanding woman, Sabine Blakeman. Perhaps I should be less surprised than I am."

Sabine stopped her exploration to reach up and tap his cheek, putting some genuine force behind it. "Hey now, *Todd.* Submissive women don't outbid evil bitches and save a guy's pretty ass."

Laughing at her passionate and colorful declaration, Koka grabbed her wrist mid-tap the second time. He used his hold to push Sabine off his chest and to her back. It was so much fun to see her mild shock at his show of strength that he trapped the other wrist too. He pinned her to the mattress thinking of future sensual torture while she glared at him.

"Maybe submissive women get a hot dessert more often," he said softly, diving into her mouth to taste her resistance to him teasing back. But surprising him once more, she arched her soft body and rose up to meet his mouth again. Kissing Sabine to subdue her quickly turned into a passionate exploration of tongues and teeth. A few minutes of it and his erection was straining against her again.

"I am not sure who just seduced who," he marveled.

"Now be honest. Do you really want me to be submissive in bed?" Sabine asked.

Koka shook his head as he slowly released her wrists. "No. If you were submissive, what would I have to conquer? Ancient warrior blood runs through my veins. The truth is—I just want your desire—whatever form that takes."

Sabine stared at his serious eyes. "I think I started desiring you the first time you laughed at my teasing. However, for this sex thing to work out in your favor, you need to accept the fact that I like being on top as well as the bottom. I don't know what kind of blood runs in your veins, but what you did—the whole flipping me over with perfect timing—that was incredible. So conquer away if you want to keep doing that."

Koka hid his face in her neck as he smiled about Sabine's cloaked praise. "I want you again, Sabine Blakeman."

Sabine laughed at his semi-amazed tone. "Oh, is that what's going on with that piece of iron poking my stomach? Wow, you had me worried there for a minute. I didn't know what that was."

Her belly laughter echoed off the walls as Koka tickled her to get revenge, but it was her thrashing legs that gave him access to what he really wanted. She melted and molded around him again as he slid inside her.

Koka's rough whispered words made his ancient warrior claim seem almost real to her. Sabine sighed in welcome as he moved inside her. Oh the fantasies she was going to have about seducing this man.

"Na'u `oe, Ku`u Lei. No Keia La, No Keia Po, A Mau Loa."

Sabine let her hands roam the bronze hardness of Koka's shoulders and arms as she closed her eyes in pleasure with each stroke. "Right now, the hell I suffered for the last two years of my failing marriage seems like a small price to have paid for my freedom to do this with you. Does that make me a bad woman?"

Koka went still as Sabine's eyes closed in bliss. His throat was clogged with declarations that demanded to be said, but he would let the choice be hers. "Do you want to know what I just said to you in my language?"

Sabine opened her eyes at the seriousness in his voice, staring into his gaze as he rocked smoothly and steadily into her. "If I tell you I can't make up my mind about hearing how you feel, will you be hurt or upset?"

Despite the fear in Sabine's question, love still flooded his heart with hope. "No, I will not be angry," Koka whispered. "I will be patient and wait for my sunshine to come out from behind her clouds."

Beneath him, Sabine snickered at his poetic promise even as she dug her fingernails into his backside while he pushed into her. Hissing at the passionate pain, Koka kissed her fiercely and had his way with her until she screamed.

CHAPTER 11

Blanche stared at what Sabine was sighing over and shook her head. "If you didn't take on so many social losers for clients, you wouldn't be holed up in here sighing over plans gone wrong to make them publicly presentable. At least your taste in men is improving. Speaking of men, drop what you're doing. Anthony wants to see us both in his office."

Sabine pulled her readers down to glare at Blanche over them. "I know you're technically my boss, and Anthony's technically yours, but lately you've both been crossing every imaginable employer-employee harassment line with me. Is this a trend I need to be concerned about in this company?"

Blanche laughed at Sabine's complaining. "Maybe I'm cranky and jealous of your new boyfriend. Now move your *Sexy Chef* charming ass because the company president wants to see us both as soon as we can get there."

Sighing, Sabine pulled her readers off her nose and tossed them on top of her desk as she stood. "Oh . . . well. . . since the company president wants to see us both about my social life outside the company, we'd better go right away."

Sabine felt at least a little satisfied when Blanche huffed as she choked on her shock.

"You were always sassy, but what is with your total snarkitude lately? You do one guest spot on a small, local TV show and now you're too special to talk with Anthony?"

Sabine made a growling sound as she joined her boss and they headed down the hall. "Every conversation I've had with Anthony lately has started with '*So how's Todd doing?*' Well, I'm tired of answering that question. Todd doesn't work for him. I do. He hasn't asked me how I'm doing lately. No one has."

Blanche shrugged. "That's because we all know how you're doing, Sabine. We hear you humming in your office all day. Sound carries well down the hall here."

Sabine shook her head. "If I'm humming, it's because my ex finally got the last of his belongings from the garage. Now I don't have to see him or his new wife's fake breasts again until one of our kids graduates college. Hey, Anthony should ask me about Clarissa's breasts. Technically, the retirement he gave me paid for them. He might want to know if he got his money's worth."

Beside her Blanche laughed as her eyes got huge.

"Sabine, that is an excellent deflection. I remember teaching you how to change the subject and you are now quite the master. But wake up and smell the PR goldmine of your situation, darling. You're dating the most sought-after bachelor in Seattle. Inquiring minds—especially those in our company—want to know all they can about it. It's okay to be jealous of the other women chasing him for his hot body, but you really need to get used to your boyfriend's popularity. Unless Todd Lake loses those muscles of his, or forgets how to cook, I don't see that waning too much."

Sabine settled for a dirty look instead of a retort. She refused to give in to Blanche's torture and confess anything significant about the last two weeks with Koka.

"He and I are friends, Blanche. If you're looking for dirt, all you're going to find out is that Chef Lake is teaching me to cook. My ex and my kids would be laughing their asses off if they found out I was taking gourmet cooking lessons after all my years of burning macaroni and cheese."

Sabine told herself that burning last night's dinner when she and Koka had stopped to make love didn't make a single word of her statement less true. Koka *was* teaching her to cook. She had mastered grilled pineapple and pork chops. It was beside the point that she had also mastered how to make her cooking teacher moan in pleasure with just a few pleasurable strokes of her hand.

"Sabine—you stopped walking and stared off into space. Are you seriously that afraid of talking to Anthony?"

Sabine rolled her eyes at the question. *Great. There went her professionalism, sacrificed for memories of hot sex with an enthusiastic man.*

"No, I'm not afraid of talking to Anthony. If you must know, I was thinking about the grilled pineapple and pork chops I made last night. I missed lunch today and my candy bar high wore off hours ago."

Blanche glared in disgust. "You're the only woman I know who gets more blissed out by the prospect of food than by dating the best looking man in Seattle."

Sabine laughed at Blanche's comments, her sense of humor finally winning out over her annoyance. She thought of Koka wearing her *Kitchen Diva* apron and no shirt as he had tried to rescue their dinner. It had been sexy as hell, even if the diva moniker also fit him when he was in chef mode. Blanche was right about one thing. Any woman would have enjoyed cooking around that kind of inspiration.

Anthony stood as they entered his office and waved two DVD cases triumphantly in the air. "Guess what I have? Early copies of your guest appearance on *The Sexy Chef*. And these babies don't have the commercials added either. Here Sabine—this one is for you."

Dazed, Sabine walked forward and took her copy. "Thank you. Why did they send you a copy of my appearance?"

Anthony grinned at one of his favorite employees. "I bought an advertising spot. It's not on this recorded version of the show—something to do with the network reserving the right to splice spots in as needed. I got these because they send a show sample to new clients so they know what customers will be watching when the spot runs. I asked for two copies of your specific show. Nice, huh?"

Sabine let her breath out slowly hoping to mask her exasperated sigh. "Yes. That was really thoughtful of you, Anthony."

"No problem. So how is Todd doing this week?"

With Anthony busy loading his copy of the DVD into a player, he didn't see the glare she gave Blanche who was laughing behind her hand.

"Chef Lake is fine. He's giving me cooking lessons," Sabine said, keeping her tone even. "I made grilled pineapple and pork chops mostly by myself last night. He's a really good teacher."

She pasted an all business smile on her face when Anthony turned and beamed at her. How the hell had her work associates gotten so involved in her personal life? Anthony's nod and wink in her direction was like having her father approve of her high school boyfriend.

"So do you call him *Chef Lake* when he's teaching you to cook? Why don't you call him Todd?" Anthony asked.

Sabine schooled her face into the most stoic expression she could manage. "Actually, I don't call him at all because his schedule is much busier than mine. Chef Lake usually calls me when he's free and wants to get together for a cooking lesson."

Anthony's face twisted in confusion as the show began to play. When all of them turned to watch, Sabine's face heated at the sight of her gigantic smile as she stared up into Koka's TV face. She blushed as she watched herself paying close attention to everything he was saying.

And was that actually a giggle coming out of her mouth every time he showed her how to do something? "Oh my God," she said finally, bringing up a hand to cover her face. "I can't believe I giggled like that on TV."

But Blanche and Anthony didn't comment or even look at her. Their gazes were glued to the screen where Koka was now feeding her a bite of grilled pineapple from his fork. She blushed quietly thinking about sitting in his lap while he did that same thing last night. Curling her fingernails into her palms, she squeezed hard trying to stop the sexy thoughts. It was nearly impossibly to keep her mind from drifting to every intimate moment she'd had in the last two weeks with the man on the screen.

When the show finally ended, Anthony raised the remote and clicked it off. He turned an inquisitive gaze to her.

"If you think that's bad, Chef Lake is a lot more bossy off camera when he's showing you how to cook something. He enjoys ordering people around," Sabine joked, trying to shake the shock from Anthony's gaze.

"Are you sure you two are just friends?" Anthony asked.

Keeping the blankest expression in place that she could, Sabine nodded, hoping she wasn't going to go to hell for lying to her boss. "Yes. Why do you ask?"

Sabine swiveled to face the woman at her side as Blanche laughed loudly and swore.

"People who watch that show are going to need a cold shower afterward," Blanche exclaimed. "Just how many times did his arm graze your breast? I stopped counting after twenty."

Sabine didn't reply to Blanche. She couldn't. Lying was hard for her and it had taken all she had just to get one good one out to Anthony about only being friends. She opened her mouth, but was saved by Anthony butting in.

"All I can say is *The Sexy Chef* actually looked sexy for once. Usually he looks serious and all business no matter what's written on his apron," Anthony said.

"Do you watch his show often?" Sabine asked, a bit surprised at Anthony's comment.

Anthony shrugged. "Actually, I do. My wife tapes it. She loves trying Todd's recipes."

Sabine eased out another breath. "So do I. He's definitely a great cook. That's not just hype for the show. It's really true."

"What did you think of his producer?" Anthony asked.

"Edwina? She's fine to work with. Tough-minded where Chef Lake is concerned, but she was nice enough to me," Sabine reported.

"I called her and asked if she thought Todd might cook for our Melting Pot fundraiser this year. I pitched them filming a live show during the event, but she didn't seem very interested in the idea," Anthony said.

Sabine blinked. "The fundraiser for the homeless shelter is too large an undertaking for one person. We usually get a catering service."

Anthony nodded. "I know. I'm not saying he wouldn't need help if he agreed. Ms. Winston said she would run a personal request by Todd even if the network didn't want to do the live show. If you get the chance, give him a nudge in our direction, will you?"

Sabine blinked again. *Give him a nudge?* Was her boss really asking her to use her connection to Koka to get something out of him for the company? "What kind of influence do you think I have over Chef Lake?"

"The kind where the man kept touching you every three seconds of his show," Blanche replied, answering for Anthony. "Unless he does that to every woman, it means he's really interested in you."

Sabine sighed. "I'm sure he doesn't do that intentionally to any woman. The set kitchen was very small. And in case you're trying to be tactful, don't bother. It's obvious that neither he nor I are miniature people. Those body brushes were the result of insufficient space."

"And I thought my ex-husband was bad at flirting," Blanche said. "Yours left you clueless about men."

Sabine answered Blanche's mean jibe with a glare. But when Anthony and Blanche both just continued to stare at her, she finally shrugged. "If cooking for the fundraiser comes up in any conversation, I'll talk to him."

Cringing inwardly at her capitulation, she promised herself that she would definitely talk to Koka about it—just not the way they thought she was going to. Under no circumstances was she going to let him be used by Anthony, or the likes of Blanche, whose ethics she was starting to question.

But she would definitely have to come up with some kind of excuse for his decline that wouldn't negatively impact her job.

***

Rising from the table, Koka gathered their empty dishes and carried them to the sink. "Pekala's declining health has made it harder for me to travel. Edwina pushes me to do local events so she can at least broadcast those to national viewers. I decline most offers, but I could do this one for you."

Sabine shook her head. "No, and don't even give it another thought. One of the reasons I went to work for Anthony is that he seldom plays tit-for-tat games with our clients. Besides—I like that you and I are outside all that. I don't want you to think I like you because you're good for my PR career."

Koka loaded the last of their dishes before he returned to his seat at her table. "I appreciate that you feel that way, but I liked Anthony too. I hope I wasn't misjudging his character."

Sabine smiled at him. "You weren't. Anthony's a good person. I think it's my direct supervisor who's acting like a publicity fiend in this case. I think Blanche has been planting ideas in Anthony's head about you and me because she suspects we're closer than I'm saying. I've been playing down our relationship because I don't trust her."

"I don't expect you to keep us a secret. Are you ashamed to be associated with me?" Koka asked. His gaze took in her wide eyes over his direct question, but he wanted to know.

"Are you kidding? Ashamed—*no*. Protective—*yes*," Sabine said. "Negative press might hurt your career, Koka. At the very least, it would be embarrassing to Pekala and Halia."

Koka crossed his arms as he studied Sabine's pensive frown. "What could be negative about my association with you? It's not like I'm planning to brag to the world about how talented you are in bed."

Sabine laughed at his sideways compliment and rolled her eyes as she stood. "Okay. Negative is probably the wrong word, but getting laughed at publicly can feel negative. I've seen my clients go through it often enough to know."

"I still don't understand," Koka said. "We're consenting adults. It's not like you're married or dating anyone other than me. Are you?"

Rolling her eyes again at his worried tone, she gave him the don't-be-stupid look she normally only used on Joe. "No. I wasn't dating at all before we got together. I guess technically I was trying to date, if you count trolling coffee shops and wishing."

"Humor is not going to save you from this discussion, Sabine. I want to know what puts that furrow between your eyes when you talk about us being together," Koka demanded.

THE WRONG TODD

Disbelief that he cared as much as he did was the real cause, but Sabine didn't feel that was confessable. Unable to formulate any worthy answer, she turned away from the beautiful man at her table with his dark hair, darker eyes, and white shirt partially unbuttoned. It was hard not to go to him and indulge the urge to undress him completely, especially now that she knew he would let her.

Distracting herself to improve the odds of resisting temptation, Sabine added detergent to the dishwasher. She closed and locked its door before she turned back to Koka again. She mentally drew on her forty-plus years of life so she could offer the most positive explanation she could.

"I'm fine with who I am—most of the time—but I'm just not the kind of woman your fans expect *The Sexy Chef* to be dating. They might find my presence in your life to be alarming."

"I didn't know my cooking fans had any say about who I go out with," Koka said, crossing his arms.

"Wait—hear my whole opinion before you get your shorts twisted up about this. You know how our society works. But as an image consultant, it's my job to call it as I see it. An incredibly fit man who looks like you being associated with a not-so-fit woman who looks like me might not be so great for your current image as a sexy bachelor."

Koka narrowed his eyes. "Why? Because you're a real woman with a real body, instead of sporting fake everything and looking plastic?"

Sabine nodded as she leaned against her cabinets. "Yes. My body is a little more female reality than most women want to accept, while you and your muscled form are every woman's fantasy. Think of any celebrity and then tell me what happens when they pack on a few pounds. Now compound that with the celebrity being a chef. There are automatic assumptions that go along with that. You and your perfectly toned body are miles outside those assumptions and they have helped make your career what it is. Your fans' expectations about you are important. I'm not willing to risk your popularity."

"So if I were overweight, you're saying you think no one would pass judgment on your appearance as the woman in my life?" Koka asked.

Sabine bit her lip at the anger in his voice. "I'm not saying that exactly. And it's hard to know for sure. But it would be less likely if you looked like just some average man, instead of a muscled god. Depression and divorce made the body I have at the moment. It would take a couple years for me to get myself

83

back into any kind of shape that would look worthy of standing next to *The Sexy Chef* in public."

Koka shook his head. "So this is why we always go to your house or you come to mine. You're afraid to be seen in public with me."

"Afraid is not exactly the right word," Sabine said.

"What is the right word then, Sabine?" Koka demanded, crossing his arms and glaring.

"*Worried,*" Sabine whispered. "I don't want anything to change what I've found with you. These last two weeks have been like a wonderful dream and I'm not ready to wake up yet. The moment I'm seen with one of Seattle's most famous bachelors, it will change things for both of us. Everyone will start speculating. In our case, that speculation might not be so great for your popularity."

"But you don't know that will happen for sure," Koka said.

Sabine walked to where he sat. Reaching out, she ran her fingertips inside the collar of his shirt and down to where the first button gave under her fingers. "I may not know for sure, but I'm a pretty good guesser about things like this. It's part of my job."

Koka raised his hand to take hers. "I find you beautiful just as you are. Nothing anyone says can change that. But your opinion of yourself must be high enough to believe you deserve my devotion. If it isn't, I am just wasting my time trying to lure my sunshine out from behind her clouds."

Sabine groaned as she bent to kiss him. "Quick. Tell me the worst of your flaws before I fall at your feet and beg to be your sex slave forever."

Koka reached out a hand and grabbed the front of her shirt. He yanked down hard and held Sabine at eye level. "I'm insatiable where you're concerned."

Sabine closed her eyes at his words and let herself fall to her knees while he still gripped her. Spreading his knees wider, Koka leaned forward and fastened his lips hotly to hers. She ran exploring hands down to his ankles over his slacks, back up his calves, and over his knees to grip his thighs. When Koka finally released her mouth, she leaned forward and buried her face in his lap, kissing the hard length of him through fabric as she made plans in her head about what to do to him. "Come to bed with me," she ordered.

Koka's hands under her arms lifted her to her feet when he stood. Before she could take a breath, his mouth was on hers again, greedy and demanding. His desire was such a perfect match to what she felt in return that the rightness of them together brought tears to her eyes. She couldn't imagine feeling that perfect feeling for anyone but him.

"I cannot wait to be with you, but afterward I want you to come home with me," Koka said. "I need to be near Pekala, but I can't bear the thought of sleeping without you when my heart is this full of concern about us."

"Okay," Sabine said quietly, not bothering to fight as she led him down the hallway to her bedroom. She'd talk him out of the idea afterward and send him on his way, like she did every time.

Her plans of seducing Koka evaporated after he removed her stroking hand and flipped her around to face away from him. After undressing her, Koka bent her over the bed and cupped her breasts as he entered her from behind. Her groan earned her a hard squeeze from both hands. Lost in feeling owned, she missed Koka's whispered question in her ear.

"What?" she asked.

"I said—*this* is another flaw," he whispered.

"It's not a flaw if I like it," Sabine said, rasping the words.

"No," Koka said, laughing roughly. "The flaw is that I like to be in control. Always."

Sabine moaned over the pleasure of Koka's hands squeezing her large breasts as he plunged in and out, his large body forcing hers to adapt to his rhythm.

"What kind of control?" she asked when she could.

Koka plunged deeply, stepped forward to shift his weight, and toppled her down until her face was pressed into the mattress. He pretended to ignore her pleased laugh at his domination.

"The kind of control where you do exactly as I say," he whispered. "Starting with telling me if this really feels as good as you're making it seem like it does."

Sabine quivered at his muscled body holding hers spread and captive to whatever he wanted to do to her. "Yes—it feels amazing. I just hope you can make me scream in this position."

Bending over the back of her, Koka's masculine moan of approval rumbled through them both as he rocked her and the bed with his hard thrusts. He hoped his motions weren't using more force than was pleasurable for her. Sabine wasn't talking as much as usual, but her moans and straining body reassured him as they always did.

"Sabine, this unquenchable desire between us is because I'm falling in love with you," he whispered.

Her rippling orgasm prevented Sabine from saying anything more than Koka's name in reply as he groaned and ground himself into her trying to prove his words were true.

CHAPTER 12

Looking around the messy bedroom with clothes, shoes, and other items littering every surface, Sabine groaned softly in dismay. Koka's bedroom was a complete disaster area.

Then she looked back at the king-sized bed with her naked king-sized lover still face down across it. *Oh, who was she kidding? If ever there was a man totally worth picking up after, it was the one that spent the night making love to her.*

Rolling her eyes at her willingness to forgo both her common sense and her feminist leanings for great sex, Sabine rummaged through the strewn clothing until she found sweatpants that tied at the waist and a t-shirt that would hang to her knees. Throwing them on, she crept from the room and thanked God it was Saturday.

She followed her nose to the kitchen and the smell of strong, black tea. What she found was Pekala wheeled up to the small table, sitting alone. Pushing aside the morning-after embarrassment that heated her face, she put on a smile as she padded barefoot into the kitchen.

"Good morning," she said, pretending to belong.

Pekala turned and smiled. "I see the sunshine has finally found its way to the kitchen again. Thank goodness. Koka is not a pleasant man without you around."

Sabine laughed. "Sunshine again? Well, I don't know about that this morning. I'm too used to waking up in my own house."

"Have some tea, Sabine. My night nurse Renee made it before she left," Pekala said.

Sabine opened a cabinet above the teapot and found a cup. Liberally filling the bottom with honey, she finally poured the dark black liquid over it. She carried it to the table and took a seat.

"Smells as strong as coffee."

"I had to give up my Kona coffee earlier this year. That was a very sad day, but I have learned to drink black tea," Pekala said.

Sabine looked into Pekala's cup and saw it was empty. "You want a refill?"

"Please," Pekala said, nodding. "The day nurse called and will be late. I couldn't reach the counter on my own."

Frowning at Pekala's limitations, Sabine went back to the counter and brought everything she could hold in her hands to the table. "There. If we drink the pot, I'll make some more."

Sabine poured a refill of tea for Pekala, grinning as Koka's grandmother ladled more honey into hers than even she had used. Afterward, the woman studied her over the teacup as she sipped it.

"Normally Koka is awake by now. I'm glad he had a reason to sleep in this morning," Pekala said.

Sabine laughed and smiled over her own cup. "Is that your gentle way of telling me you don't mind me being here?"

Pekala smiled. "Only a foolish woman would chase sunshine from her kitchen."

"Thank you," Sabine said softly, sighing over how important the older woman's acceptance was to her. "If you're hungry, I could make you some breakfast. It might not be what you're used to from Chef Lake, but I can do scrambled eggs and toast with some proficiency."

"I have a sweet tooth in the mornings. How about French toast?" Pekala asked.

Sabine thought her grin might just split her face. "French toast is my specialty. I have a family recipe unlike anything you've ever tried before. And I bet Koka will have all the ingredients."

She bounded up and headed to the kitchen. It took opening almost every cabinet before she found everything she needed. Her swearing when she went to get a skillet was too much an honest reaction to prevent in time. Embarrassed at cutting loose in front of Koka's grandmother, she looked up sheepishly when Pekala laughed.

"Sorry. I've just never seen thirty different kinds of skillets in one cabinet before. How mad is he going to be if I use the wrong one?" Sabine asked the laughing woman.

"Live dangerously," Pekala ordered. "I'm starved."

Turning back with a grin, Sabine released a slow breath and shook her head. "Okay. Let's do this."

She pulled out a skillet from near the top of the first stack. "I wonder what he thought about my pitiful, well-used cookware. It's obvious he's not used to roughing it."

But Pekala didn't respond to her concerns, she just sat at the table smiling.

Finding her cooking zone at last, Sabine mixed the egg batter and coated several large slices of multi-grain bread before laying them into the melted butter that was dancing in the skillet. Humming, she flipped the slowly browning slices and watched carefully as the other side cooked to perfection. Plating everything onto two plates, she carried them to the table.

Pekala's eyes, lighting with delight, made her smile as she slid the plate onto the table. She went back to the kitchen and returned shortly with several bottles of syrup. "I have big-refrigerator envy now too. Knowing Koka has corrupted me."

Pekala smiled as she worked her way through one slice of French toast. "Delicious," she pronounced.

Sabine laughed and nodded, her own mouth full. At the sound of a masculine throat clearing, she swung a guilty gaze over her shoulder. Koka was standing in the kitchen doorway wearing an identical pair of sweatpants to hers and a shirt that left nothing to a woman's imagination. When Pekala laughed, Sabine knew the older woman had heard the sigh of longing slip out of her throat.

"His grandfather looked like that too. I'm old and dying, and still remember the man. The sixty years I knew him was not enough," Pekala said.

Pulling her attention back, Sabine reached out and poured more tea into Pekala's cup. "Did you always have that little dancing butterflies reaction?" she whispered.

"Until the day he died," Pekala whispered back. "Even when I was mad at him."

Sighing without attempting to hide it this time, Sabine stood. "I'm going to make some more tea and fix him some breakfast."

Pekala nodded. "Take yours to the bar or it will get cold, Sunshine."

Sabine barely fought off the urge to lean over and kiss the older woman for just being wonderful. Turning toward the source of her fluttering stomach, she carried the teapot in one hand and her plate in the other.

Koka put out a hand to stop her and peered into the plate. Leaning down, he sniffed. "What is that supposed to be?"

Sabine looked at him in shock. "French toast. What did you think it was?"

"Is that really food?" he asked. He leaned in to kiss her mouth, smirking when she backed away without letting him.

"Pekala seems to thinks so. What's your problem with French toast? If you're going to go all snobby chef on me, at least tell me why you hate breakfast food."

Snorting at Sabine's irritated tone, he climbed on a bar stool. "I don't hate all breakfast food. Okay. Perhaps I am being a snob. Convince me that your soggy bread is worth eating. I'd like a couple slices of ham in case I can't choke it down."

Sabine snorted as she walked into his kitchen. "You want a side of nice to go with it too? I think I found another flaw. You are way too blunt in the mornings."

Koka burst out laughing. "I am so much in love with you already that it hurts me, Sabine Blakeman. When are you going to admit you love me back?"

Sabine set down the teapot and the plate, shaking her head. "And you just had to say that right after you insulted my family recipe, didn't you?"

Koka shrugged. "I'm being nicer than you know. I didn't say anything at all about the skillet you're using. That's not the best one for your purpose."

"Sorry," Sabine said dryly. "I didn't go to skillet school. Do you have a skillet fetish or something?"

"Or something," Koka agreed, grinning at her laugh. "Want help making your soggy bread crisp up better?"

"No thank you. Don't move from that stool," she ordered. "And it's not soggy bread."

Busying herself with getting ham from the refrigerator, she practiced deep breathing to get her racing heart to slow down. She had glossed over last night's declarations of love during sex. Ignoring it was harder to do this morning. Her hands shook as she unwrapped the meat tray and selected several large slices.

"Two or three?" she asked.

"Two." As he waited, Koka studied Sabine's backside encased in his clothes. Sabine was sexy in an uncomplicated, liking-herself kind of way. She was like that in bed too. The marketing actually matched the package in her case, which thrilled him enough to be planning how to keep her. Pekala's presence was the only reason he wasn't trying to wrestle the sweatpants off her and show her several good reasons beyond what they had already done.

"I see you found something to wear around the house today," he said, trying to get his mind off morning sex.

"Barely. How do you ever find anything in that room?" Sabine demanded.

"Is that yet another of my flaws?" Koka demanded back.

Sabine laughed at his unrepentant answer as she dipped bread and put it in the sizzling skillet. Wow, she had it bad. Muscles and knowing how to kiss well should not exempt a man from being a slob. "Yes. A pretty big one, actually. How come your kitchen doesn't look like a war zone?"

Koka grinned and shrugged. "I don't know. I never really thought about it."

Sabine deftly flipped the French toast. "Pekala? Want another slice?"

"No thank you, Sweet Sunshine. I'm so full now I need a nap. Koka, will you help me until Denise comes? She is delayed this morning."

"Yes of course, *Kupunawahine.*"

Koka slid off the stool and went to wheel Pekala to her room. He had given her the master suite downstairs and modified the bathroom to accommodate her wheelchair. He tucked her in with a kiss and a smile as she scolded him for teasing Sabine.

When he returned to the kitchen, his breakfast was sliding onto the counter in front of his stool. Sabine carried her plate around and climbed onto the one next to his. The rightness of it resonated through him. Was it really only two weeks since Sabine had rescued him at the auction? It felt like she'd been in his life forever.

He climbed up again, pulled the fork from her sexy mouth, and kissed her sweet lips good morning. Laughing at her tight mouth, he pulled back. "Swallow," he ordered.

When Sabine obeyed, he laughed again and dove into her syrupy mouth to feast on what he really wanted for breakfast. Pulling away before the temptation got bad enough to drag her back to his bedroom, Koka sighed in regret. "Thank you for cooking for Pekala."

Sabine blinked at his sincere gratitude, still too dizzy with lust after that sweeping tongue kiss to do more than nod. She forked up another bite of French toast and chewed thoughtfully.

"Don't you think we're moving a little fast?" she asked.

Koka shrugged. "I'm thirty-seven and you're forty-three. We're moving at the pace that is right for us. What is in this? There is something in your soggy bread recipe that I don't recognize."

Sabine smiled at his confusion and the fact that he'd wolfed down a whole piece already. She lifted the spare slice from the side of her plate and put it on his. He glanced at her sideways, a move she was growing attached to, and then leaned over to kiss her lips again. When he pulled away, he licked his lower lip. "I don't know what tastes more delicious this morning."

Sighing, she attacked her French toast and shoveled two pieces into her mouth to keep from blurting things best not said yet. When she finally relaxed again, she gave him a disbelieving glare.

"Why aren't you married? You're grumpy and arrogant and difficult and messy and think you're always right. But you're also honorable and loyal and caring and affectionate and just about the most wonderful man I've ever known, including my friend Joe. And all that doesn't even cover the fact that you're more good-looking than any male has a right to be. Plus you talk like a poet . . ."

"Sabine . . ." Koka began. He had been gearing up to argue until he saw her wide, scared gaze on him. Then he laughed because his need to make her feel better outweighed his irritation that she wasn't falling into his arms like he wanted. "I think I must have been waiting for you to finish your other life. I haven't been lonely or bored a single moment since we've met. Don't ask me to give you up. I can't."

"See? That's what I mean," Sabine declared, laying down her fork. She covered her face with her hands, but sniffles and tears snuck through her fingers.

Laughing and groaning, Koka laid down his fork and leaned over to hug her. He kissed her forehead as she tucked her face into his neck and sniffled.

"I am so unprepared for you," Sabine complained. "You were a dream I had when I was a teenager, but I never thought I'd actually find you. Your messy bedroom and skillet fetish are the only reasons I can bring myself not to run away."

"If you did, I would just come after you," Koka said, his voice raspy with truth. "Now eat. When Denise arrives, we're going shopping today. You are not allowed to argue with me about it."

"*Allowed?*" Sabine repeated, sitting up.

Koka shrugged and grinned. "Want to come to my messy bedroom and try to convince me that it's going to be worth my time to hide in my house with you all day? You could try and make the decision *hard* for me."

"Wow. You actually said that—emphasis and all. Was that a Hawaiian dirty joke?" Sabine demanded, giggling at his responding laugh.

Koka shook his head. "No. Want to hear my favorite Hawaiian dirty joke?"

Sabine snorted, but nodded. He looked so wicked. And that smile . . . God, she loved that smirky, smartass look on him. "Sure. Tell me."

"A newly married couple celebrated their first night together by making love all night long. Morning comes and the groom goes into the bathroom to take a shower. When he forgets the towel, he calls to his new wife to please bring one. When she does, she sees his naked body for the first time. Her eyes fall to his feet, then rise slowly stopping midway. The bride stares shyly and asks, *What's that?* pointing to a small part of his anatomy. The groom, also being shy, thinks for a minute and then answers, *Well, that's what we had so much fun with last night.* And she, in amazement, asks, *Is that all we have left?*"

Sabine leaned her face into a hand as she laughed. When she glanced at Koka, his pleased smile nearly took her breath away. "I suppose you have a right to look smug, since that's a problem your bride will never have."

Immediately after making the comment, Sabine turned her head and saw a fast walking woman moving behind them through the kitchen. Her face heated as she wondered how much the woman had heard.

"No rush, Denise. Pekala is sleeping. I'm sure she will be out for hours because Sabine fed her sugar for breakfast," Koka said.

Sabine reached over and smacked his arm as the woman chuckled and headed through. "I didn't use that much sugar. It's the vanilla and almond extracts together that make it taste so sweet."

"Almond. Of course. That was the flavor throwing me off," Koka said, sliding down. He took their dishes and carried them to the sink. Rinsing them efficiently, he loaded everything into the dishwasher, then turned back just in time to catch the glazed arousal in Sabine's eyes. She had been staring at his ass. He was sure of it this time.

"Let's take a shower. Before you announce the size of my attributes again, I think you should check my anatomy in the broad daylight just to be sure," Koka declared.

Sabine's swearing preceded her swinging backside out of the kitchen as she headed back to his room. Koka trailed behind her, humming in contentment as he followed her up the stairs.

CHAPTER 13

Joe leaned over and grimaced. "I'm so sorry. They're usually a bit more restrained than this."

Todd laughed softly. "They're fine. No one has made me uncomfortable at all. So Martin is the brother that was married to Sabine?"

Joe nodded. "Yes. And I know what you're thinking. Seeing him with Clarissa is still a bit of a shock for all of us. Mom avoids the woman, but it's not Clarissa's fault. Martin became an ass shortly after his fortieth birthday."

"He certainly didn't trade up well, did he?" Todd said, studying the giggling younger woman.

Joe sighed and put an arm around the back of Todd's shoulders. "If there was ever a woman I would have gone straight for, it was Sabine Blakeman. Since I always knew what I really wanted, that kind of relationship would never have worked out between us. Even as friends though, I often thought I loved her way more than my younger brother Martin ever did. He loved her for the first half of their marriage, but made it hell for her the second half."

"You strike me as the kind of person capable of great love and loyalty," Todd said.

Joe looked at the man at his side. Everything about him was perfect and he wanted him in his life. He wanted him even if they ended up with a platonic friendship like his and Sabine's. Todd Masterson brought out the best in him and made him happy.

"Other than Sabine, there's only one person that I ever took one look at and knew exactly how I felt about them," Joe said. When Todd smiled and looked away, his chest tightened. "I know. I promised no pressure but it's hard."

Todd turned back to him and laughed louder. "Your mother is staring at us. I hope like hell that was just innuendo."

Grinning, Joe pulled his arm back and sighed at Todd's teasing. "Mom doesn't know what to think about you. You're the first guy I ever brought home to meet her."

"No kidding?" Todd asked, grinning as his gaze flicked to Joe's mother.

"No kidding," Joe confirmed. "I never saw any of the other men lasting long enough to torture my family—or me—in this manner. Jacob and Alex are mostly normal, but since he left Sabine, Martin is a nut case."

A sudden blaring TV had Joe grabbing his ears. "Damn it, Martin. Since when do you have to have the six o'clock news blaring? Bad news is hard enough to hear. It doesn't need to break ear drums too."

He saw his brother's evil grin as Martin found the local station he wanted. Top of the hour stories were being reported. Suddenly, he was leaning forward when a photo of someone very familiar was plastered across the screen. Another showed Koka and Sabine holding hands as they walked through the mall just yesterday. Todd's whistle beside him had him swinging his gaze.

"What did they say about them? I missed it," Joe said.

Todd shook his head and frowned. "They're talking about Sabine and her weight. It was a subtle dig, but it didn't really come off as a joke to me. Poor baby. I bet she wants to crawl into a hole somewhere."

Joe huffed. "Stupid shit news." He felt supported in his anger when Todd reached over and patted his leg. "Let's go. She's going to need a shoulder or two."

"Sit. Not yet," Todd ordered, his grip on Joe's knee not letting him stand. "There's more about them coming up. We don't want to miss the rest."

Joe nodded and settled back down. After watching the latest traffic accidents, upcoming weather, and Supersonics' scores, the news finally got back around to Sabine and Koka. She was being touted as Todd Lake's new girlfriend. After showing several pictures of other sexy women *The Sexy Chef* had dated over the years, they came back to Sabine's professional picture from work, making tiny digs about her obvious enjoyment of eating and how much that probably appealed to a chef. Then suddenly up popped a more alluring photo of Sabine in a bright red camisole showing lots of cleavage beneath her sexy smile.

Joe knew all about that picture because he had been sitting in the reception area of the photo studio while she'd had it taken.

He'd even helped Sabine choose the proofs. The boudoir photos had been a fortieth birthday gift for his lousy, ungrateful brother who was now pissed because Sabine was dating a guy hotter than Martin could ever dream about being.

Martin had asked for her to take those photos, and no one had copies but Martin. Which meant there was only one way they could have gotten into the hands of the media.

Joe was out of his chair and rushing to drag Martin over the back of the couch and onto the floor. Amid Martin's protests about it being none of his business, Joe's fist connected with his younger brother's jaw before he stopped to think about it.

"You lousy bastard. Those were a damn love gift from your wife and you just had to shit on her for it, didn't you?"

Martin's fist, sneaking up to connect with his eye, didn't even snap his head back. His younger brother obviously hadn't used his weights enough to put any real strength behind it. After a couple more well placed punches to the side of Martin's face, Joe felt Todd dragging him away as he watched his older brothers, Jacob and Alex, pulling Martin to his feet.

His mother yelled to throw Martin out of the house while Clarissa started sobbing and gathering up their things to leave. Jacob and Alex walked Martin to the door and did just that, tossing the youngest Kendall sibling out into the yard in the middle of a busy Sunday evening. Punishment was served swiftly, but the damage was already done to Sabine.

After Jacob and Alex grabbed their families and left, Joe stood in the middle of his mother's living room, fuming and furious, unsure of what to do with the rest of his anger.

"They're divorced and he's already remarried. Martin had no reason to hurt Sabine like this. And what are the girls going to think of their dad when they see what he's done? I don't even think they knew Sabine had made those pictures for him. She only did them because Martin wanted them done."

His mother walked over and hugged him tight. Swallowing both fury and tears, Joe bent and whispered an apology into her ear for losing his temper. She rubbed his back, hugged him again, and then switched her hug to a surprised Todd who was still standing at his side.

Joe looked sheepish as he turned to him. "I'm sorry. You didn't need to be part of this craziness. I just wanted you to meet my family."

Todd snorted. "Are you kidding? Seeing you jump to defend Sabine was the hottest thing I have ever seen anyone do in real life. Would you fight over my honor that way?"

Joe laughed as he nodded. "Yes—I would."

"Glad to hear it. Now come on," Todd said, grabbing his arm. "Let's go give Sabine a couple shoulders to cry on. Then you and I need to talk."

Calmer at last, Joe nodded his agreement. "So tell me the bad news. How's my eye look?"

"Blackening as we speak," Todd said bluntly, looking Joe's face over. "Your knuckles are swelling too."

Joe lifted his hand, looked at his bloody, puffy knuckles, and sighed. "I hate my brother."

***

Sabine shook her head. Butterflies danced in her stomach as she put healing salve on Joe's knuckles. Her worst fears had come true after one day of actual dating. Of course, it had been accelerated by Martin, but in her heart of hearts, she had known it was coming.

"Those boudoir photos were taken the year I moved into the guest room. I was still trying to save my marriage so when Martin asked for the photos, I caved. After I gave them to him, he didn't even look past the one on top of a stack of twenty. He told me it had only been a ploy on his part to encourage me to do something about my weight. It never occurred to him I'd have them taken as I was."

"Wow. Your brother really is an ass. Next time, I'll hold him down for you Joe," Todd said.

Joe laughed softly. "Mom told Jacob and Alex to throw him out of the house."

Sabine sniffed and fought not to cry. "I always did like your mother."

"She always liked you too. Martin may be totally kicked out of the Kendall clan after this. His timing on this was the worst ever," Joe said. "Mom still isn't over Clarissa and her giant fake boobs yet."

Sabine shrugged. "It was only a matter of time. What did the other women Koka dated look like?"

When Joe clamped his mouth shut, Sabine stopped dabbing and waited. "I want to know how bad it is. I need to know."

"They showed four other women. Three looked like models. One looked like an aerobics-addicted soccer mom," Todd reported, knowing exactly how Sabine's mind was trying to work through it.

"Any woman in the group bigger than a size ten?" Sabine asked, looking at Todd this time.

Todd shrugged, then studied his hands to avoid Joe's glare. "I'm not very familiar with women's clothing sizes, but if you're asking about their weight, none of the women were packing any extra pounds."

Sabine reached up and tapped Joe on the jaw. "Stop glaring at the love of your life that way. I didn't ask so I'd have more material to cry over. The degree to which those women are less real looking than me is the degree to which the media will run with my extra pounds as something shocking and surprising. They're just trying to stir everyone up about it to gain media attention—one way or another. Scandal draws reaction—no matter how large or small the matter."

"What are you going to do about this?" Joe asked.

"Nothing," Sabine said softly, but firmly. She stood and bent down to kiss his cheek. "Thanks for beating up Martin for me, but I'm not going to do anything. I'm just going to wait and see if what I told Koka turns out to be right. I'll either garner the support of every real-sized woman who hears about it, or I'll be a joke. What concerns me is what's going to happen to Koka's popularity. Being seen with me is going to affect *The Sexy Chef's* image."

She walked to the cabinet over the sink and pulled down three shot glasses. Then she reached into another cabinet for the bottle of cognac stored there. Walking back to the table, she poured a shot for each of them. She downed her first one and poured a second one for herself.

"Do you know what we bought at the mall when that picture was taken? We bought another skillet. The man has a whole cabinet full of just skillets, and not just four or five. He needs a twelve step program for them," Sabine complained.

Todd and Joe both laughed. She held out the bottle and they pushed their glasses forward again. Snorting, she poured another round.

"So when did you get to see the man's skillets?" Joe asked.

Sabine looked at him as she sipped her third shot. "I saw them when I cooked breakfast for his grandmother Saturday morning. Then I saw them again this morning when I got a mini-lecture on types and their uses. When my eyes glazed over, Koka said he was going to designate a cabinet just for me, starting my cookware set with the wrong pan I used yesterday morning."

Todd laughed at Sabine's story and downed his shot. "Is the man really worth all that aggravation?"

"Abso-fricking-lutely," Sabine said with enthusiasm. "And so is the rest of his family so far."

"Then he ought to be worth riding this media crap out too," Joe said.

"Doesn't matter if he is or isn't," Sabine said, the three shots finally dulling the internal pain. "I'm crazy in love with a man I met less than a month ago. It's too late to pretend I'm not. Once all of Seattle sees us together on his show, there will be no keeping that a secret anymore."

"Welcome to the club," Joe said firmly, lifting his shot glass while the man he desired merely looked back at him and smiled. "Sometimes it happens fast."

CHAPTER 14

Koka arranged the pans and bowls in strategic places on the set as he thought about how much he hated Mondays. When he opened his restaurant, he was going to be closed on Mondays. Mondays would be a day to play. Today he was forced into setting up for taping his show, but his mind was still on the disturbing news Edwina had shared with him.

Neither of them had seen the newscast Sunday evening, but Edwina had gotten a courtesy notice from the network that Todd Lake had been mentioned. The only reason he hadn't gone tearing after Sabine was that she hadn't come sobbing to him. This was everything she had worried about, but nothing of real concern from his point of view. It didn't change anything real about them, other than they might have to be more careful about going to the mall on Saturdays.

He looked up and stood straighter as he saw Joe Kendall walking across the set toward him.

"Nice black eye. Did you win or lose?" Koka asked.

Joe laughed at the man's quick humor. It was a good match for Sabine's laser wit. "Let's just say my younger brother Martin looks a lot worse than I do."

"So it was Sabine's ex who provided the photos? I shouldn't have shown him I was the better man so soon," Koka said. "It's obvious now he took it as a dare."

Joe laughed. "No, Martin was an ass to her long before you came along. After I beat a confession out of him over releasing her photos, my mother disowned him and my two older brothers tossed him out in the street. Everyone in my family is tired of him hurting Sabine, not to mention how his daughters are going to feel. What kind of message is he sending to them?"

"How hurt is Sabine?" Koka asked.

Joe sighed and shrugged. "She went all PR Barbie on me when I told her. It's hard to tell. This betrayal from Martin is like number two hundred thirty-five or something over the last decade, but it's worse than even parading the other women he slept with in front of her. This time the attack was even more personal and she has to make peace with herself all over again. Though the good news is Martin's new wife found the entire folder of Sabine's boudoir photos and burned them all in their barbeque grill. She called my mother and bragged about doing it."

"It is almost a pity about the photos," Koka said. "I would have liked to have seen them. I imagine she was quite beautiful."

Joe nodded. "She was. I was there when she took them." He stopped talking for a moment and studied the attractive man flexing muscles as he prepped his cooking set. "I hope you don't mind, but I really need to ask you a serious personal question. I consider Sabine part of my family as well as one of my best friends, so think of this as a concerned brother inquisition."

Koka stopped his work again and nodded. "Okay. Ask anything you want."

"The news showed several of the women you've dated in the past. None of them were remotely like Sabine. They were all polished and accomplished, not the warm, huggable mother type at all," Joe said. "If Sabine is just a novelty to you, I'd just as soon you cut her loose before this goes any further. She's going to survive her divorce from Martin, but she's already falling in love with you. If you hurt her, I'll probably try to break your nose, even knowing you're going to fold me into a pretzel afterward."

Koka smiled broadly, put his hands on his hips and laughed. "I pray to the goddess that you are right about Sabine Blakeman falling in love with me. She refuses to say it back when I say it to her. I can't even tell if I'm wearing her down. She makes jokes to throw me off."

Was that really an answer? Joe rubbed his face as he circled back to his original concern. "So back to those other women you dated—what was the allure with Sabine? Tell me a damn good story and convince me this is the real thing for you."

Koka nodded, smiling again. "Real is a good word, Joe. Sabine stood up at the bachelor auction, yelled at a clone of one of those women you probably saw, and chastised her for being disrespectful. Then she spent her entire savings to buy me. And she did all that without knowing I was *Todd Lake* or *The Sexy Chef*. In one of the worst evenings of my life, I became a real man to a woman again."

100

"Like a grown-up version of Pinocchio?" Joe asked.

Koka laughed and nodded. "Yes—something like that story. I also love Sabine's sense of humor. She has a sexiness which any sane man would be elated to find in a lover. No offense, but your brother was crazy to let Sabine Blakeman out of his bed. I assure you I will not be making the same mistake."

Joe snorted. "Sabine said you were poetic. Now I'd like a plain answer to my question. Are you in love with her too?"

"Yes. I think I fell in love with her when you two were arguing about her buying the wrong man. After you left us, she kept apologizing for me overhearing about her mistake. I had to stop myself from kissing her then. For our date I was supposed to take her here to the set, but instead I took her to my home because I wanted to get to know her. I probably scared her that night, but my pull toward her has been very strong from the beginning."

"I think her pull to you was equally strong. I bet once her daughters get used to the idea of their mom being with another man, they're going to love you," Joe said.

"Do you think so?" Koka asked.

Joe nodded, liking the sincerity in the man's face. "Yes. They are both very much their mother's children even though they look like their dad."

Koka smiled. "I think my daughter will like Sabine as well. Halia is coming to visit this week. Her school is on break."

"I hope this whole situation works out for all of you then. Sabine deserves a happily ever after. I sincerely hope you manage to give her one," Joe said.

"If you have any suggestions for how to help Sabine deal with this media nonsense, I am willing to hear your advice," Koka said. "I stayed away this morning only because I can't bear yet to hear her gloating over being right about what would happen. Maybe I am also avoiding the argument that she might make, which would only make me angry with her lack of faith in me. I am not willing to let her go. We will work this out—one way or another."

"Well hold on to that he-man thought and let her cool her heels for a day or so. For all that she sounds flip at times, Sabine is actually a careful thinker. Just don't give her too long though or she'll think you're put off by the negative publicity," Joe advised.

Koka snorted. "We are too new to each other still for Sabine to understand just how determined I can be when I want something. I want her in my life. It really is that simple to me."

Joe laughed. "Thanks for talking to me. It helps to know how you feel."

"Good. I may need your help again later when I decide to talk Sabine into marrying me. I want Pekala to be at my wedding, so it must be soon. It is my first time to marry. I'm finding it hard not to rush my future bride."

Joe laughed loudly. "Dude, now that is outright crazy talk. You've known her less than a month and Sabine just got out of a marriage. Talking her into marrying you is going to take an absolute miracle."

Seeing all the rest of the crew starting to bring equipment to the set, Joe lifted a hand. "Looks like you're about to get really busy. Take care, Chef Lake. Happy cooking show today."

"Thanks for coming by, Joe. I forgot to ask. How are things going with *the right Todd*?" Koka asked.

"He got to watch me beat up my brother yesterday. Since he's still talking to me, I consider that a good sign for us," Joe said, waving as he walked away.

"*Aloha*," Koka called. He hummed as he returned to work.

102

CHAPTER 15

"You're home early, Halia. It's only Wednesday. Did you drive all night to get here?"

Pekala watched her graceful great-granddaughter balance precariously on a chair as she searched in the top of the closet for her memory box. The content inside it had changed over the years, but she had not added anything much since her husband had died. Now she hoped to add one or two more photos to it before her life ended.

"I left early and drove most of yesterday because I wanted an extra day at home. I am skipping only one class this morning to be here. Don't tell Dad," Halia said.

"I won't tell. The box should be near the back, ku`uipo. I haven't looked at it in a long time. You may have to ask Denise where it is. I think she was the last person to put it up for me because I still don't trust your father enough to let him touch it," Pekala said.

"Wait—here it is way in the back," Halia announced. She pulled an ornately carved wooden box from behind a stack of cotton blankets and then climbed down from the chair.

"Mahalo," Pekala said with relief, patting her lap. She smiled when Halia set the box on her legs and climbed into bed beside her. Flipping through the box's contents, she finally found what she was looking for and handed it willingly over to the girl who shared her sentimental heart.

Halia smiled as she took the photo. "I remember when you first showed me this picture and asked me not to tell Dad you had it. I was eleven. To this day, I still have never told him. Mom doesn't have any pictures of them together. I've treasured knowing you had this."

"Koka went through a phase of wanting to burn the past and remove all traces of it. I think it is important for you, and for him, to know where you come from."

Pekala peered at the couple in the photo. "See how they touch so lovingly. You came from love, Halia. Your father was young and foolish, but he once loved your mother with his whole heart. It was no one's fault that she couldn't love him back in the same way. Sometimes it just turns out that one person in a couple loves more than the other. We can only hope that never happens to us. Have you fallen in love yet?"

Halia laughed at the gentle, probing question. "No, *Kupunawahine*. My heart has not been captured yet."

"No matter child. You will fall in love eventually. Nineteen is young. There is plenty of time for you," Pekala said, knowing well she might not live to see it come to pass. She was already surprised to have lived so long. "What is important today is that your father has finally found love again. I had almost given up on anyone softening his heart. He was becoming hard-hearted as he got older."

Halia didn't know how to answer that, so she said nothing. "I found the news broadcast you had Denise email to me. I watched it last night before I fell asleep. The woman is not as perfect as the others they showed Dad dating. I don't think I even remember him with any of those women. Is Sabine Blakeman as nice as she looks?"

Pekala chuckled. "Her heart is very kind, but I would say Sabine is nice to everyone except your father. They balance each other in interesting ways. He insulted the French toast she made me for breakfast Saturday and she harassed him back about the number of skillets he owned. When he laughed at her rebuke and told her he loved her, she ignored his declaration. Who could blame her? But he did not get mad over her using his kitchen. When she is around, he smiles constantly. She is like sunshine compared to his dark cloud nature."

Halia giggled at the description, and at how much her great-grandmother obviously approved of the woman. "Dad certainly is a dark cloud at times."

"But not when Sabine is around," Pekala exclaimed. "That's why you need to get involved."

She pointed a shaky finger at the man in the photo. "Your father still sees this man in the mirror, so he is not properly understanding Sabine's concerns about not being as perfect as those other women. He is using his masculinity as a weapon to get his way. I'm worried that he will try to bully her into what he wants. His insistence without true understanding will only chase her away."

Halia reached over and covered her great-grandmother's hand. "I don't mind helping if you feel it's that important. After what you've told me, I want to meet her anyway. What do you want me to do?"

"Take the picture and show Sabine the past. I think it will help her see things more clearly. She is a sharp woman," Pekala said. "I wish I could go with you."

"We could take the van. Denise could drive us," Halia offered.

Pekala shook her head and leaned back on her pillow. "Too tired today, *ku`uipo*. I'm glad you're here though. It is an important thing to help keep the sunshine in our family. Seattle can be a very dreary place."

Halia leaned over and kissed the cheek of the wisest woman she had ever met. "Sleep, *Kupunawahine*. I will go do what you ask. I just hope she's as nice as you say she is."

***

"What is this? A PR intervention?" Sabine asked.

"Call it anything you like," Anthony said. "But the fact is— you need to do some image repair on yourself. You won't let Blanche help. You won't let me help. I don't like seeing you depressed like this. You just got over that jerk you married."

"Oh . . . so you did notice my divorce. You never said anything." Sabine tapped her pen on the stack of papers while she listened to Anthony's lecture.

"It seemed a little insensitive to congratulate you on your divorce. Dating Todd Lake on the other hand infused some life back into you and had you humming. So yes, this is a PR intervention because I want to hear you humming again. A happy worker is a productive worker," Anthony declared.

Sabine snorted at the platitude and gave him her best disbelieving glare. He'd earned it. "And this has nothing to do with the fact that you just happen to like Todd Lake."

"I don't need your association with the man to make friends with him. He's called every day checking on you. And I waited until today to confront you about your silence with him," Anthony said.

"I'm your employee, Anthony. You don't get to have an opinion about my boyfriends, whether they call you to spy on me or not. Even if you agree with the rest of Seattle that I'm the pudgy band geek dating the physically fit quarterback, this is not high school," Sabine said tersely.

"So Todd Lake *is* your boyfriend," Anthony declared, brightening to hear Sabine finally admit it.

Sabine shook her head, dismayed that Anthony had gotten her to say anything at all. "I don't know what he is, but you wouldn't be the first person I told."

"Do you know why I haven't offered you a partner position yet?" Anthony asked.

Sabine glared openly, not bothering to soften it. "Because I didn't have a high profile man in my life that you might extort for charity until now?"

Anthony laughed. "No. Because you lack self-confidence, Sabine. Your insecurities hold you back. I doubt you even realize that you get intimated by every beautiful client that comes along. For all her aggressive traits, Blanche never lets anyone intimidate her, not even you. We all know you could give lessons in witty comebacks, but you need to step up and own your power to change anything you see that needs changing. That's what we have to convince every client we can do. This situation is your opportunity to react differently than you ever have before."

Sabine sighed and nodded. "Okay. My insecurities could be holding me back. I guess those comments are fair. I wish you had saved the lecture for my yearly performance evaluation, but what the hell. The week can't get much worse."

"My comments were not a judgment on your personal life. And your reaction to what I said is exactly what I'm talking about," Anthony exclaimed.

A knock on her open doorway had Sabine's gaze lifting. Blanche stood there with a young, dark-haired girl. "Sabine, you have a visitor—a Ms. Halia Whitman. She says you were expecting her."

Blanche towered over the girl by a foot in her four-inch heels. Sabine hadn't been expecting her, but she did know who she was.

"Yes. I forgot to have Jan put it on the group calendar. Anthony, I'm sorry. I really need to talk to Ms. Whitman about something," Sabine said, using her most professional voice.

"Of course—we'll finish our talk later."

Anthony gave her a look that said this was just a reprieve. Ignoring him, Sabine shut the door on both him and Blanche.

The girl had already entered her office before she could issue an invitation. By the time she turned back, she was sitting in the chair Anthony had just vacated. Obviously, Koka's child had inherited his directness.

"Hello," Sabine said, walking back around to her desk chair. "You must be Koka's daughter. Your father told me you were beautiful, but I think for once his poetic descriptions fell short."

"*Mahalo*," Halia said. "My dad's college degree was in Comparative Literature. He intended to be a poet, but said he could not support raising a child on it. Cooking was his hobby at the time. He went to culinary school and came out a chef. But he loves the work. Now I can't imagine him doing anything else."

"He still has the soul of a poet. Sometimes the things he says are so beautiful they make me cry. Please don't tell him I confessed that. He's so arrogant now I can barely talk honestly to him," Sabine said. "So did you just come here to meet me? Or did Pekala send you to check on me after the newscast Sunday evening?"

Halia smiled. "*Kupunawahine* said you were a sharp woman."

Sabine laughed. "Pekala is the sharp woman. I'm just treading water and trying to keep my head up where there's air. Some days that isn't so easy a task."

"I noticed your co-workers call him Todd Lake, but yet you know his real name," Halia said.

Sabine shrugged. "I'm used to looking after the true identities of clients. Sometimes, especially with celebrities, it's easier to keep your private life private if you have a different name."

"Koka means Todd in Hawaiian," Halia explained.

"Oh, I know," Sabine said, smiling in recall about how she found out. "When your father told me that, I thought he was joking at first."

"The network didn't think his Hawaiian name would be easy to pronounce or remember. So they gave him *Todd Lake* to use. I don't know why they chose Lake though. He didn't argue. Pekala was just starting to get sick then. The job allowed him to provide for her," Halia said.

Sabine nodded as she smiled. "Your father is a very, very good man, especially when it comes to taking care of his family."

Halia smiled, but shrugged. "He is also quite bossy and inflexible about certain things. Plus he is terribly messy about his clothes. I don't know how he ever finds anything in his room."

Sabine laughed at the youthful echo of her own disgust. "Is that your clever-tongued Whitman way of asking me if I've seen the inside of your father's room?"

"No. Pekala already told me you cooked breakfast for her Saturday morning. I assumed this meant you slept with him," Halia said.

Sabine sighed and ran a hand over her face. "Okay. I slept with your father. Since I have daughters your age, I'm also used to personal questions. So tell me . . . why are you here?"

"I came to meet you and because Pekala asked me to share something with you," Halia said.

Sabine smiled. "Tell her I'll be fine, so long as being seen with me doesn't tank the ratings for your father's show."

Halia frowned. "So your concern is for him?"

Sabine nodded. "I met your father less than a month ago. I'm still pinching myself that we're dating. And yes—I often wonder if he's going to wake up one day and want one of those other women back."

"He won't," Halia said with confidence. She removed the photo gently from the envelope where it was stored in her purse. "My father looks at women differently than you would think. Now I know why Pekala sent me with the photo of him and my mother."

Mentally rolling her eyes at Halia's pronouncement, Sabine took the photo she was handed. She stared at it in complete disbelief, then raised it closer to her face. *"This is Koka?"*

Halia nodded. "Yes. He and my mother were both grossly overweight when I was born. When I was three or four, my father decided his weight was setting a bad example for me. So he found someone to help him lose the weight. You know the rest. It is all hard work. When I start to gain a few pounds, I watch his cooking show. When I see him, his appearance reminds me that food is for sustenance. If I'm lonely, I go do something with friends instead of eating."

"The change is absolutely amazing. Koka must have lost more than a hundred pounds," Sabine said.

"Closer to two hundred I think," Halia said. "It took a long time. He didn't get to his current weight until just before he and Pekala moved to Seattle. My mother eventually lost some of her weight too, but she is not obsessive about it like Dad is. My stepfather loves her anyway. He was never overweight. My mother found two great men."

Sabine looked at the picture. "Koka looks so young, but also very happy in this picture. I think he must have loved your mother very much."

Halia nodded. "Pekala has told me the story of their love all my life, but my mother was unable to love him back. It had nothing to do with her or his weight. She just loved my stepfather more than my actual father. Dad has burned all the old photos of himself except the ones Pekala hides. She says the past makes us appreciative. I think she also saves them for me."

"With what your father has accomplished, I can see why he wouldn't want to see any reminders of the past. He's incredibly attractive now, however he got that way," Sabine said.

"My great-grandmother says Dad still sees this man in the mirror. That's why he's like he is—I think she means the arrogant, sullen, moody stuff," Halia said.

Sabine nodded. "But when he smiles, he transforms. And when he does his show, he is amazingly confident. You immediately feel at ease with what he says. Not to mention the fact that he's an exceptional cook. I'm sure his restaurant will do great when he opens it."

"The restaurant—that's his big dream," Halia said. "What is your dream?"

Sabine laughed. "What is my dream?" She shook her head as she thought. "I don't know. It's been a long time since I had a dream. But one thing I do know is that your father is one of the best men that ever walked the earth. For all his male posturing, Koka always seems to know just the exact right thing to say when I need to hear it. Plus, you can forgive a lot, even a messy room, when a man has the ability to make you laugh all the time."

Sabine handed the photo back to Halia and smiled at the girl. "Thank you for sharing the story of your parents with me. I agree with Pekala. The past makes us appreciative."

"So do you believe he loves you now? *Kupunawahine* said you had doubts when he told you," Halia said.

"Well if I do, that's really between me and your father to work out," Sabine said. She admired the girl's nerve for coming to see her, but wasn't willing to let Koka's daughter push her into completely admitting her feelings. "I understand the message Pekala is sending me with the picture. I understand now that Koka probably doesn't judge me as much as I'm judging myself."

"So will you at least continue to date my father then?"

"What if I say no?" Sabine asked. She chuckled at the thought of any Whitman she'd met actually taking no for an answer.

"*Kupunawahine* will be gravely disappointed that Dad has chased away his sunshine," Halia said dramatically, wishing her great-grandmother could hear the Hawaiian in her voice. "Dad and I will have to listen to her lecturing about you until she has taken her last breath. You would be saving us all if you could at least pretend that you like him until she returns to the goddess. She is old. It shouldn't be too many years from now."

Sabine laughed loudly and long. "Okay. You've worn me down. I'll continue to date your father if you'll tell me the real reason the man collects so many damn skillets."

"I honestly don't know. I think he's just weird about them. Don't tell me—Dad made you go the mall so he could buy another one," Halia said with sudden understanding. "Well, better you than me. I was hoping to stay home this break and just eat his cooking for two or three days. Maybe his trip with you has saved me the trouble of going. Better yet, maybe he'll be afraid to go again because you made the news."

"I'm not going again either. Indulging his skillet habit has already cost me several ounces of public humiliation," Sabine said, being agreeable.

"Well, at least you didn't say it cost you 'pounds'. That's the kind of joke my father would make about what the news implied about you," Halia declared.

Sabine's laughter rang out through the office. "Yes—he would make that kind of joke, especially if he thought it would embarrass me."

"Thank you for seeing me, Sabine. Are you going to lie to your work friends about why I came to see you?"

"Yes. But only until I decide what to do about your father," Sabine said. "Give Pekala a hug for me. Tell her I'm going to be fine."

CHAPTER 16

After Pekala had echoed the same sentiment as Joe about leaving Sabine alone, Koka had given her a week to ignore his phone calls. They still hadn't talked about the newscast, but his greatest disappointment was that Halia had gone back to school without even getting to meet Sabine. He pulled his attention away from his disappointments and back to Edwina as they planned the next week of shows.

"Have you even looked at her book yet?" Edwina asked. "If we do this, you're going to have to talk to her about it, at least a little bit. It's not a novel so you can probably skim and pick up enough."

Brooding over keeping his promise to Edwina, Koka accepted the book she handed him. *"Sandwiches Don't Hug Back,"* he read. "Strange title."

"Not strange—catchy. It's about the emotional relationship many people have to food. The author offers lots of advice for eating healthy, but also some pointers on how to stop using food to fill emotional needs," Edwina said. "I thought you could fix some vegetarian dishes that were low-fat and healthy."

Koka nodded in reply to Edwina's food suggestion, as he flipped the book over and looked at the back cover. "No one overweight will believe her. She's too skinny. What could she possibly know about the struggle of losing weight?"

"A lot—actually. She wasn't always skinny. She used to weigh over two hundred pounds. I know because I was her roommate in college before her dramatic change into a fitness guru," Edwina declared.

Koka felt his eyebrows go up. "Why didn't you tell me she was your friend? I wouldn't have fought so hard about having her on as a guest. I also might have been kinder in expressing my disbelief."

Edwina grinned and shrugged. "Because I wouldn't exactly say she's my friend. It's more like I feel a need to make up to Ellen for all the ugly things I once thought and felt. She was a perfectly nice person, but I wasn't always kind about her issues. I was just as direct with her as I am with you. Weight was never a problem for me. And teenagers are much too selfish to appreciate anyone's struggles but their own."

Koka looked at the woman on the book cover with new eyes. "The change is certainly dramatic."

Edwina nodded. "During our initial interview, she told me it took her eight years to reach a size and weight that she was comfortable with. I can't imagine the kind of effort that must have taken. Along the way, she had married and had a family. She said pregnancy was the only time she ever backslid and packed on the pounds again."

"I was overweight as a teenager too. It took me over a decade to lose the weight, but by the time I was twenty-five I was okay with how I looked, or at least I was in my head. Lifting weights has taught me body sculpting, but I sometimes think I have only replaced one obsession with another," Koka said.

"Well, you've done a great job sculpting yourself. Your body is a machine. How overweight were you?" Edwina asked.

Koka lifted his gaze from the book to Edwina's. He searched her eyes wondering how much he should admit. He rarely told anyone, and when he did, almost no one ever believed him.

"I lost two hundred eighteen pounds. What I have gained back in weight since is mostly muscle," Koka said.

"Wow," Edwina exclaimed. She stared at his nearly perfect body sitting in the chair. "If I didn't know how incredibly honest you were, I would think you were lying. But you're not, are you?"

Koka shook his head. "No. I lost the weight as Halia grew up. For the first ten years of her life, she watched me reinvent my physical self year after year. The muscle building was just one of the tricks I tried, but I liked the results of that most. What I didn't account for was the very different way I would be perceived once I got to what I look like now. I think I am still adjusting. And I admit I think poorly of those who think they know who I am by judging the way I look."

Edwina laughed. "Now I get it. Sabine Blakeman's mistake at the bachelor auction is exactly why you liked her so much. And in her line of work, I imagine she sees right past a person's

112

exterior anyway. Combine that with her beautiful face and quick wit and you get the perfect woman."

"I won't argue your conclusion. Sabine is unique, and nearly perfect in every way," Koka said. "Tell your author friend I'm happy to have her on my show. I'll look through her book tonight. Maybe we can schedule her later this week if she's free. You're going to have to modify the set though if I'm going to keep having guests. Sabine and I were okay with the tight space, but I don't imagine others will take my arm swipes so graciously."

"Depends on how attracted they are to you," Edwina said, laughing at the glare she received. "I'm teasing. I'll have the guys work on it after today's shoot. I imagine it won't take much to expand the set two or three feet. It's the camera guys who'll have to make the real change. We'll have to do fewer close-ups of that pretty face of yours."

"I plan to marry Sabine," Koka said, annoyed when Edwina laughed again.

"*Marry her?* Didn't the woman just get divorced?"

Koka sighed. "Yes. But not from me."

Edwina shook her head. "I can only imagine the two of you debating that demand. She's a forty-three-year-old mother of two who needs to drop about thirty pounds. I'm not saying she's not pretty, but it's obvious to everyone that she's not as pretty as you. I bet she has doubts every moment of every day."

"I cannot worry about changing what others think. It's hard enough to change what Sabine thinks," Koka declared.

Edwina steepled her fingers on her desk as she pondered something risky, but interesting. "What if we could change what everyone thinks?" she asked.

"What do you mean?" Koka asked back, not trusting the calculating glint in Edwina's gaze on him.

"I have an idea, but it will only work if you think Sabine is worth the embarrassment," Edwina declared.

***

"I promise I will not steal any pictures from you," Koka swore, crossing his heart.

Pekala lifted her chin. "Even if I had such a picture in my memory box, what do you want with it?"

Koka sighed and sat in the chair Denise had put next to Pekala's bed. "I'm going to use it for my show. I'm having a guest on this week who lost over a hundred pounds. I'd like one of myself when I had a similar amount to lose."

"I don't know if I have any of just you alone. You burned most of those," Pekala said.

"Then I'll take one of me and Leileiana. I know you and I fought over those. I'm sorry I was so mean about it. You were right that Halia has a right to understand her parents and know the past."

Pekala frowned. "Begging is not like you, Koka. What's wrong? Are you upset that your sunshine still stays away?"

"Yes," Koka admitted. Pekala was the only person who could truly understand.

"Then you are allowed to be upset. I miss her too," Pekala said sharply. "But she is coming back. I think Sabine just needs a little more time."

Koka's sigh echoed through the room. "Well, she is taking too long. I'm lonelier now than before I met her."

"Now that sounds more like you. Maybe you will make it after all. This has taught you appreciation," Pekala declared.

"*Kupunawahine*," Koka said sternly in warning, but ended up sighing again when she laughed.

"You are so like your father and his father when you boom out in that big man Hawaiian voice. Sabine likes it though. You are a very lucky man," Pekala said, nodding.

Koka sat quietly and stared at her for what had to be five minutes before his grandmother finally relented.

"Very well. The box is in the top of the closet behind the big stack of blankets. Be careful picking it up. It is as old as I am. The lock does not work well anymore," she ordered.

A few minutes later, she passed him the only two pictures she had of him.

"*Mahalo*. These will do just fine," he said.

"Swear again that you will return them to me," Pekala ordered.

"I can do even better. I will scan them into my computer and not even take your copies from the house," Koka said softly.

"You can do that?" Pekala said in amazement. "Wonderful. Send the one of you and Leileiana to Halia."

"That's a good suggestion. I guess I should talk to my daughter before I confess on TV," Koka said.

Pekala snorted. "Halia has been looking at this picture of you and her mother since she was a young child. It was helpful to her to know the past so I showed it to her."

"She has seen this picture? Why did she never tell me?" Koka asked.

Pekala shrugged. "Probably for the same reason you have trouble seeing why Sabine is struggling. Women are complex creatures. Their confidence does not come from lifting heavy things."

"I never said women weren't complex," Koka denied. "And I'm not ashamed of the man I was. I just had to keep focused on where I was going. Lifting helped me."

Pekala reached out and patted his hand. "You have a right to be proud. For women, the journey to their true self is an emotional jungle. But hopefully Sabine will realize that a big Hawaiian man with a machete wit might have his usefulness."

"Sabine is fine like she is. I have no wish to change her. I just want her to forget her hurtful past and be happy with me," Koka said.

"For Sabine, great patience and great love will be necessary for *Pilialoha*. You are capable of both," Pekala said firmly.

Koka nodded. "The question is how long shall I wait to use my big man Hawaiian voice on her?"

Pekala laughed at her grandson's teasing. "Your heart will lead you. Do what you plan. See her after." She shrugged at his frown. "The clouds can move, but no one can tell the sun when to shine."

Koka snorted. "Are you going to call her that when she moves in here with us?"

"Yes. She likes it. I will make her feel appreciated. Her first family did not do well with that," Pekala said.

"You just want her to fix French toast for you again," Koka said, laughing when Pekala smacked his arm with a strength that surprised him.

CHAPTER 17

The call from Edwina inviting her to watch today's show had come at the same time Sabine had finally cleared the cobwebs from her brain. She had planned to come by earlier though and get the initial confrontation over, but the timing hadn't worked out. For one, it had taken most of the morning to find another dress that fit well. She hadn't seen Koka in over a week, and the weekend had been miserably long and lonely while she prowled her house and thought.

Now she stood behind privacy curtains chewing her lip while watching him set up for the show. He was probably too busy to talk at the moment, but once she had made up her mind, she decided seeing him again was too important to wait.

"Somehow I didn't see you as the hiding behind the curtains type," Edwina said, stopping beside a wide-eyed Sabine Blakeman. "Thanks for coming. I was waiting until I saw you to tell him. He's been a little more high-strung than usual lately."

"It's been a week since I talked to him. I'm being a coward. What if he's mad at me? Maybe I waited too long before coming to see him," Sabine offered in explanation.

Edwina snorted. "I'm sure that's not the case. Koka has only chewed through three spatulas this week. But there's really only one way to find out how he's feeling. Ask him, Sabine. You know he's not shy about answering direct questions."

"I tried to get here earlier, but it didn't work out. How bad is my timing?" Sabine asked.

Edwina checked her watch as she laughed. "Depending on what you have in mind, there's forty minutes left before we start the intro. Want me to send him to my office to meet you so you have some privacy?"

Sabine shook her head, knowing they would attack each other. "No. It wouldn't be a good idea for us to be alone until after his show. Just take my word for it."

Edwina laughed again. "Okay. I think I will. Go and say hello while I find you a seat. He's got a guest coming—one he didn't have to blackmail this time. I think you're going to see a whole different man today."

Sabine laughed. "I think I'll keep the current version just as he is, but thanks."

Laughing harder, Edwina walked through the set and on to her other tasks.

After Edwina had disappeared, Sabine turned her attention back to Koka. She took a deep breath, pushed aside the déjà vu making her apprehensive, and walked toward him. The click-clacking of her heels on the cement floor had several gazes turning in her direction, but not the right one. She was almost in front of the counter when she stopped and cleared her throat loudly to get his attention.

"Hello Chef Lake," she said, swallowing hard when Koka's gaze finally lifted to hers.

The spatulas, spoons, and other cooking implements in his hands went clanging to the cement. Several interns and grips rushed over to scoop them up, scrambling on the set floor around his feet while he just continued to stare. Her laugh was nervous, but not forced when it finally escaped. And she prayed fervently that she would always have the ability to stun him with her appearance.

"Another very nice dress. Blue looks really good on you, Sabine. And your curves are . . . not something I can comment on at the moment and keep my dignity," he confessed.

"Blue looks good on you too," Sabine replied, pointing at his shirt.

Koka looked down. "That's right. I wore blue today. We match," he said, raising his gaze to hers again.

Sabine snickered. "Well you know, that's what I decided too. We match and that's why I'm here. I've decided I want us to try dating . . . *real dating* . . . and I don't care who knows. If you like the way I look and who I am, then that's all I'm going to care about. And I won't let your career suffer for it because I know how to fix those kinds of things. I also promise you that I'll eventually lose the weight and look more like I belong with you. Until that happens though . . . I'm still here. I missed you like hell this week. So what do you say? Want to be *my right Todd*?"

Another anxious intern came running up with clean replacement utensils. Koka nodded at the clean ones and said thanks, asking the wide-eyed young woman to just lay them out on the counter.

Then he walked around the set kitchen and straight into the open arms of the woman he loved. Sabine's happy laughter at his action brought all faces to them as he put his arms around her and hugged as hard as he could. Sabine truly was like sunshine when she was happy. He was going to keep her that way.

"'O Ku'u Aloha No 'Oe," he whispered.

"I love you too. Later you can translate all those things you've been telling me. I'm ready to hear them now," Sabine whispered back. "And thank you for waiting this week while I did my soul-searching."

"Will you come home with me after the show?" he asked.

"Yes," Sabine said. "Edwina offered me a seat for it. Can I stay?"

Koka thought about his plans, but nodded anyway. "So long as you do not run away. Promise me."

"Why would I run away?" she asked.

"Promise me," he insisted.

Sabine nodded. "Okay. I promise." She was rewarded by a lip-tingling kiss just as insistent as his command.

Then she was free and he was striding back around the counter.

***

Unsure what to do next or where to go, Sabine turned and saw Edwina waving and pointing to an empty chair next to a man sitting behind a stationary camera. Nodding, she headed in that direction, hoping all the spandex she was wearing would allow her to sit. Unlike the full red dress, the new blue model was fitted and outlined her generous curves. She had wanted to look as sleek as possible today. She had wanted to look like a sexy older woman with her life on the mend.

The tall heels she was wearing helped maintain the illusion of lean as she walked, and Sabine glanced up to see several people in the audience smiling and waving at her. The thumbs up signs she got from several women made her laugh, but she got the gist of their support. They had obviously seen Koka hugging and kissing her. Rather than the envy she'd felt from the auction bidders, the fans in his audience seemed warm and accepting.

Smiling and thinking she might just manage this high profile relationship after all, she sat in the chair and turned her legs to one side, crossing her ankles in a way that emphasized the length of her legs. When she got herself adjusted, she looked up to find Koka's eyes following her every movement. Ducking her head, she smiled at how completely feminine she felt.

So maybe she wasn't his typical sleek woman, but when that sexy man looked at her that way, she always felt like one. Almost from the first moment, Koka had made her feel sexy and vital and worthwhile to him. With someone less demonstrative or less romantic, it might have taken her years to get over the damage Martin and his affairs had done to her. But her damage simply wasn't there with Koka. Lust and laughter and love overrode it.

Halia's visit had given her a lot to think about. Koka had made himself into both the father he wanted to be and the man he wanted to be. Skillet fetish be damned, she wanted to be the woman in his life. Now the messy room—well, that would have to change eventually—but she could save reality for another day. No man was perfect, no matter how many muscles he had.

Music queued up and the intro played. Then Koka started introducing the woman that the assistant director had walked to the set.

"I'd like to introduce my special guest for today's show. This is Dr. Ellen Lighthouse, author of *Sandwiches Can't Hug You Back*," Koka said with a flourish.

He stopped and raised his eyebrows when the audience laughed. He waited a few seconds for it to die down before continuing.

"I know. I had the same reaction when I first saw the title, but it's actually a very insightful book about how many of us use food to feed more than just our bodies. I finished reading my copy last night. Welcome, Ellen."

"Thanks for having me on your show, Chef Lake. It's my pleasure to be here," Ellen said.

Sabine snorted when Koka smiled as he addressed the attractive, smiling woman. *Look at him*, she thought. *He's such a big flirt when he wants to be.* She pulled her attention back to the conversation, just as Koka addressed the audience.

"As I was preparing for today, I discovered Ellen and I have something in common. If you read her book or visit her website, you'll find that her personal story is very inspiring. I only wish I had known about her when I was starting my own fitness journey. She's agreed to let me show you a picture of her past, but what she doesn't know is that I am including a picture of myself as well in this reveal. Can we get the handheld camera in for a close shot on these please?"

119

Koka reached under the counter and pulled out a giant double frame with two photos, as the camera zoomed in for a shot.

"Believe or not. This . . . is us," he said simply.

He pointed to the overweight man on one side and the overweight woman on the other. The audience groaned in dismay and shook their heads in disbelief at the images projected on the giant screen across from them. Sabine noticed that even the grip holding the audience prompt cards was staring. It was a very real moment, one that took a lot of courage from both the woman and Koka. She sniffed a little, feeling proud.

Koka let his gaze rise to the audience and then go back to the counter and photo. "This is me at age nineteen, overweight from all my bad habits. The woman is Ellen at age twenty. But look at us both now. Proper diet, exercise, and perseverance have transformed us. What do you think? We've really made some changes, haven't we?"

The audience broke out in cheers and Sabine saw Ellen Lighthouse reach out to touch Koka's arm. He nodded at something she said as the audience clapped and cheered. When they quieted, he went on.

"I lost over two hundred pounds. It took me a decade of my life to do it. The reason I did it was to give my daughter a healthier, more fit example to follow as she made her choices about life and food. How about you Ellen? Want to tell them a little of your story?"

"I lost just over a hundred pounds. I spent most of my teen years and my early twenties feeling bad about myself. It took me five years to lose the weight and some serious internal reflection to kick that emotional baggage that went with it. I think women especially have a hard time," Ellen said.

Koka nodded. "I know what you mean. My new girlfriend is a sexy woman with a healthy body, but she's not skinny. And truthfully, I don't want her to be. I like her like she is. Do you think as a society we're ever going to ease up on comparing everyone to some ideal of thin that only a small percentage of people ever achieve?"

Ellen smiled and nodded. "I'm certainly trying my best to make it happen. As a fitness specialist, I tell my clients to work toward their happiest, healthiest selves. For many, that is not going to be a body like they see in magazines. But toned and fit is achievable for everyone. I think you can get to a place where your inner voice will stop responding so dramatically to the negative opinions of others. Or at least you can dial them down to a tolerable level."

"Well, I'm no fitness guru, but I do know a thing or two about cooking healthy. My daughter is in college now and I worry sometimes about what she's eating. She tells me she watches my show, so I hope she's watching this one. Want to help me fix a mouthwatering, vegetarian meal?" Koka asked.

"Can I also help you eat it afterwards? I love to eat," Ellen said.

"Excellent. I like to eat also. Let's do this then," Koka said.

As Koka and Ellen Lighthouse cooked, Sabine sat in her chair and studied him. Though she hadn't been his guest for this show, she felt like she'd made an appearance. Everything he had said or done, including showing the unflattering photo, had been for her. Koka really knew how to put action behind all those romantic words of his.

She laughed, glad the audience chattering above her drowned it out. Now that he had bared his soul to the world, it was going to be a long time before she was going to be able to complain about his underwear and shoes all over the bedroom floor. *Damn the man.*

Jarred out of her daydreaming, she realized Edwina was lifting her arm and trying to get her to stand.

"What do you want me to do?" Sabine asked.

"He wants to show you off to Ellen," she whispered.

Swallowing her shock, Sabine lifted her chin and walked toward Koka. Applause rose in the air behind her. She walked slowly and carefully toward his smile of welcome, taking the hand he offered as he came out of the small set to greet her.

"Ellen, this is Sabine Blakeman, my personal sunshine," Koka said.

Sabine felt him pull her behind the counter with a firm grip on her hand. His gaze connected with the cameraman's thumbs-up sign that she was in the frame well enough.

"Wait—I know you," Ellen said excitedly, jumping up and down. "I saw you bidding on Chef Lake at the bachelor auction. You even argued back with that woman who was yelling at you. You were amazing."

"That's the night we met. Our secret is that Sabine was bidding on the wrong man when she won me," Koka said proudly.

Ellen laughed and looked around him. "Is he kidding, Sabine?"

Sabine winced, forgetting the camera was watching. "No. It's true. I didn't know who he was then. I went to bid on Todd Masterson. I got my Todds wrong."

When Koka turned to grin at her honesty, Ellen Lighthouse shook her head and mouthed "no you didn't" behind his back and made the audience laugh again. Sabine bit her lip to keep from laughing herself.

"Or maybe you got your Todds right," Koka declared, making everyone laugh again. "Though I have met Todd Masterson also. He is a very nice man, but I doubt he cooks as well as I do."

"Oh . . . do you know how to cook?" Sabine asked, pretending shock and getting her own laugh from the audience. "Prove it, Todd. I want a bite of that vegetarian dish. It looks wonderful. I didn't know you could cook without using pork."

Koka glared while everyone laughed again. "Maybe you need to come on my show again. Next time I'll teach you how to make real French toast instead of that soggy bread you like to make."

"That's my family recipe." Forgetting where they were, Sabine whacked his arm. Then mortified, she looked at Ellen. "I'm sorry. His insults always make me want to hurt him."

"Are you kidding? This is the most fun I've had on any show before. Can I come back again too?" she asked.

"Deal," Koka declared. "And unfortunately extracting a promise of tomorrow is all the time we have left for today. Thanks for stopping by. Come on ladies, *Kiss The Sexy Chef* and we'll all sign off."

Giggling, they each took a cheek as the music rose and Koka laughed.

Seconds later, Sabine let out a sigh when Edwina yelled, "Cut. That's a wrap."

But she knew the end of the show was just the beginning for her and Koka.

CHAPTER 18

"Oh, dear God. Please, Joe—tell me you're wearing shorts under that," Sabine demanded.

Joe laughed at Sabine's fearful expression while Todd was busy adjusting the grass skirt around his waist. "Koka came in a little while ago and told us how to make it hang correctly. Just remember it wasn't my idea to have a Hawaiian-themed wedding, or for me to be your *Man of Honor*. You seriously need to get some girlfriends so I can have my dignity back."

Laughing, Todd turned to look at Sabine. "Nice flowered sarong," he said, admiring her from head to toe. "Giant red hibiscus suits you."

Sabine smiled and ran a hand down the front of herself. "Nice and loose too."

Joe snorted. "What are you worried about after all those workouts? Your boobs have never looked better. No one is going to blame you for wearing a flowered bra instead of real clothes to your wedding. If I had those, I would show them to the world too."

Sabine shook her finger at him. "This is not a flowered bra. In Hawaii, this is the top of my dress. You're just mad because I refused to wear the plastic coconuts. I wore them at my bachelorette party and they fell off twice. That was enough humiliation for a lifetime."

Todd laughed as he deftly shifted the conversation away from a party they were all better off forgetting. "Okay, I don't care if this is your wedding. I've been waiting two whole days to ask this. What did Anthony say about the Rundgren contract?"

Sabine stepped back and flicked her fluffy blonde locks over her lightly tanned shoulders. "You are now looking at Anthony's latest partner—thank you very much. My promotion is effective immediately following my honeymoon. Since Anthony has a terrible man-crush on *my Todd*, he's holding out to make sure I go through with the marriage."

Todd clapped his hands. "Excellent. My boss adores you, by the way. He said you were the most upbeat, no-nonsense public relations specialist he'd ever met."

"A woman can never hear enough sweet flattery," Sabine said with a smile.

Three giggling girls dressed similarly to her rushed into the room. Her youngest was vibrating. "Mom, there are at least twenty nearly-naked guys at your wedding. Before the music started they were dancing in grass skirts and tossing fire staffs around. One of them was Koka. But don't worry, he's not wearing a skirt anymore. Halia fussed at him. Now he's wearing the shorts and shirt you wanted, but he was twirling a fire staff too—a lit one."

"Any of the skirted guys look better than your Uncle Joe here?" Sabine asked.

"Only like all of them . . ." Sabine heard her oldest say, making everyone laugh, including her. Grinning, she looked at Joe, who was sporting as much of a tan as he could for the occasion.

"Hey now. Be careful with those insults. You might hurt my sensitive *Man Of Honor* feelings," Joe exclaimed. He yelled mild obscenities and sent his grass skirt swishing madly as his two nieces attacked and tickled his naked chest and belly.

"Now is not the time for hula practice, Joe," Todd said sternly. "Maybe after the wedding."

Sabine shook her head as Todd's laughing gaze met hers. Halia looked on, blinking quietly as her soon-to-be stepsisters acted too crazy for her to join in. Sabine could only hope they didn't embarrass the more conservative girl too much. The three had gotten along almost too well since they first met. It was so hard to believe that almost a year had passed.

"Todd, you're going to have to fix me. It's twisted again," Joe ordered. He sighed in relief when the girls finally let him alone and rushed out to go take their seats. "You will owe me forever for this, Sabine."

"What are you complaining about? I made sure there was no chance of you burning off your skirt. Only the groomsmen will be fire dancing at the luau afterward. The rest of us get to watch and admire the show," Sabine said.

And she'd seen the nearly naked version of Koka's fire dance during his practice in the backyard of his house. Grateful for the seclusion of a tall privacy fence, she had enjoyed the show immensely.

Denise suddenly appeared in the doorway pushing a familiar wheelchair. "Aren't you ready yet, Sunshine?" Pekala demanded. "You need to hurry before Koka and his cousins burn the house down with their practicing."

"I'm ready," Sabine said, walking to her.

Pekala lifted the bouquet of white orchids, jasmine, and assorted colorful flowers. "These are not completely traditional, but they suit you. Come now. He waits impatiently."

Sabine buried her face in the fragrant bouquet. "These are beautiful and they smell amazing."

"Come," Pekala ordered, but she smiled.

"Boys—it's show time," Sabine called when she lifted her head.

Rolling his eyes, Joe gave a head nod to a still laughing Todd. "If we ever decide to do this, and I use the word 'theme' in a sentence, remind me of Sabine's wedding."

"Yes, honey," Todd teased, snapping the elastic that held up Joe's grass skirt as he walked around him.

Despite the not so graceful beginning of their march, the two men grew quiet as they walked ahead of the bride and her escort, slowing more when they heard the music.

The walk down the sand-covered pavers was slow with the wheelchair, but Sabine hardly noticed. All she saw was the brilliant white smile of the man with ancient warrior blood who waited for her. He stood by the side of the walkway he'd created for his grandmother.

Denise rolled Pekala to the side and waited while Koka stepped onto the pavers and took a position facing her. Sabine fought back a giggle when he cleared his throat and took a deep breath. It made her smile to see that he was as nervous as she was.

"For our friends from the mainland and our family, we decided to start our ceremony with exchanging our declarations in front of you first," Koka said. He watched Sabine's smiling face with his heart beating hard.

"*Mahalo nui loa.* Thank you for your prayers and for bringing my sunshine to me today," Koka whispered. He bent and kissed Pekala's cheek, then straightened to hold out his hand formally to his bride.

"*Ke Aloha*—I am calling Sabine Blakeman my beloved. *Aloha No Au Ia 'Oe*—I am saying to Sabine that I truly love her—and I do very much," Koka said, explaining to everyone as Sabine put her hand in his.

"*Aloha Au Ia 'Oe*," Sabine replied, grateful for the language lessons Pekala had given her. "I am saying back to Koka Whitman—I love you too—and I always will."

Overwhelmed with emotion that simply had to be expressed, Koka bent his mouth to Sabine's for a kiss that rocked them both more than was wise. When he lifted his head, she stumbled back a little. He instantly reached out and caught her, unable to stop his masculine chuckle. "Whoa—don't fall."

"I wasn't going to fall. I just wasn't prepared. You weren't supposed to kiss me yet," Sabine complained.

"Do you expect a warning every time I kiss you?" Koka demanded.

"Not now, children. We have guests. No fighting until this is over," Pekala yelled as loudly as her old voice would rise, clapping her hands for extra sound.

"Sorry, Pekala. But Koka started it," Sabine said, snickering and pushing against her handsome groom's chest with the hand that held her flowers.

"Consider yourself warned then, bride. If you think I won't kiss my wife when I please, you are definitely marrying *the wrong Todd*," Koka said sternly. He pulled a squealing Sabine into his arms and kissed her neck while everyone listened to her protests.

Finally pushing free of her demanding groom's hold on her, Sabine glared at Koka's happy face. He was so absolutely beautiful. It was still very hard to believe a man like him could want her as much as he did. Overwhelming emotion with the force of a tidal wave swept through her every time she looked at him.

Afraid she might burst into stupid bride tears any second, Sabine buried her red face in her flowers and turned to the only person she could for help. "Don't just stand there, Joe Kendall. It's your job as *Man of Honor* to fix this awkward situation."

Joe crossed his arms and spread his legs to look as intimidating as possible. "What is there to fix? Your embarrassment over fighting with your groom cannot be greater than mine wearing this grass skirt for you. Go say 'I do' to the bossy Hawaiian you adore and let the man feed you grilled pineapple for the rest of your life. You're just afraid to say 'I do" again, sweetie. But there is no reason to be in this case."

When Sabine shook her head and wouldn't raise her face from her flowers, Joe sighed and turned to the now suddenly worried groom. "Trust me, Koka. Your bride doesn't mean that head shake one bit. Instead of fighting with her, try saying something romantic and poetic. Sabine loves that stuff now. She goes on and on about it."

The wisdom of Joe's request hit him in a rush, and just as hard as his bride hit her *Man of Honor* in the chest with her bouquet over his request. Koka laughed loudly at Sabine's actions, but he finally understood what was needed. He cleared his throat loudly as Joe forcibly turned his suddenly reluctant bride to face him again.

He stepped closer and smiled into her wary eyes. "Sabine Blakeman—there is a man standing by the ocean with the power to marry us. He is waiting for us now as anxiously as I have been waiting for you all my life. Will you marry me today? Will you become my wife? I know you're worried, but I swear your heart is safe with me. I promise to love you and only you until I take my last breath. *Aloha Aku No.*"

Raising her head at the sincerity that was always in his lovely words, Sabine nodded and smiled at the only man who could have ever talked her into remarrying so soon. "Okay. I love you too. I'm sorry I panicked. Now I'm so nervous that I've forgotten Pekala's lessons. How do I say a simple yes in Hawaiian?"

"Let your heart say it for you, Sunshine. I will hear it," Koka whispered, tugging her hand until Sabine laughed happily and followed him.

# # #

NOTE FROM THE AUTHOR: If you enjoyed this book, please consider leaving a positive review or rating on the site where you purchased it. Reader reviews help my books continue to be valued by distributors/resellers and help new readers make decisions about reading them. I value each and every reader who takes the time to do this and invite you all to join me on my Website, Blog, Facebook, Twitter, or Goodreads.com for more discussions and fun.

You are the reason I write these stories and I sincerely appreciate you!

Many thanks for your support,
~ Donna McDonald

GLOSSARY OF TRANSLATIONS

Most of the Hawaiian in this book came from internet research. I found one very good site that was geared to weddings which was full of phrasing for love and romance. I'm not including it because sites have a tendency to disappear or change. Instead, I am including the translations of the phrases I used.

aloha is a greeting used to say hello or goodbye. Aloha can also mean love.

kupunawahine ~ grandmother, grandma,, granny, grammy

ku`uipo ~ sweetheart

Ke Aloha ~ beloved

Mahalo E Ke Akua No Keia La ~ thanks be to God (or the goddess) for this day

Mahalo ~ thank you

Mahalo nui loa ~ thank you very much

Nau ko`u aloha ~ my love is yours

Na'u `oe ~ you're mine

No Keia La, No Keia Po, A Mau Loa ~ from this day, from this night, forever more

Nou No Ka `I`ini ~ I desire you

'O Ku'u Aloha No 'Oe ~ you are indeed my love

Pilialoha ~ to be in a bond of love

Aloha Au Ia 'Oe ~ I Love You

Aloha Aku No, Aloha Mai No ~ I give my love to you, you give your love to me

Aloha No Au Ia 'Oe ~ I Truly Love You

KEEP READING in this book to
read extended excerpts from several of my
first-in-series books.

Some are still FREE to download in ebook
format.

See www.donnamcdonaldauthor.com for
more information or to subscribe to my
newsletter.

CONNECT WITH DONNA MCDONALD

WEBSITE
www.donnamcdonaldauthor.com

EMAIL
email@donnamcdonaldauthor.com

TWITTER
@donnamcdonald13 and @scifiwoman13

FACEBOOK
Donna McDonald Contemporary Romances
Donna McDonald SciFi Romances
Risky Readers

CONTEMPORARY BOOK BLOG
www.donnamcdonald.blogspot.com

PARANORMAL/FANTASY/SCIFI BOOK BLOG
www.donnamcdonaldparanormal.blogspot.com

OTHER BOOKS BY DONNA MCDONALD

Visit my website at **www.donnamcdonaldauthor.com** to see a
complete list of my books including
the following bestselling series:

NEVER TOO LATE SERIES

ART OF LOVE SERIES

NEXT TIME AROUND SERIES

FORCED TO SERVE SERIES

If you want to hear about new releases and planned books,
please subscribe to my newsletter.

Thank you for Reading my work! You are the reason I write.

~ Donna McDonald ~

EXCERPT FROM NEXT SONG I SING

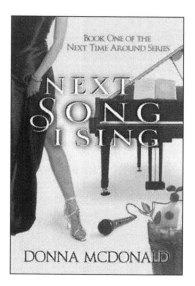

CHAPTER 1

Chloe sighed heavily when she saw a magazine with earmarked pages being pulled from the bright red overnight case tossed on the roll-away cot next to the window. She hung her head and groaned like a woman dying, eliciting a wicked laugh from the bag's owner. "Emma Wallace, I can't believe you still do those silly quizzes. I will not be answering any questions about my favorite position during sex, so don't even ask."

Emma studied her friend Chloe and then pointed the magazine at her, punching the air with it for emphasis. "I'll take it easy on you because your divorce is still fresh, but you need soul-searching more than any of us, Chloe. You stayed with a man who cheated on you for more years than I did. This is not just a quiz. It's part of your journey to self-discovery."

"Journey to self-discovery? Jeez, Emma, you're starting to sound more and more like those greeting cards you write," Taylor Baird said, dragging an expensive black leather overnight case on wheels into the room behind her.

Emma and Chloe smiled at the svelte blonde who looked all business in her suit. Chloe ran over to hug her, surprised to be getting all choked up over how happy she truly was to see Taylor.

"Thank God you're here. Emma brought a *quiz*," Chloe complained, saying it as if it were a dirty word.

Finally letting Taylor go, Chloe returned to her unpacking, a little embarrassed about how incredibly happy she was to be with her friends again. God, she should never have left.

"Command some authority here, Taylor, and tell Emma no quiz questions. I moved to the West Coast to get away from being emotionally tortured," Chloe said.

Taylor laughed, her voice husky. "Remember in college when Emma got the idea that we needed to get our belly buttons pierced to be sexy?"

"Unfortunately," Chloe said, remembering the trauma all too well.

She had screamed in pain while Emma had laughed and Taylor had winced in sympathy. But ironically, Chloe had kept the piercing over the years. Mostly because it had cost her so dearly to get it, but also because it made her feel sexy even when her husband Aaron hadn't liked it. Wearing jewelry in her belly had been her way of rebelling against him when they fought, which ended up being often during the almost five years they had been married.

133

"Earth to Chloe? Where are you?" Emma called, waving a hand in front Chloe's face.

"That piercing hurt like hell, Em," Chloe informed her, glaring hard as she remembered the pain.

"Everything worth doing hurts a little, even exercising. And who was it that ran around in navel-revealing shirts all that year? I'll give you a hint. It wasn't me or Taylor showing off our piercings," Emma reminded her, not a bit embarrassed to gloat.

"What else could I do but show it off? I figured I might as well enjoy flaunting it after going through hell to get it done," Chloe insisted, glaring at Emma, who stuck out her tongue.

"I bet you still have your piercing," Emma said with a knowing grin. "I don't. Taylor doesn't. Tell us the truth, Chloe."

"A woman has a right to some keep some secrets, especially from nosy friends," Chloe announced, turning away from their knowing smiles.

When both Emma and Taylor laughed, Chloe rolled her eyes because...well, she had kept her piercing. And it had felt very brave to take a healthy chunk of her savings and buy a tiny real diamond-studded ring to wear there. It made her feel a lot younger than forty. She had needed help to feel better about her thirty-six-year-old husband replacing her with a skinny woman half her age.

Taylor laughed at Chloe's and Emma's bickering, thinking five years living on opposite coasts hadn't changed the dynamic between them much. Back in college though, Chloe's programming to please people she cared about had practically guaranteed she would never outsmart a determined Emma hell-bent on a makeover. Helping people improve themselves was practically a religion to Em, and she and Chloe were usually favorite converts.

"We were twenty-one not sixteen when we got those piercings, Chloe Zanders. You could have said no about the belly button ring. You can say no to the quiz now. That was my point for bringing it up. It's time to learn to command your own authority," Taylor said with a laugh.

"Trust me, Baird. I'm not the pushover I was in college. I command authority when I need to nowadays, but you're not fooling me. If I don't play along, you and Emma will think I'm just as boring as my ex did," Chloe said, turning away to shake out her clothes from the exercise duffle she had brought.

She glared at the plain black gym bag. It wasn't red and perky like Emma's or sleekly black like Taylor's. It was black and old, not to mention well-used, but her good luggage had been too large for a simple three-night stay in a resort, so Chloe hadn't bothered with it. Everything that worked for California fit in the one small bag she'd carried on the plane.

"You are so not boring, Chloe. Your ex was just a selfish jerk like my mine was. Own it, girlfriend—and then let it go," Taylor said flatly, snorting in derision. "Trust me, you didn't lose anything divorcing a man who didn't appreciate you. One day soon, you're going to be nothing but relieved that Aaron is out of your life. It just takes a while to feel it."

Taylor unzipped her case and started looking through her clothes. "Now come on. We're going shopping for sexy new dresses to kick off our weekend. For once, I'm looking forward to letting Emma try to fix me with her quizzes and questions. I haven't had a decent date in three months. I obviously need an attitude adjustment."

"It's been two weeks since my last date," Emma recounted, "but I've been sexually abstaining for several months. I'm balancing my chi and preparing for a better relationship. I want to be in an open and receptive state of being when I let the next man that far into my life."

Chloe snorted. "Balancing your chi? Wallace, you crack me up." She shook her head and sighed heavily again. "Well, don't try to balance mine, Em. I like my chi like it is. I'm still too mad at my ex to even think about sleeping with another man right now. I just want to enjoy my freedom for a while and be grateful I can stop worrying about what some guy thinks of me."

Taylor laughed, rich and full. "Well, speak for yourself. I don't even remember the last time I had sex. I think I would like someone to unbalance my chi—and soon. What I need right now though is some minor lubrication, a late lunch, and some good old-fashioned girl fun."

"Taylor, I booked us appointments in the spa like you asked," Emma said, speaking to her very savvy business friend who had placed her order for the weekend with specific instructions that she would be picking up the tab for their fun. "Full works on all three of us tomorrow at ten, including massages. We're going to be buffed, fluffed, and stuffed. I hope that's what you had in mind."

"*Stuffed*? What do you mean stuffed?" Chloe demanded, gripping her most slimming black dress in her hands. "Just what kind of massages did you arrange for us, Emma? I told you I'm not ready for anything yet."

Taylor fell back on the bed laughing. "Would you listen to her? The woman who used to date three guys at once has now been replaced by an uptight version afraid of getting laid. Will you tell her sexual massages are not on the spa menu at this five-star hotel? I swear I am never going to visit the East Coast if Chloe is an example of what happens to people out there."

Emma put her chin on her chest and sighed heavily as she looked at Chloe. "I can see unwinding you is going to take some time."

"Yeah? Well, I'm about to show you two skinny blondes how much authority big women like me command. I'm going to sit on Emma's tiny butt until she tells me what she means by *stuffed*," Chloe said firmly, shaking out the five-year-old black capris that she hoped might still tame her curves.

At an extremely healthy size fourteen, Chloe was not all that big by East Coast standards. But in southern California where tanned and toned bodies were the norm, she was twice the size of her two skinny friends.

"Stuffed as in lunch, Chloe. Lunch is included in our treatment. Relax, will you? When was the last time you had any fun?" Emma demanded, shaking her head sadly.

Chloe stopped sorting her clothes. When *was* the last time she had fun? Good grief, she couldn't even remember. Sex she'd had, if you could count sleeping with her cheating ex-husband, but fun was sorely lacking. How pathetic was that?

"The last time I had fun was in college," Chloe answered finally. "Despite Aaron's time out here, he and his family had very different ideas about fun than I had. Honestly, I don't know now why I married him. When it came right down to day-to-day living, we didn't have much in common."

"I know why you married Aaron. You were almost thirty-five and thought the world was ending because you were still not married. It was easy for you to cave-in to the sexy, semi-retired football player who spent all his time trying to get you into bed," Taylor said wisely.

"That's the truth, and Aaron is still very sexy," Chloe said wistfully, sighing again. "I didn't leave him because the sex was bad."

"Oh—please. Stop mooning over leaving a repeat adulterer," Emma ordered, her tone fierce. "Trust me, it's a total waste of time."

Chloe opened her mouth to tell Emma that Aaron wasn't as bad as her ex, but Taylor chimed in first.

"You married Aaron for the same reason I married Lewis and in the same year. Being single at thirty-five sent you right into the arms of the first sexy man who popped the question. Lewis was good in bed too, but that didn't make up for his lack of morals. Luckily, my opportunistic ex-husband moved on to his next victim when the business failed. I don't even think I was a woman to him. I was just an investment plan. God—the business failing put me on the right track in a lot of ways."

Taylor looked over at Emma, who hadn't said anything. She was sitting cross-legged on the bed in a meditative pose, listening and looking serene. Unfortunately, Emma was always serene, Taylor thought, and it wasn't healthy to hold the hurt in that tightly.

"I guess when it comes down to it, Emma is the only one of us who even came close to finding real love," Taylor said wistfully

"Real love? What are you talking about? Brad got another woman pregnant before I even found out for sure that I couldn't have children. A bad marriage doesn't get much more pathetic than that," Emma said lightly, not breaking her pose. "But I've separated myself from his energy now. He's already working on baby number two with his new wife, who is also a twenty-something. So I know how you feel about being tossed out to the curb because of a younger woman, Chloe."

Chloe looked at Emma and blinked. Aaron's defection had nicked her pride because she hadn't wanted to fail in her marriage, but it hadn't affected her heart much. Emma hadn't been so lucky. Though divorced the longest amount of time, Emma had loved her husband sincerely, and there had been no serious man in her life since.

Chloe bit back her first response of denial. Emma didn't need more pain.

"Fine. I concede we all need help with our love lives, but if I'm going to have to answer those dumb quiz questions, it's going to require more than mild lubrication. I think I'm going to start at lunch and do a follow-up drink every hour to make sure I maintain a buzz all day to get through it," Chloe said, gracing Emma with as sincere a smile as she could manage. "It shouldn't take much though. I haven't been inebriated in years."

Shaking off her mood, Emma stood to wiggle her hips and her eyebrows as she looked at Chloe. "Does alcohol still make you want to get extra friendly?"

"Yes. So if I do get tipsy, don't let me run off with some strange man. That's a bit more self-exploration than I'm ready for right now," Chloe said, letting herself find the humor in it at last.

Listening to both her friends laughing at her plea, something inside Chloe eased. She hated being defensive, hated that she'd brought that attitude to these two women who had been true friends to her through thick and thin. They didn't need her angst on top of their own. She was the fixer not the fixee in their group.

Taylor laughed at Chloe's confession and sighed at the kindness and caring on her face as well as the return of ease to Emma's expression. "I have missed you something fierce, Chloe Zanders. The California sunshine is going to melt all that East Coast angst away soon. By the time you get your tan back, you'll be a new woman."

"Wow. Aren't you the optimist for once? Saving a business agrees with you," Chloe teased. Then she sighed. "I'm glad to be back. It was way past time to make a change."

Taylor sprang up from the bed, lithe and confident in her dress clothes, which she intended to shed right now for crops and the tightest T-shirt she owned. "Wear something easy to get out of, girls, and bring slut shoes if you have them. We're going shopping."

CHAPTER 2

"I just love this place," Emma said, flipping through the racks. "Upscale consignment, and just look at all these wonderful recycled clothes. I've said it before, but Taylor—you really are amazing."

"Yes, well you know I became very resourceful during the two lean years I was working to save Pink Link Sports. This place was a financial godsend for schmoozing wear when I had to go to sponsor parties. Are you still a twelve, Chloe?" Taylor asked.

"I wish. Now and again I can squeeze into a really, really large twelve bottom, but I'm always a fourteen on the top," Chloe replied. "I moved from a D to a DD cup a few years ago so I need the boob room."

Taylor stopped to study her. "This will be perfect then." She handed a two-piece outfit over to Chloe. "This will let the girls peak out and say hi to people. Your breast size is an asset. You need to use it."

"It's a harem girl outfit," Chloe declared in horror, laughter choking her as she looked at the jewel toned top and skirt Taylor had passed to her. "I'm not wearing this in public."

"Come on. You're a little soft, but you still have the waist for it," Emma said briskly. "I watched you change clothes. You look great, just pale. Try it on."

"I agree," Taylor said, smiling. "Try it on."

Chloe rolled her eyes, then tossed the outfit over her arm with the other two she'd found. "You two are as nuts as ever. I know I used to be the primo slut among us, especially when it came to clothes, but those days are long gone. I don't flash my cleavage or anything else at the world anymore. I was only a size ten in college. There's a big difference in flashing now."

"Why?" Taylor asked with a grin. "If there's one thing I've learned in business, it's that it's hard to find the right customers without good advertising."

Chloe tilted her head and looked at Taylor as Emma laughed in the background. "Says the five-foot-seven woman with the body of a skinny model. I bet you barely wear a size eight."

"Six sometimes," Taylor said, eyes twinkling. "What can I say? Despite working out regularly, it's mostly genetics. I kiss my mother for it whenever I see her, which is fortunately only twice a year."

Chloe rolled her eyes. She had never met her own birth mother, but Chloe would bet money the woman hadn't been less than a size twenty. She was watching her hips and thighs spread with every passing year. The thought of being even bigger than she was now did not make her cheerful.

Emma laughed at their banter over weight. Her proportionate size eight body on her five-foot-four frame had never much mattered to her so long as her health was good.

"All this fixation on weight is bringing me down. How did you lose touch with your inner slut, Chloe? I only met your ex a couple of times, but he seemed like the type that would have liked the sexually liberated side of you. I remember him being tall, broad-shouldered, and very handsome," Emma said.

"All true—and Aaron did like my slut side," Chloe said, irony dripping from the words as flipped through the racks. "We were in bed more than out the first year we were married. He was really good in bed too. For a couple of years, I thought I had found the perfect man."

"So what went wrong?" Emma asked, trying not to exude too much sympathy because she knew Chloe didn't like pity. "Your husband never came with you when you visited, but I guess I always thought that was your choice."

What went wrong? Chloe stopped flipping through the rack of beautiful clothes to ponder her answer.

"It seems like I spent the last four years trying to figure that out, Emma. For one, Aaron's family was always critiquing me— us—no *me*," she corrected. "They frequently complained about the way I dressed that first year I lived there. To get them to shut up about it, somewhere in the second year I started wearing clothes with no cleavage, flat shoes, and pants in the summer to work. And then I found out about the first woman Aaron cheated on me with. She was my age, but she looked like you two, including the blonde hair."

Chloe looked at the sympathy in their faces but also saw a glint of steel in both gazes aimed at her. *That's what I came here for*, she realized. Under their sympathy was support of the best kind. Chloe knew they would never let her wallow too long in self-pity.

"Even though it killed my pride to know Aaron had slept with someone else, I still loved the jerk, so I told myself that I wanted to work out our problems. For a while, I even went back to normal until he asked me to tone it down again for his family's sake. So back I went to wearing my conservative clothes and dark colors. That would have been—oh, early in year four I think—just before woman number two entered the picture."

Emma stopped to stare. "Chloe, that's awful. Your husband wanted you like you were, but then wanted you to change just to please his family? That seems kind of dumb of him, don't you think?"

"Well, I do now," Chloe said emphatically. "I should never have let anyone tell me how to dress or what to like or what was funny or not funny. By the time Aaron actually left me for the last woman—a nubile twenty-three-year-old I heard—well, I didn't even recognize myself except for the belly button ring hidden under my drab clothes."

Taylor was shaking her head. "Well, screw that. Try on the harem-girl outfit. That's who you really are."

Chloe laughed. "Right—I'm a giant-sized harem girl," she said wryly, rolling her eyes. "You know, the sad thing is that only the first woman hurt. The other two just seemed inevitable and as much my fault as Aaron's. If I would have left after the first woman, then the other two would never have happened."

"Why did you stay?" Emma asked softly, wondering if Chloe had loved Aaron as much as she had loved Brad. She hoped the answer was no for Chloe's sake.

Chloe thought how falsely attentive Aaron had been when he'd been cheating, how great the sex had been when he'd felt guilty, even when the real intimacy had died. Even knowing it wasn't enough to hold her relationship together, she had swallowed the hurt and told herself it was what adult women did to make their relationships work. It was pathetic to think about now, but at the time it had seemed a lot less trouble than starting over at her age. Now she was doing it anyway...at forty no less.

"Why did I stay after I knew there were other women? Laziness," Chloe answered firmly. "If Aaron hadn't moved out, I probably would still be there."

"Oh, you'd have found the energy to leave eventually," Taylor said, laughing when Chloe laughed. "Emma and I both know you better than that."

"Honestly? Even though Aaron moved in with his girlfriend before the divorce was final, I didn't really care by that point. On the plus side, my in-laws were incredibly nice through it all, and I know Aaron caught hell over leaving me for her," Chloe remarked. "They begged me to stay on at the company. Thank God I wasn't that desperate for work. Having savings meant I could totally leave."

"Of course they wanted you to stay," Taylor said. "You were working in the family business for a fraction of what you're worth. I intend to hire you as soon as I can afford you."

"I love you for saying that, but no thanks, Taylor. I'm on sabbatical from being a money genius. I haven't had a real vacation in years, so I'm not even looking for work for three months. And when I do start looking, I'd like to do something very different in my next job," Chloe said cautiously.

"*Singing?* You're going back to singing?" Emma asked excitedly, almost dropping her clothes. "Oh, Chloe, that would be simply awesome for you."

Taylor paused to study Chloe as well. She wasn't fooled by her pretended interest in vintage evening gloves. She'd seen her friend's eyes light up at Emma's comment.

"I did not say I wanted to sing for a living," Chloe protested. "I haven't sung in years—well, not really."

"That's a sacrilege with your talent. We'll rectify the not-singing-thing tonight. There's a piano lounge at the hotel with a very nice looking pianist," Taylor teased. "I had a supplier who was staying here a couple of weeks ago. We met for drinks in the lounge. If I hadn't been working, I might have even talked to Mr. Hunky Piano Man."

"Ply me with enough alcohol and I'll sing my thong song," Chloe teased. "That gets a rise out of most men."

"No, I want to hear you *really* sing and quiet the whole room like you did in college," Taylor insisted, narrowing her eyes at the startled gaze Chloe sent her way. Oh yeah, she was interested.

"Give it up, Ms. Optimist. College was a long time ago and so was singing in front of an audience," Chloe told her sadly.

"Not that long," Taylor denied easily, "and you were more than just good. You were extraordinary. I never fully understood why you went into accounting instead of music."

"I was young, just out of the orphanage then, and wanted security. If I hadn't gotten the scholarship I would never have met you two. My left brain and stomach won the debate over what to major in," Chloe said. "I've made some good investments with my degree and don't regret my accounting work. It gave me security, which I badly needed in my life even if the work wasn't very fulfilling otherwise."

"Or fun," Emma said, cringing at the idea of sitting behind a desk for days on end with no movement. "I'm with Taylor. Singing tonight will be like the old days. We'll do back-up. It will be fun for all of us. We'll all pretend we're twenty again."

"Twenty? Don't make me laugh. I don't intend to spend my sabbatical money on the amount of lubrication it's going to take for me to get up the nerve to sing in public after all this time," Chloe informed them with a laugh.

"Lubrication is on me then," Taylor said, laughing. "I want to hear you sing, Chloe. If you can sing again, then I will believe anything is possible, including me finding a decent straight man in southern California."

Chloe held up a one-piece black bathing suit that had more cutouts than material. "Well, if this bathing suit can cover all the important parts, then I'll believe anything is possible." She looked at Emma, who was smiling at her. "What are you smiling about?"

Emma shrugged. "I always believe anything is possible. And I would like to hear you sing tonight too. That bathing suit is going to make you look dangerous, Chloe. Be careful wearing it."

"Dangerous?" Chloe repeated with a laugh, holding the suit to her body in front of a mirror. "Yeah, all my fat will squish out the holes and I'll probably look on the verge of exploding."

"Fat?" Taylor exclaimed, choking on the laugh. "You have the body of a centerfold. God, those Easterners did a number on you. I remember when you used to brag about your curves, especially the ones falling out of your bra. Emma and I couldn't even get an interested look from a guy until you were hooked up for the evening."

Chloe looked at the clothes over her arm and snorted at the irony. Everything they had pushed on her to try on looked like clothes a more confident woman would wear.

What happened to her over the last decade? Had she truly become a different person?

"You two crack me up. I've gained at least thirty pounds since college, and I wasn't skinny then. Was I really like that?" Chloe asked.

"Yes," Emma and Taylor both answered firmly, exchanging a look that had them both laughing. They used to complain to each other all the time about how lucky Chloe was with her curvy body.

"I guess I don't remember it the way you two do," Chloe said, realizing it was true.

"Your new sexy clothes will put you back in touch with your inner slut," Emma told her. "Wear the short belted dress to lunch. Work your way up to harem girl. The shock would be too much for the men in this hotel."

Taylor plucked a blue halter dress off the rack. "I love this. Look at this," she demanded, hooking the hanger over her head.

"Everything looks like that on you Taylor," Chloe said, grinning.

Emma laughed. "I love it. It matches your eyes perfectly."

"And thanks to the tanning bed I put in at the gym, I have no tan lines," Taylor said gleefully. "Did you find anything, Em?"

"A few things," Emma said, shrugging. "I brought my white strapless dress. I think I'm wearing it tonight. What do you think about this little vest to wear over it?" She held it up to her chest for Taylor to see.

"Love it," Taylor said, noticing Chloe was smiling at them. "I think Chloe likes it too."

"Chloe likes everything today," she said, her grin spreading. "This is more fun than I've had in a long time. I hung out with Aaron's family so much that I never really made friends where I lived. I've missed you both. I'm really glad I came back to California."

"That's because you came back to us—people who love you," Taylor said, while Emma nodded in validation.

Chloe laughed. "That's very sweet, Taylor, but I'm still not working for you."

Taylor narrowed her eyes, making Chloe laugh. She didn't care so long as the woman went back to being the feisty friend she really was under all that self-effacing garbage she was spouting.

"I was not flattering you for that reason, Zanders. In fact, I'm changing tactics totally. I'm going to wait for you to run out of money and then offer you half of what I would have today. I've become very shrewd," Taylor said.

"Would you really do that to Chloe?" Emma asked, shocked.

Taylor sighed and snorted. "No—of course I wouldn't. I'm ruthless, but not where you two are concerned. I love you like sisters."

143

Relieved to know her friend wasn't becoming as heartless as she had sounded for a moment, Emma walked over and hugged Taylor, who just laughed.

"Come on, let's try on clothes," Taylor ordered. "I need lunch. I'm starved."

CHAPTER 3

Jasper's gaze kept being drawn to the three women sitting on the patio drinking mai tais. From his table by the café window, he had a prime view of them, especially the one with her top unbuttoned for comfort who looked ready to bust out of the short dress any moment. She was a lot of woman for a city that regularly produced dozens of tanned and toned clones like her tablemates.

He shifted in his seat, surprised at his reaction to a stranger—and a hotel guest.

"I bet I know which one you're looking at," Max said with a grin, forking up a bite of his meatloaf.

"I'm not looking at anyone. I was checking out the pool," Jasper denied, his gaze going immediately back to the woman's breasts as she laughed, her voice full and rich, the movements of her body mesmerizing to him.

"There's not a single woman in the pool with breasts like the laughing brunette's. I'm your brother. Why are you lying to me?" Max asked. "I like the taller of the two blondes, the one with the short hair. She was in here a couple of weeks ago in a sharp business suit. I'm intending to sleep with her. Go for the brunette. She's just your type."

"Max, you *can't* sleep with hotel guests," Jasper said sternly. "We talked about this before you decided to recuperate here. It's not ethical. Neither Sam nor I have ever violated that rule."

"Jasper, I haven't slept with a woman in four months. I bet what's going on in your pants isn't ethical either. You're forty-five, not eighty-five, so stop waiting and go after those breasts. You don't have to settle for being your ex-wife's booty call," Max said fiercely, staring at his brother over his food.

"It's complicated," Jasper told him. "When you're older, you'll understand."

"I'm thirty-one, not thirteen," Max joked. "And I aged a lot those two months in the hospital before I came here. I realize now that life and luck can change in an instant. The one with breasts looks fun, sexy, and like she'd be nice to touch. Go for it."

"She looks like she's enjoying the company of her friends, relaxing for the first time in ages, and smart enough to sue the hotel if I offend her," Jasper commented, having to shift in his chair when she leaned over the table. He *was* having a strong reaction to her, but it wasn't worth risking the hotel's reputation to follow the urge.

"Those three are going to end up in the piano lounge tonight with me. If you don't come join us, I'm going to seduce all three of them, even the one with big breasts," Max bragged, settling back in his seat and looking at his older brother with a definite challenge in his gaze. "I will not spare your feelings just because you're too old to go after what you want. It's not my fault I'm a menopause baby and have the advantage of youth on my side."

"Menopause baby? Where do you get that crap? Those women are all probably a decade older than you and way too smart for your lame pick-up lines. Plus, they haven't been looking at anyone but each other all through lunch. They are not here on the prowl for men, much less younger men," Jasper predicted, looking at Max's grin in disgust. "Fine. I'll take that bet. You won't get even a friendly kiss out of any of them."

"Bring cash. Twenty each since you're so sure," Max warned, standing and getting the attention he was used to from the rest of the dining room occupants.

The physically fit body that made him a successful hockey player also came in handy in gaining him all the female attention he wanted, and then some. Since he wasn't limping anymore, no one could tell he'd even been hurt. He might have failed on the ice, but Max never failed with a woman he'd set his sights on seducing.

***

Chloe had laughed so much in the last hour that her face hurt. And several mai tais had put a humorous haze over pretty much everything.

"Emma, those quizzes are all going to say that I can't get a guy because I have some sense of decorum about not groping a guy's crotch in public. Do women in their twenties actually follow that advice?" Chloe demanded.

"Yes," Emma said firmly. "And I think they have a lot of sex."

"But do they ever find a genuine love-that-lasts kind of relationship?" Taylor asked, trying to sound wise.

Emma scrunched up her face. "Well, two of them found mine and Chloe's husbands, so I think the answer is yes in some cases. Of course, this is assuming they actually love our ex-husbands and vice versa."

145

Chloe snorted. "Well, I say good luck to them for trying. My ex's new woman better stay skinny for the rest of her life."

They laughed again and took another sip of their drinks.

"Okay—okay," Emma said more soberly, "one more question and I'll quit." She paused until she knew Chloe and Taylor were paying close attention.

"You and your best friend are having lunch. She tells you there's a hot guy checking out your breasts," Emma said seriously. "What do you say in reply? Taylor—you go first."

Taylor laughed, the drinks having worked their magic on her by loosening her tongue. "Well, I would dip into the sarcasm I hold back just for these special situations. I would say 'Sure, him and every other guy' in my best, most confident voice. Then I'd do this."

Lifting her small breasts in her hands like an offering to the gods, Taylor pursed her lips in a smooch, and leaned over the table to her friends. They laughed so hard and so loudly that all the people in the pool starting leaving.

"Just like the old days," Taylor said. "We're clearing the area."

"Okay Chloe—what would you say?" Emma said, swinging an innocent gaze in her direction.

"If the man is checking out my breasts, it's because he's not used to seeing so much untanned flesh in the state of California," Chloe declared, laughing and holding the edges of her lapels open as wide as she could to peer into her dress. "Look—the girls and I haven't seen sunlight in five years. It will take me months to tan all this."

They all looked at Chloe's large and very white breasts, giggling without denying her statement. It was the truth after all.

"Maybe you can start with one of those self-tanners or a bronzer. You have to work your way up to a real tan again," Emma said with a laugh.

"Emma—that question didn't sound like the other quiz questions," Taylor commented, looking at her not-so-innocent friend who was giggling softly and looking guilty.

"Okay—fine. It wasn't a real question on the quiz. There's a good-looking guy in the dining room who has been admiring Chloe's cleavage since we sat down to have lunch," Emma said, laughing. "I think she should practice her subtlety theory on him."

"Well I'm certainly in the mood to practice after three mai tais. Show him to me," Chloe demanded on a tipsy laugh.

Emma's eyes grew larger as she giggled and whispered. "Okay I will, but just don't turn around. He's headed to our table. Just smile at Taylor and pretend to be fascinating."

Chloe's eyes widened as she heard the deep voice at her side.

"Good day, ladies. I'm Jasper Wade, hotel manager. I hope you're enjoying your stay. If you need anything while you're here, please let me know," he said gallantly, his gaze taking in all of them before coming back to Chloe and her breasts.

Chloe, full of mai tai and happy laughter, turned her head and smiled into his very nice face, sighing with ego happiness as she watched Jasper Wade's gaze straining to stay away from her cleavage. The day was certainly turning out to be a very nice way to celebrate her return to California.

"Well, aren't you sweet, Mr. Wade? I was just going to look for the ladies room," she said, laughing. "Can you point me in the right direction?"

"It's in the hallway just outside the dining area. If you like, I'd be happy to show you," Jasper said, his heart beating rapidly as she rose slowly to her full height.

Jasper couldn't remember the last time he had been so excited by a woman he didn't even know. She was tall, smiling, and quite an alluring woman altogether. It was all he could do not to reach out and put his hands on her to assure himself she was real.

Chloe purposely stayed bent over the table until the last minute, and then straightened slowly, her breasts following her slow moments. "Sorry. I seem to be a bit tipsy. Too many mai tais."

"Lovely way to enjoy a sunny afternoon by the pool," Jasper said with a smile, placing a solicitous hand on her arm, or at least he hoped it was coming off that way.

Chloe took two steps and stumbled slightly, forcing Jasper to catch her, which momentarily squashed her ample cleavage against the front of him. "Oops—sorry."

She watched his eyes darken and had to restrain the giggle fighting to be set loose. Behind her, Chloe could hear Emma and Taylor's in-drawn breaths at her boldness.

Turning innocently to look at them, she had to fight laughter at their obvious surprise. She didn't need a damn quiz to tell her how to interest a man. She just needed the good-looking motivation currently with his hands on her. It was the most wickedly confident thought she'd had in years, and it brought an equally wicked smile to her face.

"I'm fine girls, but I guess I need to walk off a little of the buzz. Don't worry. Mr. Wade seems quite dependable. I'm sure he won't let me fall," Chloe said, winking at their wide-eyed expressions.

Chloe turned back slowly, brushing her breast lightly across his sleeve as she put her arm through Jasper Wade's. He inhaled sharply at the contact, but Chloe pretended not to notice or hear, though of course she had. It was all she could do to bite back a sigh of happiness. "Sorry again. Can't believe I'm so tipsy. Thank you for helping me, Mr. Wade. You really do have a nice hotel."

"Really?" Jasper asked, his voice breaking on the word so he cleared it. "Sorry. I mean—thank you."

They walked off then, with Jasper walking slowly and watching every step Chloe took. Taylor and Emma watched them weaving through the dining room, with Chloe acting like she couldn't walk straight and Jasper Wade carefully holding onto her.

When Taylor thought they were far enough away not to hear, she leaned on the table and laughed into her hands.

"Emma," she said contritely, "you and I should have gone for shorter dresses. It seems the slut we used to loathe and love is back."

"Good," Emma declared, not caring a whit. "That ex-husband of Chloe's did a number on her head. I don't like hearing her get all defensive over her body or anything else. Jasper Wade looks like a fun fling."

"I don't know if he'll settle for a fling. I think he's in love with her breasts already. That's pretty serious for some guys," Taylor said with a laugh. "I prefer leg men myself. They look you in the eye unless you're naked or wearing a short skirt."

"I like men who appreciate the whole package, but they don't exist," Emma declared.

"You know how it works. Breasts, butt, or legs. You pick one asset and play it up," Taylor ordered.

"Too much work," Emma said, laughing at her own lack of interest. It had been a long time since she had been interested enough in a man to try luring him. The last guy had left before she'd found her nerve. Now she was content just to watch Chloe, glad her friend was getting back in touch with the woman she was meant to be.

Visit **www.donnamcdonaldauthor.com** for more info

EXCERPT FROM CARVED IN STONE

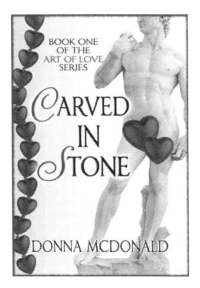

CHAPTER 1

Will Larson watched the batter bubbles burst before he flipped the current batch of pancakes. When he heard the motorcycle roar up outside, he knew Shane had finally arrived for breakfast.

"Good morning," Will said, smiling as his youngest son came through the door sniffing the air like a hungry dog.

"Banana walnut pancakes," Shane said on sigh, walking into the kitchen of his brother Michael's house. "Those are still my favorite."

Will tossed a grin in the direction of his son and then smiled when Shane walked over and dropped an affectionate kiss on his unshaven cheek.

Shane looked like his blonde Nordic-looking mother, but had definitely inherited his father's size, exceeding Will's height by several inches and the width of his shoulders even more. It would take the same quantity of pancakes he and Michael ate together just to fill the twenty-seven-year-old up, so Will poured out batter to make another six.

"So how's the graphic novel business? Has the Winged Protector solved any more crimes or saved any more damsels in distress lately?"

"Nah. His alter ego, Eric Benton, is mostly a monogamist. He's still enjoying the last damsel. I did get offered a deal for action figures last week," Shane said, going to the coffee pot and pouring himself a cup.

"Action figures? That's cool. Was it a good deal?" Will asked, impressed that his son's creative work was gaining popularity. He was doubly glad now that he hadn't let Ellen discourage the boy's comic book drawing too much.

Shane shrugged. "It's a toy company working with my publisher. My agent said they're offering enough to buy a small house, plus a percentage of sales over time. I guess that's pretty good."

Will stopped and stared. "Pretty good? I would say it's pretty great, Shane." He went back to flipping pancakes, smiling and proud.

"Well, I like the idea of getting a house," Shane admitted. "Guess I'm tired of condo living."

"When you get your house, maybe I can come live with you for a while. I think your brother is tired of me already," Will said, wanting to laugh at the pained expression on Shane's face.

It would be hard for his youngest to bring home his one-nighters with his father in residence. Will was seriously tempted to do it for a while just to disrupt Shane's habitual womanizing.

"Yeah, I am tired of you," Michael confirmed, walking into the kitchen, stretching and scratching the six-pack abdominal muscles he worked to maintain. It had been harder since his father had been in his house and doing most of the cooking.

Will laughed at his oldest son's comment about being tired of him because it was half teasing and half-truth. The month he'd been living with Michael had been an interesting social adjustment for both of them. He had been relieved to have some company for a while, even if it was reluctant. The last year in a house with no family had been a really lonely one for him.

When he looked at Michael now and smiled, Will had the same thought he always had that it was like looking in a mirror showing him a picture of his past. Michael had inherited his muscular build but not his height, which his son complained about still at thirty-four.

At five-ten, Michael was average in stature, but his wide shoulders, broad chest, and muscled arms only emphasized the passionate nature promised by his dark brown eyes and equally dark hair that hung nearly to his waist. Will's Celtic heritage had branded his eldest hard, but it looked good on him.

"Why exactly are you tired of me?" Will asked, grinning at Michael's snort.

"You've been moping around my house, not dating, and barely working on your art. I'm sick and tired of being greeted by a giant marble penis every time I go out to the courtyard to work. Carve a damn leg or something, Dad. No matter how artistically impressive, a giant marble penis by itself is still creepy as hell," Michael complained, making his father blush.

To soften his words, he patted his father on a shoulder, sniffing the pancakes with appreciation. He loved to tease, but would never outright criticize his father's art. God knew his mother had done enough of that when she and his dad were married.

Shane was laughing so hard at his brother's comments that coffee was threatening to come out his nose.

"So how long has the marble penis been leading its solitary existence?" Shane asked, pulling a coffee cup out of a cabinet to pour Michael a cup.

"Practically since Dad sold the house and moved in here," Michael said, answering for his father.

Shane laughed harder as he handed his brother the coffee.

151

"Thanks," Michael said, savoring that first bracing sip. "I think Dad's depressed."

Despite his father's amazing financial success as a sculptor, his mother had never thought his father's art was as important as his other work. As the oldest child, Michael clearly remembered all the fights his parents had had about the time his father had spent carving. Selling the house, which was also the place his father was used to working, had been as bad as the divorce itself.

"Stop talking about me in the third person. I am in the room, not deaf, and not depressed," Will denied, sighing over their concerns, which were way too close to his for comfort. "I just haven't felt like carving. Throw a cover over it if it bothers you so much, Michael."

"Maybe the state of the statue is trying to tell you something, Dad," Shane suggested, his amused but serious gaze on his father's face. "Maybe the marble penis isn't the only penis leading a solitary existence. The divorce was over a year ago. Mom and Luke married a few months after it was final. You're not even dating yet."

Will turned off the griddle and set the mountain of pancakes in the middle of the table he'd already set for three.

"Listen, Mr. All-But-Dissertation in Psychology, when you actually finish that million-dollar doctorate at Johns Hopkins, then you can analyze me and my man parts. Until then you're just my smart-ass son. Sit and eat—both of you laughing hyenas," Will ordered, only partially minding their amusement at his outburst.

"Dad, you know Michael and I love you. At least let me give you my best dating advice," Shane said, sliding into the nearest chair.

He heaped six pancakes on his plate and covered them with a lake of syrup before he paused and schooled his voice into the businesslike tone he had learned from the man he addressed.

"Shave your head, get an earring, and ride your bike around town. Your body is great for a man over fifty. You could be picking up the kind of women I do. Look, I got a tongue stud. You need to get one of these. Women love this kind of stuff."

Shane stuck out his tongue to show his father, who only rolled his eyes. He heard his brother snickering around a mouthful of pancakes, but merely ignored his jealous sibling.

Will studied the tongue stud with a mixture of horror and shock.

He looked at Michael, who only laughed, shrugged, and went on eating. His eldest son was crazy in love with a woman

152

he couldn't get along with for more than two minutes at a time. But even though the woman wasn't in his life the way he wanted, Michael wasn't always out with nameless, faceless blondes like Shane favored doing. Sure he dated, but he also tended to bury himself in his work.

His oldest son had only done that kind of mindless dating when the woman he loved got married. When she got divorced, which was remarkably often, Michael stopped chasing other women and resumed chasing her, which was the stage he was going through currently. While it seemed fruitless to Will to want a woman so badly who so obviously didn't want you back, he still never worried about Michael as much. At least Michael cared deeply about someone. Will wasn't sure Shane even had the capacity to genuinely love a woman.

"Shane, you're missing the big picture. Do you even remember their names, what they did to you, what you did to them? Do you ever want to go back to any of them so bad you ache?" Will asked.

"No. But I've not been looking for that kind of experience," Shane said, shrugging away his father's disapproval.

Will pointed his fork at Shane. "Yes, you are. I raised you. You know I felt that way about your mother because I made sure you did. So I know you're at least subconsciously looking for that whether you realize it or not. There is nothing like finding that one incredible woman who changes everything. There is nothing like exploring the full range of lovemaking with an equally devoted partner."

"What happens when that one incredible woman changes so much that she leaves you and marries a younger man? Do you just give up?" Shane asked sharply, daring his father to answer his question less than honestly.

He and Michael both knew their father had taken the divorce very hard. They knew he had sincerely and faithfully loved their mother. Neither of them had really understood what had gone so wrong between their parents that it couldn't be fixed. The divorce had not been easy on any of them, but their father was the one who hadn't moved on.

"Look—every relationship is a risk in some way. I had thirty-three good years with your mother. We grew apart, and she fell in love with someone else. I don't know why these things happen. They just do," Will said, getting up and refilling his coffee. "I am sad about the divorce but not really depressed. When the right time comes, I'll find someone and start dating again. I have an open mind about it."

"Good. When?" Shane asked, watching his father walk back to the table and sit down heavily with a resigned sigh. He wanted to laugh at his father's irritation with him, but he held it in. There was too much at stake to risk his father thinking it was just a joke.

"When I'm ready and I meet someone, I will start dating again. There's nothing wrong with waiting for the right woman to show up. I don't need to fill the interim with tall, leggy blondes half my age," Will said firmly.

"Fine," Shane agreed easily, his tone dripping with fake resignation. "I'll take care of chasing all the leggy blondes half your age, Dad. Geez, you're hard to satisfy. No wonder Michael is tired of you."

When his father glared at him, Shane turned to look at his brother, his gaze full of wickedness. "What kind of women does Dad pawn off on you?"

"None—and I'm totally pissed now," Michael said, putting as much anger in his voice as he could over the urge to laugh. "Dad's always liked you better, Shane. When you buy your house, he's definitely moving in with you."

"Oh, shut up and eat—both of you," Will said, stabbing his pancakes viciously, tired of being harassed by his adult children. "I'm getting my own damn place as soon as I can."

"When? Mom said you gave all the money from the house sale to her," Shane said sadly, shaking his head side to side in pity. "I guess that means you're broke. That marble penis better grow a body soon."

At the vicious swearing following Shane's comments, Michael shook his head at his father as well and made sympathetic noises with his tongue. "Did you ever even use the f-word when you were a principal, Dad? I don't remember you swearing in front of me or Shane, until *he* ran over your Harley with his car."

Michael used his fork to point accusingly at Shane, whose glare matched his father's, and made him want to laugh.

"Thanks, Benedict Arnold. Did you have to remind Dad about me killing his bike?" Shane asked, pancakes all but falling out of mouth. Backing over his father's beloved Harley was the only thing Shane had ever done in his life so bad that his father had been truly disappointed in him.

"You're the one making Dad mad this morning, not me," Michael said, laughing at Shane's pained expression.

Since it was his house, Michael reasoned he could say anything he wanted to defend himself under his own roof. This included shifting his father's irritation in his brother's general

154

direction and away from him. His obvious success at having done so made his smile even wider.

"I'm definitely getting my own place soon," Will said to his pancakes, even as both his sons laughed harder. "And I'm not inviting you two over for breakfast."

Shane pointed his fork at his brother. "If I never get banana pancakes again, you are a dead man."

Michael grinned and gave his brother the finger to let him know how afraid he was of him and his threats.

"I am serious," Shane warned, stabbing the air between Michael and him with his fork like it was a weapon.

Will rolled his eyes to the ceiling and shook his head. Sometimes he wished they had both taken more after their less passionate mother.

CHAPTER 2

Though celebrating her birthday in the dreary March weather had been depressing, Jessica Daniels didn't mind being forty-seven because she was mostly happy with her life. She was close to retiring from her teaching position, and her daughter who dreamed of being an eccentric college professor was finally about to graduate with a PhD in Philosophy from Ohio State.

While her daughter was just beginning her career at thirty, Jessica had started teaching high school art right out of college at twenty-two. Now she found herself constantly longing for a different life. She wanted to get back to her own art—whatever form it took now—before she got too old to want to do it.

In fact, she wanted to get back to doing a lot of things she hadn't done in a while, before she forgot what it was to want them too. So when one of her favorite former art students, Melanie Simpson—now Melanie Madison—had suggested she come to the café to scope out the biker guy who was fast becoming a regular, it hadn't taken much to talk Jessica into it.

Seeing him now in the flesh, Jessica totally agreed the balding biker was all tall-and-firm-body hunky, except for the massive arms and shoulders on him. The man looked to be six feet tall or better, which was not so intimidating for Jessica's five-foot-ten height. She preferred tall men anyway. But the man looked big as well, which was a welcome deviation from the lanky, lean intellectual men she usually dated. You didn't come across tall, big, and well-toned bodies very often, especially in men over forty.

As Jessica listened to him chat with Melanie, she decided that the biker was very articulate, polite, and well-spoken. She also concluded there was a sort of raw power in his assertive tone. The man had the kind of authoritative voice that was just instinctual to obey, unless you had trained yourself otherwise. Being a teacher of wild and unruly high school students, Jessica had a lot of respect for anyone who could speak with authority and command.

Yes, the biker was definitely intriguing to her, so Jessica stood and walked to perch on the bar stool beside him. She was very glad they were the only two patrons in the café at the moment. Jessica found it easier to flirt boldly when there was a smaller audience.

"Hey, big guy, I'll pay for your coffee if you take me for a ride," Jessica offered, instantly drawing his full attention to her.

His gaze traveled the length of her body before returning to her face and hair. "Very nice offer, but no can do. You need a helmet to ride and I don't carry a spare."

Jessica blinked and grinned at his refusal, but only laughed low in her belly.

Will noticed his body absorbed the sound of her laughter and vibrated pleasantly. Her reddish hair streaked with silver blonde strands revealed her age as somewhere over forty, but no more than his shiny dome revealed he was way over forty himself.

"Well, I wasn't necessarily talking about your bike," Jessica said on a laugh, liking the way his face actually flushed at her innuendo. The man was certainly not accustomed to flirting or playing games, she thought. It was a fact she found enormously appealing, and she appreciated the edge it gave her.

"Well, I don't have any safety of any sort, but could fix that if you can wait a bit while I go shopping," he said on laugh, bringing his mildly embarrassed gaze back to her face, the amusement in his hazel eyes evident. "Does your offer have an expiration date?"

Well, well, Jessica thought, her smile broadening at his teasing tone. There was a fun guy in that great body somewhere, and she was immediately interested in finding him. There was also a little something buzzing between them causing arousal to flare. She really loved that first flaring of genuine attraction. Even though she dated a lot of men, it had been a long time since she'd felt the real thing.

"Well, I'd say my answer depends on what you intend to go shopping for," Jessica said sweetly, leaning an elbow on the ancient counter, intentionally letting her shirt front gape to show both her breasts and the blue lace bra she wore.

Ignoring the cleavage, which Will figured she knew damn well he noticed, he instead studied her intriguing face and the fullness of her hair. Then he let his gaze drop to her jean-covered legs. She had very long legs encased in well-worn jeans that fit snugly and intimately to all of her.

"I would buy a spare bike helmet, of course," Will said sternly, keeping his laughing gaze focused in her lap as he spoke.

Jessica laughed loudly and squirmed in her seat. Suddenly all of her was really interested in what that look of his was promising. Okay, the biker was good, very good, she reluctantly admitted. He just seemed out of practice, and Jessica couldn't help wanting to know why.

"Ms. Daniels, don't be teasing Mr.—" Melanie began.

"—Williams," Will interjected firmly, interrupting Melanie's introduction to introduce himself. "I'm Everett Williams, but you can just call me Will."

Melanie raised her eyebrows, but did not correct the proffered introduction. She did give William Larson—still Mr. Larson, her former middle school principal, to her—a questioning look and grin. He had just recently confided in her about his artistic *nom de plume,* and that he had used it to separate his art from the rest of his life.

Today he evidently wanted to play the bad biker artist for Ms. Daniels. How interesting was *that*, Melanie mused? Brent was going to love this story, and she couldn't wait for his return tomorrow so she could share it with him.

Jessica put out a hand for Will to shake. "I'm Jessica Daniels. Sorry for teasing you. Melanie was my art student a couple years ago. I like to shock her with my flirting. It's the cheapest entertainment I can find."

"Ms. Daniels, I was your student almost ten years ago," Melanie corrected with a laugh.

"Shush," Jessica said, laughing. "I'm sure it was just two. What do you do, Will?"

She ignored Melanie's laugh as the girl wiped the counter.

"I'm an artist—a sculptor. I carve people out of stone," Will said easily. "What medium do you work in, Jessica?" He decided he liked her name and the way it sounded when he said it.

"Life," Jessica answered quickly, well practiced in giving a smoothly polished version of her story. "I teach high school kids to express themselves artistically. I haven't wholeheartedly pursued my own art in years. Maybe you can show me your work sometime."

"How about today?" Will asked, the offer coming from some rusty place inside him. But after issuing the invitation, he smiled at how good it felt, how natural. He really would like to show her his art. "The art center in Berea has two pieces of my work on display, if you're interested."

"Sounds like fun," Jessica said, thinking that seeing his art did sound like fun for a first date. Spending time with a man who genuinely aroused her with just a look was equally appealing.

Melanie walked back to them and slid a small tablet and pen over the counter. "I'm assuming you'll need to exchange phone numbers and addresses," she said to them both, laughing at her blatant interest in their conversation.

Jessica smiled at Melanie, pulled the tablet toward her, and began writing down her information.

Will studied her hands as she wrote, noticing the close trimmed nails and the total lack of a manicure. This was a woman who worked with her hands. He imagined her touch would be explorative but sure of its journey over him. Her grip would undoubtedly be strong.

When his jeans got tighter the longer he watched her write, Will let out the laugh he'd been holding in since she sat down. It was nice to know Ellen hadn't taken *everything* from him in the divorce. Thank you, Jessica Daniels, for being interesting, he mused, smiling at her.

"Something funny about my writing?" Jessica asked him, noticing his warm, intimate smile.

"No—something funny about being picked up by a woman in a café," Will corrected.

"*Picked up?* If that was the case, we'd be necking in the parking lot by now. Visiting the arts center with you is not exactly the same thing as taking you home with me for wild sex," Jessica said, laughing. "You haven't dated in a while, have you?"

"No. I haven't dated in a while," Will agreed, liking her laughing face and her quick sense of humor, even if it was racier than he was used to. "And I am definitely out of practice when it comes to flirting."

Will slid off the bar stool and put a five on the counter next to his coffee cup. He took the paper Jessica tore off the tablet, smiling at the address on it. She lived in the same neighborhood as Michael, sort of the artists' community in Lexington, Kentucky. She might not be creating art, but Will bet she lived the life.

"You suddenly in a hurry now?" Jessica asked, fighting not to be disappointed that the man was so anxious to leave. "You haven't even said what time we're going."

"How about three?" Will asked, smiling at the mild irritation in her gaze. It was nice to think she wanted to spend more time with him.

Grabbing his jacket, he reached over and turned Jessica's bar stool with one hand, causing her to rise off the counter and bump into him as he stepped between her legs. Score one for the old rusty guy, Will thought, when her surprised gaze met his.

"I need to run to the bike shop to buy a spare helmet. That's going to take a couple hours because going there always does. Then I've got another stop to make before I pick you up," Will said softly, looking directly into her laughing blue-green eyes.

He slid both arms into the butter-soft leather jacket, standing as close as the stool would let him as he zipped it, all the while keeping his eyes focused on her lap, and enjoying the spread of her thighs on each side of the stool. It gave him ideas he hadn't thought about in a hell of a long time.

When Will finally lifted his gaze back to Jessica's face, her color was high and her eyes were full of questions about his intentions. He smiled, his body tightening with the thrilling thought of answering even one or two of them. He might be out of practice, but the laughing Jessica Daniels was certainly inspiring.

"Is three o'clock okay?" Will asked, keeping his tone easy and his smile as innocent as he could.

"My schedule is pretty free this afternoon," Jessica told him, unconcerned with what Will might think of her not having plans. "The most exciting thing I'm doing today is laundry."

"Oh, come on—I'm not *that* much out of practice," Will jokingly told her with a snort, finally stepping away from the stool. "I'm at least a couple notches more fun than washing clothes."

He laughed as he walked to the door and grinned when he heard her sputter.

"Hey—who said I was *doing* you?" Jessica challenged, laughing openly at him now.

She'd bet fifty bucks Everett Williams would run like hell if she made a real move on him, despite the bar stool thing. She hadn't missed the quiver in his hands as he zipped up his jacket.

"You started this, lady. You still want to go for a ride or not?" Will asked back, a wicked glint in his eye.

"Yes. I still want to go for a ride," Jessica said on a laugh. "Pick me up at three. If I don't rush right down, give me a few minutes to put my laundry away. I like to take my time and do things right."

"Good to hear," Will said, grinning as he pushed the door open and headed outside.

Jessica and Melanie said nothing to each other as they watched Will pull the helmet over his head and strap it down. They didn't speak until he started the bike and zoomed out of the parking lot.

Jessica hummed in her throat, contemplating the interest she had seen in Everett Williams' gaze. "I've honestly never wanted to go for a ride more in my entire life," she said sincerely with more than a little bit of surprise.

She laughed when she heard Melanie giggle beside her.

Jessica looked over and grinned at the younger woman, whose face was now beet red. "Now how did that simple statement embarrass you? You're married. I'm not saying anything you don't know by now. If that's not the case, I'm going to have a serious talk with your husband."

"No," Melanie said, laughing. "I know what you mean, but he's at least fifty and you're what—mid-forties? Do you all really feel all that stuff at your age? I admit I had a little moment myself when he turned the stool and stepped between your legs. Brent is not going to believe he did that. We've both known him for years."

"Yes, you sweet innocent child--we still feel everything. Bodies get older, but they remain fully functional in most cases. Now what's his deal?" Jessica asked, even as Melanie shook her head no. "Come on. I want to know the biker's real story."

"Can't tell you, Ms. Daniels," Melanie said.

"For pity's sake, will you *please* call me Jessica?" Jessica insisted, making Melanie laugh. "I can't joke about sex with a twenty-eight-year-old who still calls me Ms. Daniels.

"Okay, fine, but I still can't tell you, *Jessica*," Melanie said on a laugh.

"Tell me why he's out of practice then—just that much at least," Jessica pleaded.

Melanie considered. It was probably a good thing to reveal that much. "Will was married forever. A year ago, his wife divorced him and married a younger man. He took the divorce hard. I don't think he's even been dating."

"Great," Jessica said morosely, "another rebounder. I hate being the first woman for a divorced guy. Their guilt over their ex never lets it work out with anyone new. They have to go through three or four women before they get over it."

Melanie studied Jessica. She could practically feel the woman's disappointment.

"Maybe it will be different with Will. I know the man. If he hasn't dated, there's a good reason. Most divorced men I know date lots of women really fast. Geez, you know I never even thought of him as a hot guy, and now I may never be able to see him again without thinking about the stool thing."

"Yeah, what you witnessed was a prime male putting on a show for new female. And your instincts are dead on—Will is a seriously hot guy," Jessica agreed. "What was his ex thinking? I'd bet my teacher's retirement that man knows where all the buttons are and just how hard to push them. As long as the man was married, he probably learned to make a woman's body sing the hallelujah chorus and hit the high notes. If he does anything interesting at all for an encore, I swear I may actually fall in love this time."

"Oh God, stop," Melanie begged, laughing. "Brent won't be back until tomorrow. It's going to be bad enough sleeping alone tonight as it is. If you get lucky, will you come back and tell me about it?"

"Sorry," Jessica said, laughing. "I'm an outrageous flirt, but very discreet about what I do in the bedroom. You'll have to get your vicarious thrill elsewhere tonight."

"But you are planning to do something interesting with Will?" Melanie asked teasingly. It was still hard not to call him Mr. Larson, but she was not going to blow his cover.

"If that second stop of his turns out to be to buy condoms, I am absolutely planning to ride more than his bike today," Jessica said. "That look in his eye was very promising."

Melanie's body shook with laughter, but she was afraid to ask any more questions, no matter how tempted she was. She knew full well Jessica would tell her the truth and she was missing her husband enough as it was.

"Well, laundry calls," Jessica said, going back to the booth she had left and gathering up her things. "Next time I come by, we're going to talk about some art for the outside of this place. Your food is great, honey. We need to draw in some customers. One lonely biker and a spinster do not a clientele make."

"*Spinster?* That so does not describe you. Come back and tell me about what happens. If it works out, we'll put out the word that we're a hook-up place for mature singles," Melanie joked. Then she pointed a finger at the woman smiling at her. "But this is the last guy I fix you up with. If you don't keep this one, I'm taking down my match-making shingle."

"I don't think love works like that," Jessica said, leaning over the counter. "Come here and let me hug you."

Melanie stood on her toes and accepted the hug Jessica offered. "Love is going to find you, Ms. Daniels. You're too much fun not to have a guy in your life."

"You're the sweetest thing—always were. I'm glad Brent Madison III talked you into marrying him. That boy was nuts about you since you were in that freshman art class together. Oh God, that really was more than ten years ago, wasn't it?"

Melanie laughed and nodded. "It was thirteen. I was being kind saying ten."

Jessica sighed. "Well, I'm going home now to soak my old head. How did I get to be forty-seven? Life goes by really fast." She headed to the door. "Bye, sweetie," Jessica said.

"Good luck on your date," Melanie said, sincerely hoping two of the nicest people she knew would find out they actually liked each other.

CHAPTER 3

Jessica walked to the living room window of her second-story rental home and stuck her head out when she heard a bike roar up on the street and stop outside. The man looked just as good from up here, she thought, watching Everett Williams park the black monster, step off, and unzip the jacket to reveal his impressive chest. When the helmet came off, she laughed a little at the top of his shiny head reflecting in the sun. It was only a reminder of how real he was and didn't dim her enthusiasm for him a bit.

"Hang on," she yelled, "I'll be down in a minute."

Will looked up to see a mass of red hair spilling over the laughing face smiling down on him. He hoped like hell they could be friends even if nothing else. Jessica Daniels' sunny disposition turned on a light inside him, illuminating places that had been dark for a very long time. Her cheerful attitude was as appealing as the way she looked.

"Take your time, gorgeous," Will yelled up at her, making her laugh at his attempt at charm. "But don't keep me waiting too long."

Jessica laughed again and disappeared from the opening, leaving Will to wonder what he was going to do while she made him wait. The thought had barely found its way into his consciousness when Jessica bounded out of the house, all but running down the front sidewalk to him.

He didn't know yet , how old the woman was chronologically, but he put her mental age at seventeen as she all but ran to him. She wasn't even pretending to be coy, and her excitement to see him was on her face. The closer Jessica got to him, the more Will was reminded of the attraction he'd felt for her in the café. Suddenly, a friends-only option didn't seem quite so appealing. Will ran a hand over his front jeans pocket, patting the just-in-case package it contained, glad now he'd made that second stop.

Then Jessica was standing directly in front of him, and he was surprised as he realized she was almost eye level with his six-foot-two height. Will let his gaze travel down and back up once, not missing the amusement in her gaze on him as he did it.

"You're very tall for woman," Will said, trying to justify his thorough scan of her body by stating the obvious.

"So? Are you one of those big guys who wants a tiny woman to make himself feel even bigger?" Jessica asked, crossing her arms. "I can fake a lot of things for the sake of a first date, but being short isn't one of them. I would fail miserably. I love being tall."

Will ran a nervous hand over his head and laughed softly. "No, I'm not one of those guys," he said, leaving it at that.

There was no reason to bring up his ex or her height or anything about any other woman he had dated ancient ages ago. Unfortunately, those memories were the only things Will could think about rationally with Jessica's long body so close to his.

Not used to dating, Will hadn't had to make conversation with strangers—or strange women—very much since his divorce. He could feel Jessica's energy spiking around him, jostling his nerve endings back to life. It scrambled his brain, along with some other parts of him that had him becoming more cautious around her.

Sighing at his lack of composure, Will flipped open a storage compartment on the back of the bike and pulled out a black helmet with bright blue and green swirls. He'd bought the colors because they just seemed like her, though he was unsure why he could think of only her wearing it. He had meant to purchase a spare just in case he got asked for a ride in the future—by anyone. Which could still happen, he told himself, looking at the helmet with serious contemplation.

The red-haired enigma in front him was vibrating with excitement about wearing it. She charmed him with nothing more than her enthusiasm, and Will sighed at his thoughts.

"Got a sturdy leather or heavy canvas jacket?" Will asked. "Boots would be best, but good sneakers would be okay."

Jessica wrinkled her face and hummed in concentration. "I think so. Be right back."

Will watched her dash off at the same clip she'd run out to him, and it made him laugh. The laughter died when Jessica came back out of the house in less than two minutes wearing well-worn dark brown cowboy boots and a leather jacket that molded to her impressive curves. Her comfort in her clothes and herself had his mouth watering and his hands shaking to get on her. He sighed with longing when she was standing directly in front of him again.

Jessica grinned at Will's sigh and liked him even more for being the kind of man whose passion was visible.

"I ride a lot of things," Jessica teased, the lines at her eyes crinkling under his inspection. "This is my horse gear."

Will stepped up to her with the helmet in his hand. She was even taller in her boots and was meeting his gaze full on. Jessica Daniels was literally the tallest woman he could ever remember going out with, even counting college, which was a hell of a long time ago. He pulled the helmet down on her head, feeling her hands come up to push it back and seat it more comfortably.

"How's it feel?" he asked, his hands on the straps.

She brought her hands up to Will's, brushing hers quickly over them to encourage him, trying to pretend not to be thrilled when he froze at her touch.

"Feels good. Adjust the straps. I'm ready for my ride," she said on a laugh.

Will blinked a couple times, then moved his now slightly shaking hands under her chin to secure the chin strap. She tilted her chin up for greater access and his gaze went directly to her unpainted mouth.

"Just do it," Jessica told him, her smiling gaze taunting him.

"What?" Will asked, still sliding straps to adjust each side of the helmet.

"Kiss me and get it over with," Jessica told him. "I'm as curious as you are about it."

"How do you know I'm curious?" Will demanded, trying to decide if he liked her aggressiveness or not.

She was awfully forward, almost too honest. He hadn't even decided if he was going to kiss her yet, even if he did want to.

"Maybe I'm not as curious as you think," Will chastised, frowning and trying to convince himself her suggestion was too much too soon. He dropped his hands from the straps and took one step back for breathing room.

"*Chicken*," Jessica taunted, laughing as Will all but scowled at her.

"You flirt this hard with all the guys you date?" Will asked, seriously frowning at her as he slipped on his jacket.

"Only the ones I really, really want to kiss in return," Jessica said, crossing her arms and levelly meeting his gaze.

"Good to know," Will told her, narrowing his gaze at her and wondering just how many guys that had been, not that he cared. He looked at Jessica's mouth longingly one last time and pulled his own helmet over his head.

"We're wasting daylight," he said to her, using a phrase his dad had used often in his youth to hurry him up. He turned and stepped over the bike. "You coming or not?"

Disappointed he hadn't taken her up on her dare, Jessica almost replied with a scathing comment, but in the end she decided to play nice. She wanted the bike ride. It had been twenty years and she was genuinely looking forward to it. So she bit her tongue and dropped the subject.

She walked to the bike and swung herself onto the seat behind him. "Do you want me to hang on to you or the bike?" she asked, sliding her long legs intimately beside his hips and along his thighs, putting her crotch practically against his back. Yoga kept a woman very flexible, and as a fairly large woman, Jessica appreciated being loose in her hips. With a little effort and the right motivation, she could have flattened herself against his back but figured she had already worried him enough.

It was all Will could do not to scoot backward into the heat of her. With Jessica wrapped around him, Will suddenly found himself fighting to breath normally. He started the bike before he answered, hoping the idle would cover the huskiness of his voice.

His level of interest in the woman was way too advanced for a first date, Will thought. Hell, it was way too advanced for him period. He wasn't yet sure what he even felt about dating, much less what he felt about Jessica Daniels, her long legs, or the heat at his back. It was appealing, but damn—he needed time to think about it.

"I haven't had a passenger on a bike with me since my sons were in high school. I guess just put your arms around me and hang on," Will said finally, breathing a sigh when she kept her hands above his belt line. If she let them drop, he would wreck them before they got off her street.

Doing as she was told, and feeling the firmness of his chest under her hands, Jessica thought the women of this town needed to have their libidos checked for letting this man run around alone. It was all she could do to keep her hands off the rest of him.

Not that Will seemed to be having the same problem, which was a damn shame. If she'd been younger that disappointment might have ruined her day, but at her age it was not the end of the world.

And as much as she hated to admit it, she'd been down this road with other men before. There could be only one reason, Jessica concluded, for Will not kissing her when she could clearly see he wanted to. It was the same reason he likely had for not dating up to now. Everett Williams was obviously still in love with his ex-wife.

Sighing heavily at the knowledge, Jessica hugged Will tighter. Her suspicions were depressing and sucked most of the excitement away from the ride. They were halfway to Berea before Jessica could finally quiet her disappointment enough to enjoy the air whizzing past her and the rumble under her rear.

How old had she been when she dated the last guy with a motorcycle? She had probably been twenty-something—twenty-something and still happily naïve about men. They had ridden the bike everywhere and made love on it several times. She had fond, fond memories of those previous bike rides. Riding with Will now, years later, was certainly no hardship either, even if a bike ride was all she was going to get from him today.

Sad, but feeling better about her motives, Jessica decided to just focus on being a good companion to Will. When they cruised into the parking lot of the arts center, she climbed off first without being asked, knowing it was what she needed to do. She could tell she had surprised him. It brought a smile to her face.

Will didn't comment on Jessica's actions as he set the kickstand and climbed off himself. It was obvious he wasn't her first bike ride, and he couldn't help wondering who she'd ridden with before him.

"Great ride," she exclaimed, removing her helmet on her own. "I like how you drive, Will. Bike is smooth as glass, too. It's been twenty years since I've been on a bike. Yours is great."

"Yes, it is," Will replied, basking in her praise, even as he wondered about her change in attitude.

Gone was the seducing siren who had climbed on his bike. It was like they had left her behind in Lexington. Instead of feeling relieved, Will found he was sorely disappointed. He looked at Jessica's softly smiling mouth, wondering what would happen if he kissed her now. She looked away from him, pretending not to notice his study, but Will knew she was aware of everything he did.

Damn it, he thought. The woman was under his skin already. How and when had that happened?

"So where's your work?" Jessica asked, taking a few steps and stretching her legs.

Will unlocked the compartments on each side of the bike. "You can store your gear in here if you want. Hang the helmet off the handle bar."

Jessica did as he asked and bent to check her hair in the bike mirror. "Oh God," she said, running fingers through her wildly curling hair trying to tame the worst of the helmet hair problems. "I forgot about that little side effect." She laughed as she straightened. "Got an ink pen?"

Will pulled his leather jacket back out of the side compartment and retrieved a pen from the pocket before handing it to her. He couldn't imagine what surface the woman intended to write on or what piece of knowledge was so critical she had to write it down.

"Oh, that's the perfect kind," Jessica said sweetly, taking the straight stick ink pen from Will.

Will watched, mesmerized, as Jessica twisted and wound her hair with her fingers, finally using the ink pen to secure it in place at the back of her head. When she was finished, her hair was as tame as her conversation had been since she'd climbed off the bike. It brought yet another frown to Will's face, making him wonder what kind of reaction he was having to her.

The woman was being nothing but pleasant, yet he found her sweetness irritating as hell for some reason. The urge to kiss her was strong. His regret for not doing it earlier was even stronger. Whether he wanted to or not, Will sincerely missed the aggressive woman who had flirted so hard with him before. He wanted that woman back.

"Okay, I'm ready now," she said brightly, smiling at Will without any heat, without revealing anything more than polite interest in his art. "Let's see your work."

"Sure. Fine," Will answered, wondering what else he was expecting.

Whatever it was, he wasn't getting to the bottom of it in the parking lot.

He led her to the side of the center and to a paved garden area filled with budding trees. They stopped at a white alabaster piece consisting of five large interconnected circles, each round ring looking like it grew out of the last one.

"This piece is abstract. I don't do many of these, but now and again the idea for one comes and I usually indulge it," Will said quietly.

"Wow, this is all one piece," Jessica said reverently, amazed at the smooth precision of it, the intricate, graceful design. "Will, this is amazing."

Jessica ran her hand over the piece alternatively looking between him and his art. She couldn't help wondering how Will visualized a piece like this as he was working on it.

"You definitely have a gift," she said, meaning it more than she had imagined she would.

Will watched her running fingertips over the piece, her experience of it as much in her touch as it was in her gaze traveling over it. She used her hands for tactile exploration, a touch meant to learn secrets, but still reverent and full of admiration. She was touching his art exactly how he'd imagined her touching him.

Interested parts of his body started to harden at the enticing idea that it could be next. There was shock followed closely by a deep acceptance of his desire for her, but he didn't have a clue how to tell Jessica what was going on. With erotic thoughts robbing him of the ability to speak, Will said nothing much in reply to her comments about his art, just motioned Jessica deeper into the area when she was done with the first piece.

Set in a paver circle, the seven-foot marble man Will called 'David 13' was a little too realistic to greet modest guests at the center, but he certainly had an impact on those willing to venture deeper.

Naming his work after the statue he considered the greatest of all body sculpting work, Will considered his attempts to create art were only emulation. The numbers were self-explanatory for the attempt. So caught up was he in seeing his earlier work again himself, Will hadn't realized Jessica was still moving forward until she had walked completely past him.

She appeared to be in some sort of trance, Will decided, a small smile tugging at his mouth. His amusement didn't last long. Jessica walked up to 'David 13', reached out, and put her entire right palm flat over the all-too-realistic penis, covering the majority of it with her sizable hand.

Will couldn't stop the shiver that shook him as he watched Jessica's hand travel down and back up skimming and cupping the marble, taking its measure, gauging its proportions. He was suddenly dizzy with a soul-deep longing for her hands on him, and right behind that some unnamed fear rose up that engulfed what remained of his sanity.

He couldn't make himself look away from what Jessica was doing to the statue as she explored it. At the same time, he continued to shake in apprehension of what she was concluding.

"You carve this part first," Jessica said roughly, her throat constricted by her awe of the work. "You start here and that's why the proportions are perfect. This is the most perfectly proportioned statue I have ever seen."

Keeping her right hand covering the marble male organ, she reached her left arm up to its head, out to his shoulder, across to the statue's arm and down to its wrist. She switched hands, and repeated the measurements on the other side.

"I could teach a math class with these measurements. You're incredibly precise and incredibly talented—I can't believe. . ."

Her comments were halted by Will spinning her around hard to face him.

"Stop," he commanded. "Just stop touching. . ." His words drifted off as he gazed into her awestruck face.

Jessica had one moment to register the fear and physical pain on his face, then Will totally robbed her of breath when his mouth met hers in a hard, devastating kiss. His mouth on hers could have been glorious, could have been the stuff of dreams in fact, but his anxiety provoked too fierce a response in her. She fought to free herself from his mouth's invasion of hers, but couldn't get through the anger to coax him to soften his lips.

Jessica felt the evidence of his desire for her pushing against her legs, but what should have been thrilling simply wasn't under the circumstances. In fact, it wasn't even pleasant. It was intimidating, and it hurt her to think that Will likely meant the experience to be as scary as it was. He was purposely silencing her comments, and it was working.

Passion—true passion—seemed totally gone from her as she made herself cease struggling. She let herself grieve the loss and for a few moments just absorbed all the anger Will poured into her through his mouth. And when she acknowledged his anger fully, her heart and soul—the part of her that mattered—retreated as far as possible from him.

Jessica once again exerted some force to pull her mouth from his, but Will only pressed harder, held her tighter. His tongue continuously seeking advantage and taking it, whether she was willing to grant access or not. She pushed the panic away as she'd taught herself to do with aggressive men. It had been a very long time since she had allowed herself to be powerless in the arms of any man.

Then it hit her suddenly, the realization, the understanding of where the art came from inside Will. His embarrassment, his pain, and his punishment of her for seeing it, were all suddenly clear to her.

Jessica struggled against Will with more force as she renewed her efforts to pull away, her rising angst finally giving her enough strength to fight against his hold on her. She was seconds from doing something to physically hurt him when Will finally let her go.

Free of his demanding mouth at last, and more mad and hurt than she'd been in a couple decades, Jessica couldn't have stopped the truth from pouring out if her life had depended on it. She was never, never again going to let her experience of life be silenced or controlled by any man, especially not one she might have liked under better circumstances.

"Self-portrait in stone," Jessica said stiffly, swallowing tightly, upset to have to push remnants of her reluctant arousal down, deep down inside her. "The statue is you, Will. The proportions are yours. The perfect statue of David. The perfect form. It's like I already know your body from touching your work. I'm right, aren't I?"

Will tightened his hold on her upper arms, gripping hard enough to bruise her, but he couldn't seem to help himself. Jessica had stripped away the artistic secrets of several decades from him in under ten minutes. He was suddenly very afraid of the other damage she could cause. It was too late to stop himself from hearing her conclusions, too late to wish she hadn't seen and understood.

"How?" he demanded harshly. "How do you know these things? I've been doing this work for thirty-two years. You're the only person who ever just *saw*."

"What does it matter?" Jessica asked sadly. "Why does it bother you so much?"

She stood in his arms with his hands gripping her painfully, stood there and reeled from understanding. Intuitive knowing poured into her like someone filling a bucket up with water until it overflowed. Looking into the artistic soul of this man was like looking into a mirror and seeing herself. Already she was deeply regretting her insights, and Will's bruising grip was making her sorry for speaking the truth out loud to a man so unready to hear it.

And intentional or not, Will's artistic pride was completely destroying the wonderfully sweet attraction simmering between them. Regardless of how much it grieved her, there had been nothing even remotely affectionate in Will's punishing kiss, even if it had still weakened her legs and cemented her feet to the ground.

Even now the man still looked at her with loathing, and Jessica could feel Will's panic all the way to her bones. Empathy

170

for him assailed her, but she also cursed him to hell and back for making her care. Despite the number of men she had dated and bedded, she was standing by the man's art with her heart breaking for him and for what they could have had if he had been ready for it—for her.

But she wasn't seventeen this time, though the attraction and the capacity to love Everett Williams had come just as hard and just as fast as it had with Nathan Daniels. Older and much wiser, Jessica could and would run, she vowed. This time she would not have to have the pain of loving and losing.

Jessica pulled twenty-two years of teaching around her and summoned her best, most authoritative voice. "Get your fucking hands off me or I'm going to knee you in the balls."

Yanking herself forcefully from Will's grip at last, Jessica stepped away from him in relief. She glared over her shoulder at the artistic perfection he had created, and then glared at Will as well, who seemed to finally have the common sense to look ashamed. Then she turned her back on Everett Williams and his work and strode briskly away from both.

By the time Will got to the parking lot and the bike, Jessica was standing arms crossed, gaze on the pavement, her helmet in her hand.

"You don't have to worry about me telling anyone your artistic secrets," Jessica informed him quietly, but firmly. "I teach art, Will. Go with that explanation about how I knew, and we'll both be better off. I'm ready to go home now."

Even though the apology he owed her was on his tongue, Will didn't say anything in return, just opened the compartments on the bike to retrieve the rest of their gear. Still feeling exposed from her observations, he didn't know how sincere his apology would be anyway—which was just as well because Jessica didn't look capable of hearing anything he might have to say to her.

What in the devil had possessed him to kiss her like that? He had just wanted to stop her from telling him more because he hadn't been able to bear hearing what she saw in his work. But the moment his lips touched hers, the desire that had been building for hours had ruled his actions. Will hadn't even realized how far gone he had been until she wrenched herself from his arms and swore at him. His instant remorse and shock at his actions had frozen his tongue.

Jessica was suited up, zipped, and helmet in place before Will had finished his own. He climbed on the bike and felt her settle in the seat behind him. This time she used her knees to

171

hold his hips, keeping the rest of her as far away from him as possible.

He immediately missed the heat of her, missed the intimacy of her long legs beside his. Her hands around his middle weren't shaking, weren't damp, weren't even moving. It was like Jessica had drawn her entire personality back inside herself to keep it away from him, Will thought regretfully, just as she had now positioned her body as far away from his as she could on the seat.

He started the bike and reached a hand to pat hers as a signal they were going to be moving. She didn't flinch away from his touch, but she didn't acknowledge it back either. All remnants of the vibrating energy of excitement she'd had when he'd picked her up were totally gone. In fact, it was like there was no connection between them at all anymore, Will thought, frowning.

Not only shouldn't he have kissed her when he was so upset, he also shouldn't have all but accused her of—*what*, he asked himself? What had she done? Tell him some truth he wasn't comfortable hearing? So what if all of his male statues were self-portraits? What did he have to be ashamed of?

He still couldn't explain his panic, couldn't explain the magnitude of anxiety he'd felt when Jessica told him the truth about his art. She had reached inside to places he had locked away from everyone, even his children. First he had panicked, and then he had overreacted. Now he was ashamed, but didn't know how to make things right again.

At her house, Jessica climbed off and removed the helmet, handing it to him along with the ink pen that had been in her hair. She leaned down and kissed his cheek lightly, barely a brush. The lack of any emotion in it had his gut churning.

"Thanks for the bike ride," Jessica said, breezily. "See you around, Everett Williams. It was interesting to meet you. Good luck with your work."

With a wave over her shoulder, Jessica walked slowly up her sidewalk until she disappeared behind a firmly closed door.

Maybe he hadn't dated in decades, but Will recognized her actions as a major and very final brush-off. He scrubbed a hand over the still visible part of his face, then turned around and stowed her helmet in the now empty storage compartment.

Jessica's helmet, Will thought miserably, something he'd bought for the sole purpose of taking her for a ride. He wasn't going to be letting anyone else use it anytime soon, no matter how brave he'd been earlier.

Tucking the pen she gave him back into his jacket, Will stared off down the street, letting the reality of what had happened sink in completely. He knew enough about women to know what returning the pen meant. Jessica was done with him. She wanted no reminders of their time together.

Now he wished like hell' he'd kissed her earlier in the afternoon when she had taunted him. He wished he'd just stepped into her and hungrily kissed her teasing mouth when her lips had first called to him. She would have tasted like the excitement and energy of wanting the bike ride. She would have kissed him back, laughed against his mouth, and maybe even invited his tongue to play with hers.

Instead, he'd forced his mouth on hers when he was angry, forced an intimacy she obviously hadn't wanted at that moment. As Will thought about it now, he realized Jessica had not for one moment responded with any heat to his kiss in the garden. Not that what he'd done counted as real kissing anyway. He almost wished Jessica had kneed him. Maybe it would have balanced out some of his now growing guilt.

The only thing that helped calm him at all was remembering that Melanie knew her, knew who Jessica really was and all about her life. Will decided he would just give Jessica Daniels some time to stop being so upset at him, and then he would find a way to make this right with her.

Today was not going to be the only interaction he had with Jessica Daniels.

He wasn't a bad guy. He certainly couldn't live with the idea she might think he was one.

Will sighed unhappily, put the bike in gear, and rolled away from her curb.

EXCERPT FROM DATING A COUGAR

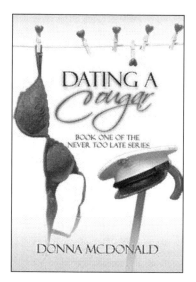

CHAPTER 1

"Why so glum, gorgeous?" Sydney unwrapped his sandwich with great anticipation, frowning when he saw Alexa was just frowning at hers. "Trust me. I made sure you got double avocado. It's just the way you like it."

Something was up. Normally, Alexa would have been three bites ahead of him by now.

"Do you think fifty is old, Sydney?" Alexa Ranger watched her thirty-five-year-old assistant and good friend take a giant bite of his club sandwich and swing his gaze to hers in shock at the same time. Then she watched him pound his chest to keep from choking as he attempted to swallow the bite around a coughing fit.

At six two with a trim waist and shoulders like a football player, the brown-haired, brown-eyed Sydney could easily be the most handsome man Alexa had ever known. He designed and wore his own line of clothes, and often looked like a male model. In her line of business, Alexa had always been proud to have someone as attractive as Sydney standing next to her, but it was his steadfast friendship that she valued most.

When he didn't answer right away with one of his usual smart-ass quips, Alexa concluded he was genuinely surprised by her question. Surprise was okay, but if he looked at her with pity, she would have to throw her sandwich at him.

"When it comes to age, it's all about the quality of the preservation," Sydney said at last, joking to give himself time to think.

In the ten years he had known and worked for Alexa Ranger, he had never known her to be truly insecure about anything, especially her age. Maybe—just maybe—a person could say that Alexa had let herself go a little bit in the last couple of years.

A lack of male companionship had taken a negative toll on her in his opinion. Alexa hadn't shown any personal interest in anyone specific in some time.

The same could be said about how little she seemed to care these last few years about making a fashion statement too. Most days the woman wore jeans and a shirt, which in Sydney's mind was barely better than a uniform.

But—*insecure*? What could cause such a foreign emotion in a woman the tabloids even feared to cross? Alexa had never been the type of person to worry about much. She was brash, boastful, demanding, and many, many other things, but the woman was not insecure.

Pulling himself from his contemplation, Sydney noticed Alexa was still intently waiting for his reply. He made himself focus on the possibility of being fifty. Naturally, his stunning life partner came immediately to mind.

"Do I think fifty is old?" Sydney asked, repeating her question. "Well, Paul is fifty-two. I certainly don't consider him old. The man just gets sexier with each passing year."

Despite being starved, he took a smaller bite of his sandwich this time just in case Alexa shocked him again.

"Yes. But it's different for men," Alexa said with a wave of her hand. She hated the dark cloud of female worry over her head. "Men get better with age, and Paul is proof. Women—well, women just get old, Sydney. Even women like me."

"Okay, this is too weird," Sydney said, putting down his sandwich. "That was definitely self-pity I heard in your voice. What is wrong with you today, Alexa? Years of good maintenance are paying off big-time for you, honey. You look great. You look my age, not yours."

Alexa shrugged her shoulders. She enjoyed her looks. In fact, she built her business on her looks. The problem was that looking younger at fifty didn't make her feel as good as it had in her thirties or forties. Now, regardless of how she looked on the outside, inside she still *felt* fifty. Why did no one understand that?

"Oh, just forget I said anything. I don't mean to whine—you know I hate whining."

Sighing over her depressing thoughts, Alexa took another bite of her sandwich.

Sydney hurriedly finished his last bite and leaned back in the chair.

"When was the last time you had a date?" he asked, inspiration striking. "I mean a real date where you dressed up and went out somewhere nice."

"Don't remember," Alexa admitted around a bite. "It's been a while I guess. Nine months, maybe? It's harder at my age to find someone interesting."

Which was mostly true, if you didn't count the attraction she'd felt shaking hands with Casey Carter last month. The retired Marine was appealing, but definitely too young, and definitely too related to her daughter's boyfriend. Her life was talk show worthy enough as it was. She certainly didn't need to add to it.

"I can't believe turning fifty is making me this crazy. Most women have their mid-life crisis at thirty or forty." Alexa sighed and picked up her water. "I may have to ask Regina for professional help again."

Sydney laughed. "Needing sex is not a crisis, honey. It's a highly solvable problem."

"Who says I need sex?" Alexa demanded, rolling her eyes at the statement.

"Sweetheart—we all do."

Alexa laughed. Okay, so maybe it had been nine months ago with a friend, and who knew how long ago with a man she genuinely desired. Maybe she even secretly worried on some level about never wanting sex again, because not dating had been a huge relief instead of a sacrifice. Determined not to sink into an even deeper funk dwelling on her voluntary celibacy, she took a big bite of her awesome sandwich and chewed.

Sydney looked at Alexa's expression and smirked. "Quit holding out and talk to me. Do you have a booty call man you haven't told me about?"

"No," Alexa said sadly. "Not anymore. I gave him up too. He started talking about setting up a regular time for us every week. I stopped seeing him about nine months ago."

"Bad call. Abstaining does not suit you, Alexa. You are a vibrant woman. You need sex." Sydney snapped his fingers. "I've got it. I could hook you up with one of my straight friends. I have several who think you're hot."

"Good lord, you're offering me a pity date?" Alexa laughed, shocked under her amusement. "Am I that bad off?"

Sydney nodded with enthusiasm. "I think the answer is definitely yes. Your insecurity is showing, honey, which is so not like you. I think you need someone in your life who will make you feel young."

"Thanks, but no thanks. I don't even let Regina and Lauren fix me up with dates. I prefer to just meet a guy and follow a little feeling that says he's worth getting to know."

"Well, I hear you there. Certainly sounds like the best motivation, but when was the last time you had a feeling about a guy?"

Sydney grinned at her guilty look and raised his eyebrows.

"Last month actually," Alexa confided. She wasn't worried about revealing the truth to someone who would never betray her. Sydney valued his life too much.

"Details please. I require proof." He made a come-on signal with his fingers.

Alexa laughed and shook her head. "Fine. It happened with Seth's older cousin, but Jenna would simply kill me if I put any moves on him."

"So? Don't tell her. Swear the man to secrecy." Sydney gave the order, laughing at Alexa's suddenly pink cheeks. That set him to wondering what kind of man could cause that level of reaction. It was utterly fascinating.

"I can't. It's totally out of the question."

The idea of asking the former Marine to indulge in a secret love affair with her struck Alexa as more funny than possible. What would Casey Carter want with an older woman like her when he could have a younger, more attractive one?

And if she did get that far with him, what would she do with Casey when they weren't in bed? There might be different problems dating younger men, but years of experience had taught her that all dating had the same depressing outcome. Plus there would be hell to pay if Jenna found out.

"Ask whatever you want, so long as it also involves asking the man out."

"Right— no problem." Alexa shook her head, her long hair sweeping her face. "You want me to date Seth's macho cousin, and convince the upright, former military man never to mention it to Seth or Jenna? That's a bold play, even with my dating history."

Sydney stood and gathered their lunch trash.

"Since when is Alexa Ranger afraid of being bold?"

Alexa shook back her reddish-brown mane of brunette hair, her eyes crinkling in amusement as she belly laughed over the challenge. If only she could find a straight man who understood her as well as Sydney. He knew just which buttons to press.

"What would I do without you, Sydney? You're absolutely right." She nodded and smiled widely, not wanting to argue further.

"Of course I'm right. Now go be bold," Sydney said sternly. "And make notes so you remember the details. You know how forgetful people are at your age."

Alexa swore at him, but blew him a kiss as he headed back to his desk.

Even if Casey Carter wasn't a good possibility, now that Sydney had all but dared her to date someone younger, the idea was churning inside her. However, a decision so important needed more than the sanction of a gay friend. Fortunately, she was meeting her two favorite dating experts for dinner that evening.

***

The food at Lucinda's was always good. If it hadn't been, Alexa would have rousted the manager for a heart-to-heart. Not just because she was part owner, but also because she truly loved meeting there for dinner. Part of what she liked was that the management trained the staff well on deflecting unwanted attention from its more famous customers. Anyone with a press badge or camera had to check their electronics at the door. Both she and Regina felt safe there, and Alexa wanted to keep it that way.

"So when was the last time you felt a genuine interest in getting to know a man," Alexa asked the two women seated at her table.

They had demolished three plates of appetizers in less than twenty minutes with no complaining about calories. It was a point of honor between them never to feel guilty about food. Regina—aka Dr. Regina Logan—was polishing off the last of the veggie pizza.

"I love pizza. It's such happy food. And all those carbs make for a good snooze after. Did you ask a question, Alexa? Sorry, I was in the middle of a pizza orgasm."

Alexa laughed when Lauren McCarthy—one of *The McCarthys* of Falls Church, Virginia—rolled her eyes at Regina's response. Lauren had the sexual sensibilities of a twenty-year-old and the sexual urges of a forty-year-old. It was not a happy combination in a woman who worried daily about what people thought of her. Stranger still, Lauren risked her prized reputation weekly by hanging out with Regina and Alexa, definitely two of the most sexually notorious women in Falls Church.

While she waited for her friends to think about the question, Alexa thought about the differences between the women she trusted with her deepest secrets. Regina and her work as a sex therapist drew the interest of the press regularly. Fortunately, Alexa's notoriety had dwindled when she'd stopped dating so much.

Only Lauren avoided the press, rarely even making the society pages. They teasingly called her 'Saint McCarthy' because the woman never did anything even remotely scandalous. The worst thing Alexa had ever known Lauren to do was buy a vibrator after her divorce. But what single woman didn't own at least one of those?

Alexa looked at Regina, smiling as she watched the most outrageous woman she knew lick cheese off her fingers.

"Come on you two. I need your opinion. When was the last time you felt a genuine interest in getting to know a man?"

Regina frowned as she wiped her hands on a napkin. "Wow. I just realized I'm stalling because I don't have an easy answer to

179

your question. That's so depressing. I guess it's been almost a year for me."

"Like you want to get to simply know him, or you want to—you know—get to know him in the biblical sense?"

Alexa shook her head at Lauren's question. The woman squirmed whenever any of them talked about sex. Only Lauren could make forty-two look as innocent as twenty. Even her daughter Jenna seemed more knowledgeable about such things.

"Biblical sense," Alexa finally answered, grinning as Lauren averted her gaze.

"I guess I'd have to say about two years ago and for yet another womanizing man. The one before him was six years ago when I first got divorced. I developed an urge to date my lawyer."

Regina arched an eyebrow. "Your lawyer? Honey, that was gratitude, not a sexual urge. Haven't you ever wanted a man so much you just went for it?"

Lauren shook her head. "Absolutely not. Technology is a much better solution and more satisfying."

"No sweetie, it's not," Alexa said gently, but with great conviction. "There's nothing like falling into a satisfied sleep after you've had a man inside you two or three times. There's no substitute for that kind of man-to-woman connection."

Regina smiled at the thought of her gorgeous friend getting lucky. God knew one of them should. "True. And I agree. So—have you been connecting to someone lately, Alexa?"

Alexa laughed and sighed. "No. I'm just a little attracted to someone, that's all. It's been a while for me too. It's complicated because the man is a lot younger."

"Younger can be good. How much younger?" Regina asked, inspecting the appetizer plates for any lingering bites.

"I don't know," Alexa said frowning. "Why does that matter?"

"Less than eight years makes you a Puma. Over eight years makes you a Cougar," Regina said wisely, grinning as Lauren nodded excitedly in agreement. She hadn't missed the gleam in Alexa's eyes either. She dialed her grin back a notch and tried for her best 'lecturing doctor' tone, even though Alexa rarely fell for that these days.

"That kind of hookup is happening a lot these days, and many older women are benefitting greatly. Biologically, it can make a lot of sense. Sometimes I wish I had an eye for younger men. They're braver and I could have a lot more dates. Unfortunately, I get irritated with their conversation long before the mating urge can take hold."

"So who's the younger guy you like?" Lauren asked, truly interested in the answer.

"I'm curious about that too," Regina said.

Alexa stared back silently, blinking as she tried to decide whether to tell them or not. Her reluctance to share his identity only made it worse for her. And her silence had both of them giggling.

"Hmmm . . . this is interesting, Lauren. Alexa doesn't want us to know. Let's ask more questions. So is the boy-toy of legal age in the state of Virginia?"

"He's around thirty-eight I think," Alexa said. Hadn't Jenna said something like that? She wished now she'd paid more attention to his back story.

"You're definitely a Cougar then, but honestly—thirty-eight is not that young." Regina laughed, rolling her eyes. "When you said young, I was picturing a twenty-something who checked himself out in the mirror every two seconds."

Lauren laughed at Regina's description because it fit her own mental image. "I was thinking the same thing. Honestly, anyone over thirty-five is fair game, Alexa. Though I'm a bit like Regina, I like men closer to my own age. Younger men seem to be too anxious and needy."

"Amen, sister." Regina held up a hand, high-fiving with Lauren, making her giggle.

Alexa repeated what she heard, or thought she heard, wanting to make sure she understood their advice. "So neither of you would pursue this interest if you were me, simply because of his age?"

Regina and Lauren looked at each other. Surprisingly, it was Lauren who piped up with "depends on the amount of attraction." The answer pleased her, so Regina smiled widely and nodded in agreement.

Alexa closed her eyes and crossed her arms. "How am I supposed to measure attraction from an encounter that only lasted about five minutes? This is not helping."

Regina removed the white linen napkin from her lap and folded it into a neat triangle before placing it on the now empty plate in front of her.

"Do not try to fool the sex therapist, Alexa," she said ominously, grinning when she made Lauren giggle again. "You've dated slightly younger men before. What's the real problem with this guy?"

Alexa bit her lip and then sighed. "The only younger man I ever dated was only two years younger than me, Regina. The term 'younger' barely applies in that case. But you're right, the real problem is the man I met is Seth Carter's cousin. It's not like Casey is Seth's exact age, but he's probably not forty either. He looked very young."

Conversation paused while Regina and Lauren absorbed the news.

"Jenna would probably kill you. Sorry—I shouldn't have said that." Lauren winced at how dramatic the announcement sounded, even though all of them knew it was the truth.

"Yes, exactly. Jenna would kill me," Alexa agreed, nodding her head. "I'm not sure any man is worth risking my life. We all know my daughter is my worst critic when it comes to dating."

Regina squinted hard as she considered the frown on Alexa's face and the disappointment reflected in her gaze. Moments ago there had been a damn twinkle. It wasn't fair.

"I agree it's a tough twist, but I wouldn't let Jenna's comfort be the deciding factor. Who knows? Jenna and Seth might not work out anyway. If you don't take this chance, then everybody loses. Sometimes it's okay to be selfish, Alexa. This may be one of those times."

Alexa nodded. But nothing they said made her want to call Casey up and ask him out. The idea of a fifty-year-old woman dating a thirty-eight-year-old man just smacked of desperation to her. If the press found out, she would make the headlines again—*Aging Model Dates Young Marine*. She wasn't ready to deal with the public or private fallout if that happened. Over the past few years, she had come to like being less notorious. As far as she was concerned, she had officially passed the title down to Regina.

"Forget I mentioned Casey Carter. The tingle he caused had 'bad idea' all over it the moment it happened. Let's change the subject. Do you think fifty is old?"

"You're kidding, right?" Lauren exclaimed, shocked at Alexa's sad tone.

Alexa sighed. Talking to Regina and Lauren was turning out to be worse than talking to Sydney. No one seemed to understand her concerns.

Regina swore and got up from her seat to gather her things. "I wish I could stay longer and talk some sense into you, but I have to go catch a plane. So let me be quick with my two cents on the subject. No, fifty is not old, and you make it look better than thirty anyway. Lauren and I are using you as our role model. And you know damn well that at forty-seven, fifty's just around a corner for me. Now stop feeling sorry for yourself. Go have sex and shake this mood, Alexa. You need the oxytocin high from intercourse to fight the hormonally depressive funk you're in right now."

Alexa blew out a frustrated breath. "Hormonally depressive funk? Is that a precise medical opinion, Dr. Logan?" Regina just gave her a look that asked if she needed a little more proof, or *a lot* more proof. She knew Regina would happily give either.

"Don't make me change my flight," Regina ordered.

"Okay. Fine. I'll take care of it," Alexa said sarcastically. "You're probably right, anyway. Sydney said the same thing."

Regina snorted as she pulled on her coat. "No, I'm *probably* right about the weather changing, and that the plane ride will be bumpy to Boston. I am *always* right about sex."

As they split the bill and debated the tip, Alexa thought about how best to follow Regina's advice. Instantly, Casey Carter's image popped into her mind and her heartbeat picked up. *No*, she told herself, consigning her longing to the realm of fantasy instead of reality.

Instead, Alexa made herself think about the ever-available Todd Lansing who was a 'friend with benefits' as Jenna would say. A couple years ago her comfortable relationship with Todd had been enough because it kept her from bed-hopping while she casually dated other men. Now, the thought of using Todd for gratuitous sex held no appeal at all.

"You're so beautiful, Alexa. Maybe you should sign up with one of the dating services online." Lauren smiled to soften her suggestion.

Regina laughed wickedly and Alexa looked shocked.

"Well, why not? Lots of older women do it. Some of the women at the country club rave about the variety of offers they get."

"Wait until I get back, Alexa. I'll sign up too." Laughing, Regina dashed ahead of her friends, hoping there was a cab waiting outside.

Lauren walked beside Alexa, wondering what she'd said wrong. "Did I hurt your feelings?"

Alexa snorted. "Variety is overrated, honey. Regardless of what your country club friends say, most women just want to find a decent guy who can inspire lust now and again."

Alexa patted Lauren's arm as they walked out to be sure the younger woman knew she wasn't mad. There was no reason to take her sour mood out on her friends. It was just bad luck that the only sexually interesting man in years had turned out not to be a good possibility. Probably just as well. She didn't need another empty sexual relationship without the remotest possibility of happily-ever-after attached.

CHAPTER 2

When he walked through the door of Eddy's Bar and Grill, Casey's attention zeroed in on Alexa Ranger sitting at one of the polished dark wooden tables with two other women. Since meeting her a month or so ago, he had evidently developed a radar for her presence.

Looking around, he saw Seth was not waiting for him as promised—no big surprise there. Luckily he was having a good day and hadn't needed to use the cane, so he chose a seat in a dark area of the bar near the door. It was as far away as possible from Alexa's table, but still offered a decent view of her.

Slipping off his sunglasses, he pulled the Marines' logo ball cap lower over his eyes, not wanting to draw attention to himself while he studied her. Alexa had to be at least forty-five years old despite the fact that she looked much younger. The intensity of his attraction to the older woman was a mystery, but he couldn't stop himself from meticulously planning what he would sexually do to her and with her if he ever got the chance. He had had that reaction even the very first time he'd met her.

Over the last month, Casey had not only been avoiding the necessity of dealing with his attraction to Jenna's mother but also avoiding even minor social contact. Jenna and Seth had finally given up trying to include him in their activities. Not that it looked like Alexa was having the same problem. Looking at his watch, Casey saw thirty minutes had passed now without her even once glancing his way. Evidently, Alexa did not have the same physical radar for him, though he still believed she had been attracted to him too.

Maybe she was just better at denial. Maybe she was seeing someone else.

Who knew?

As Casey studied her, he considered it a point in Alexa's favor that she didn't constantly scan the bar for men like one of her companions was doing, or look around in disgust like the other one. No, Alexa Ranger just kept on talking, her focus completely on the conversation.

His phone buzzing with an incoming text message finally snagged his attention away.

Can't make it after all. Last minute problem keeping me here. TTYL.

Telling himself he should have known this would happen, Casey texted back a reply.

WTF? Drinking your beer and mine then. Your fault if I don't make it home.

184

Seth's obsession with his entrepreneurial work matched any Casey had ever had with the Marines. Despite being only eight years older, Casey felt a couple decades ahead in understanding what was important in life. There had been some rough times for him during the last few years. While he hadn't let a hip replacement or a wife dying of cancer take him down for good, he had let both those things teach him about living in the moment. Life was too damn short to work seventy hour weeks. He hoped his workaholic cousin figured that out soon.

His attention came back to Alexa just as hers shifted to the door opening. Even at a distance, Casey could read the concern in her unsmiling lips pressed into a firm line. He shifted in his chair, willing his body to relax when all it wanted was to go ask her what was wrong. She was probably the most independent female that had ever crossed his path, and yet he wanted to take care of her. It was the craziest reaction he'd ever had for a woman he barely knew, certainly a lot more crazy than simple sexual attraction.

Following her gaze, his attention finally shifted to the person Alexa had watched come through the door. He ducked his head as a blur of blue brushed by his table. He got a whiff of some expensive scent that made him think of silky sheets, pulled blinds, and ceiling fans.

From the back, he saw tall heels and seamed stockings going way up to more interesting curves outlined by a skin-tight dress. Maybe he was out of practice, but the woman was a dream come true for the lucky guy she had dressed to please tonight. *That is a take-me-now-I'm-yours dress*, he thought. Though it had been a while, he still recognized them. And thank God for that—or rather thank Alexa Ranger for reminding his body of things it had almost forgotten.

Dragging his attention away from the decked out woman, Casey finally noticed pretty much every man in the bar had also been watching her trek with great interest. But instead of singling out a man, she seemed to be heading directly to Alexa's table. When the bartender yelled the woman's name, Casey swore silently. The woman was Alexa's daughter—Seth's girlfriend.

So where in the hell was Seth?

His cousin hadn't mentioned anything about Jenna in his text. What crisis had detained Seth at home if it wasn't Jenna in a seduction dress? The freaking emergency his cousin needed to take care of was here in the damn bar. Seth swore Jenna Ranger was the one, but so far Casey hadn't seen much evidence backing that up.

He drummed his fingers on the table as he thought about what to do. Some clichés were truer than others, especially where military men were concerned. All his instincts were telling him—no, yelling at him—that this situation was not good. Even if he contacted Seth, there was no guarantee Jenna would still be here by time he got downtown.

Sighing, Casey put his sunglasses back on, picked up his beer, and as discreetly as he could, moved to the other end of the crowded bar. This placed him nearer Alexa's table where he could do some further reconnaissance. Or in other words, where he could eavesdrop on their conversation.

***

Alexa's mother radar went on full alert when Jenna walked into the bar. Seeing Jenna in seductive woman gear was a thrill, but the look in her daughter's eyes spoiled the perfect picture. She sighed with resignation when Jenna frowned at all the males avidly watching her swinging curves move across the room. *Oh hell*, she thought. *What has Seth done to Jenna now?*

When Jenna stopped at the table, she put her hands on hips, mirroring a physical gesture Alexa recognized as one of her own. Her heart contracted with love.

"Is there an age limit to join this hen party?" Jenna demanded, her gaze meeting her mother's.

"Yes. Lauren barely makes the cut, but at twenty-seven you're good."

"Wonderful—because I really need a drink right now."

Alexa offered her still nearly full glass of red wine to her daughter who took it while still standing and drank greedily.

"Well, don't you look yummy tonight? If I were a lesbian, I would make a pass," Regina said in her best sultry voice, giving Jenna an admiring perusal.

"Thanks." Jenna bent forward to brush her lips across Regina's forehead. "I'm glad the dress is getting an appreciative response from somebody."

Alexa's eyebrows rose into her hairline at the comment, but Jenna looked away before she could ask the obvious question.

Lauren looked at Regina and shook her head. *"Lesbian? You?* I can't even imagine you giving up men."

"Oh, I don't know. How much harder could being a lesbian be?" Regina pushed her auburn-red waves back from her face. "When I suggested male enhancement drugs to the last man I hoped to be intimate with, he told me I needed to grow up. I told him he needed to get it up, patted him on the hand, and left."

186

Lauren stared in complete and utter shock, because that was appalling behavior, even for Regina.

"You didn't really suggest your date take male enhancement drugs, did you? Regina, you probably hurt his ego. If you'd just slipped it in the man's drink at dinner, he'd have thought you inspired lust."

"I would never trick a man into taking male enhancement drugs. Besides, drugging someone is a felony. Don't you ever talk about sex with the men you date? Communication is key, you know."

Regina laughed when Lauren rolled her eyes.

"I have no need to discuss sex with my male companions. My dates are strictly platonic, and I like it that way," Lauren insisted, saluting Regina with her mineral water. "You are the only person I ever discuss sex with, Dr. Logan."

Regina rolled her eyes and took a long drink of her pomegranate martini. "I feel sorry for you then."

Alexa breathed a sigh of relief when Jenna belly laughed at the argument between Regina and Lauren. Jenna smiled the first real smile since she'd come into the bar.

Looking at her vital, lovely daughter, she couldn't help wondering for the umpteenth time what Jenna found so appealing about Seth Carter. The man was good looking, but Jenna constantly worried about his lack of desire for her. How invalidating would that be? It eluded her how any hot-blooded woman could tolerate being sexually ignored and made her mad as hell thinking her daughter was putting up with it.

There had to be something wrong with Seth. His cousin's sexuality had plastered her over the kitchen counter with a simple handshake. She was probably the only mother in history who ever worried about a man *not* putting the right moves on her daughter.

"Sweetheart," drawled Alexa, "if your ego needs stroking, all you have do is turn around. There are at least eight pairs of eyes glued to your lovely rear right now."

Jenna sighed, walked around the table, and leaned over the stunning brunette who had borne her for a lingering hug. "Thank you, Mama. If you were standing up, you know every man would be looking at you instead of me."

Alexa crushed Jenna to her in a fierce embrace. "Not today. That shade of blue is amazing on you and matches your eyes perfectly, which is only secondary to what it does to enhance your—"

The sound of glasses dropping interrupted Alexa. It was followed by someone big hitting the floor with a loud thud and swearing.

The other women at the table giggled, and then laughed outright as Jenna straightened red-faced from the hug. "I guess I shouldn't have bent over so much."

A booming voice yelled.

"Jenna Lee Ranger, no more bending over the table. I can't afford any more losses here, cutie pie."

Several people in the bar laughed, but the women at the table laughed louder than anyone. Jenna felt her blush spreading upwards to the roots of her hair. She pulled out a chair to sit, but could barely manage to wiggle into it because the dress was so tight.

"Sorry, Eddy," Jenna yelled over her shoulder. "I'm sitting down now."

Alexa patted her daughter's shoulder in support, while she worked to stifle her own laughter. It was not nice to laugh at your child—your *only* child. But she gave Jenna mega cool points for keeping her composure.

"Well, *that* was mortifying. What makes an intelligent woman think a dress like this is a good idea?"

Jenna sighed loudly as she complained to the still laughing women surrounding her. Frustrated, she laid her head back in the chair, and slid down as unglamorously as possible into the seat.

"I can't sit comfortably. These three-inch heels are killing me. The dress is so tight I can barely breathe. I'm a freaking idiot for wearing this stupid outfit. What was I thinking?" Jenna smacked her forehead a couple of times.

In that moment, Alexa decided Jenna looked more like a pouting twelve-year-old than an accomplished woman of twenty-seven. Being an architect in a profession mostly populated with men, her daughter rarely bothered with her feminine side.

Men, Alexa fumed. *They can ruin anything.* Only a few were even worth the expenditure of hormones, and the one Jenna liked was not in that category.

"I bet you were thinking Seth Carter would want to chew that dress off you with his teeth," Regina offered, eyeing the dress with envy.

Jenna opened her mouth to reply, but Lauren interrupted and patted her hand.

188

"At your age Jenna, hormones cause a temporary form of female insanity. Men briefly look good for a few years, but the urge passes eventually."

"Stop that!" Regina scolded, smacking Lauren's hand off Jenna's. "You'll scare her. Just because you swore off sex years ago doesn't mean you get to warp Jenna."

"Ouch! Your watch scratched me, Regina. And I did not swear off sex. I swore off men. It's a different thing altogether. You of all people should know that," Lauren protested.

Regina turned to Jenna and spoke seriously. "Sex with men does not have to ever go away. Or at least it doesn't have to if you want to keep on living and not become a dried-up prune at age forty-two."

Alexa looked at her friends in both amazement and wonder. There couldn't be two more different women or two more differing views on men. Jenna certainly had unusual role models with the three of them. She focused her piercing sapphire gaze intently on her daughter's slumping form.

"Well, I bet you were thinking the dress would once and for all get Seth Carter's attention off his cell phone and focused instead on you. Just like you thought the red dress, the pink shorts, and the black lace bra I gave you would do the trick. You looked just as amazing in them as you do tonight."

When Jenna didn't reply, Alexa gave her daughter a long, knowing stare.

"Sweetheart, are you one hundred percent sure Seth's not gay?"

Jenna's chin lifted at the question and she pulled herself completely upright in the chair. "I'm sure, and—*no*," she answered, embarrassed to have to explain such a thing. "Seth's *not* gay. I don't know what his problem is, but it's not him being gay."

Alexa knew quite well the good and bad of men. She loved men, but in her experience, most men were better in bed than out of it. She watched Jenna look away from the three of them staring at her intently, only to finally swing a tortured gaze back.

"I just wanted to surprise Seth. When he answered the door, the phone rang. He took the call, turned his back to me, and left me standing in the doorway."

"*Left you standing the doorway? In that dress?*" Shocked, Regina could only shake her head and think that Seth Carter needed his testosterone checked if a phone call was that damn distracting.

189

"Was it bad timing, maybe?" Lauren suggested, choosing to believe there had to be an answer other than Seth didn't want Jenna as much as Jenna wanted him.

"It's always bad timing with Seth." Jenna sighed, upset and unable to keep the sadness out of her voice. She looked at her mother. "Earlier this week Seth kissed me good night, and I know—damn it, *I know* he was interested in that moment. I mean I'm not *completely* stupid about men."

"Jenna," Alexa scolded. "You're not stupid at all. Any man in this bar would happily take you to bed. This is obviously about Seth and not about you. Don't even go there."

Jenna looked at her with huge eyes, and Alexa winced at what she saw. She sighed and reached for her daughter's hand.

"It was an observation honey, not a suggestion to take a strange man to bed."

Of all the people who thought poorly of her dating habits, her own daughter was the worst critic. But it was a fact that Alexa would never, ever have let a man she dated make her feel as bad as Jenna felt right now because of Seth's lack of response.

"Let me rephrase my comments," Alexa said gently, well-practiced at soothing her daughter's ego. "I admire your sincere affection and longing for Seth. He's damn lucky you came to see us instead of picking up the first great-looking guy you saw. If Seth Carter is worth the emotional investment, he's yet to prove it to you. Most men would never have turned a sexy woman away. If you don't believe me, ask Lauren and Regina."

Jenna looked at Lauren who squirmed, then sighed.

"Your mother is right. Most men would never have turned you away, not in a killer dress and those heels. The message you're sending is loud and clear."

Jenna swung her gaze to Regina. "So am I being a doormat? Am I letting Seth make me feel bad for no reason?"

Regina hesitated, but as usual opted for honesty over diplomacy. "Yes. It's probably because you love him."

"This is just great," Jenna said sarcastically, leaning down and banging her forehead on the table. "I am definitely an idiot then."

Alexa and Lauren looked across Jenna's bent head to Regina. Regina tugged at her Rolex and pulled herself reluctantly into Dr. Logan mode.

"Jenna, listen. Seth may have reasons for rejecting your advances," she softened her tone, "reasons that make sense only to him. You should consider dating other men. It might at least help you decide if Seth is worth the risk of more rejection."

Jenna's forehead was still pressed to the table, so Regina leaned over and touched her hand to make sure she was hearing.

"If you keep repeating this specific rejection pattern with this particular man, you put yourself at risk of believing the problem is yours alone. Seth may be passive-aggressive about it, but he is rejecting you, not the other way around. You wouldn't even be here if he had reacted the way you had a right to expect."

Jenna raised her head and sighed in defeat. Alexa saw the decision in her eyes before she spoke, and she hurt for her daughter. Jenna reached out and Alexa linked their hands, squeezing hard.

"No matter how much I care about Seth, I refuse to spend my time wanting a man who's never going to want me back the same way. One Ranger woman already did that. I'm not repeating the same mistake."

Alexa brought Jenna's hand to her lips and kissed it in support. She was grateful there was at least some understanding between them. She was also grateful she'd always opted to tell Jenna the truth, even about her father.

"Okay—to hell with feeling sorry for myself. I'm so done with that tonight," Jenna said firmly. "It hurt so bad this time I didn't even cry."

"Maybe it's just over," Alexa suggested, letting her daughter pull away.

"Maybe it is."

Jenna stood and lifted her chin as she smoothed the dress down.

"I love you all. Thanks for letting me vent. I need to go home, change clothes, and try to forget. I'll call you tomorrow, Mama. Is Daddy coming this weekend?"

"I left the invitation open. I'll call you when I hear for sure."

Alexa watched her daughter walk out, not acknowledging the men who looked longingly in her direction.

"*Men*," Alexa spat the word like an oath. "Life is so much less complicated when you don't want one."

"I'll drink to that," Lauren said, lifting her mineral water.

Regina snorted. "Well, I'm not drinking to such foolishness. And since when have you given up on men, Alexa? At fifty, I consider you the ultimate optimist for trying so many for so long to find the right one."

"Very funny, Dr. Logan. For your information, I haven't seriously dated a man in a couple of years." She paused for dramatic effect, sipping her now meager glass of red wine,

191

thanks to Jenna. "But that doesn't mean I've given up sex. I'm not totally crazy."

Alexa winked at Lauren, who grinned back.

Regina saluted Alexa with the rest of her drink, and polished it off. "Thank God for that at least. It's *use it or lose it* after menopause starts, honey."

***

Behind them, Casey sat in silence trying to absorb all he had heard.

First, a big one for him was Alexa was fifty instead of forty-five, which made the age gap between them even wider than he had imagined. He would have to think about whether or not it bothered him. Certainly, knowledge of their exact age difference didn't stop him from wondering if Alexa would heed her friend's advice to *use it or lose it*. Since the idea of her using it with another man bothered the hell out of him, Casey supposed his reaction likely answered his question.

But *why* was the red-haired woman talking so much about sex anyway? They called her Dr. Logan. Casey made a mental note to look her up online. She was the one scanning the room for men earlier. The other woman, a polished blonde, seemed to not like men at all. The entire conversation had made Casey wonder just what kind of woman Alexa Ranger was.

Not that he was a prude or anything, he just preferred a woman with at least some modesty.

Okay, so maybe he was used to having more experience than the women he'd been involved with sexually. He had been his wife's second lover and last one. The thought still pleased him. That didn't make him sexist, did it?

He didn't even want to contemplate how many lovers Alexa had had looking like she did. It was one more thing he would have to think about before getting involved with her—IF he decided to do so.

Still, the worst bit of news to ponder was that something might be seriously wrong with Seth. Did he really send Jenna away tonight? Casey would bet his entire military pension Seth was not gay. The boy had not slept around indiscriminately as a teenager, but Casey had bought him box after box of condoms when there had been a woman in his life.

Seth was definitely not gay—incredibly stupid maybe—but not gay.

Eavesdropping had seemed like a good idea when he'd moved around the bar. Now the only part of the conversation

Casey was glad he'd heard was that Alexa Ranger wasn't currently dating anyone.

CHAPTER 3

Just a few more months was all he needed, Seth thought. The import and export business he had started two years ago was taking off at last. Soon he would have to hire an assistant to help him keep up with it. After that, he could finally slow down and enjoy what he had accomplished. And he could pursue his relationship with Jenna Ranger without constantly being interrupted by work problems.

Seth tapped his phone and ordered flowers to be sent to her home along with an apology. Tomorrow he'd call in person and apologize again. He was becoming well practiced at saying "I'm sorry. I'm a jerk. I'm crazy about you, so you have to forgive me."

Normally, Jenna didn't hold a grudge, though Seth expected this time it might take a little longer. Before, she had at least complained about being ignored. This time Jenna had just left without saying anything. In his experience, silence from a woman was never good. It meant she was too mad to trust her reaction.

After finishing his apology note, Seth pressed send on his phone just as Casey came through the door. The look on his cousin's face instantly propelled him back to being a teenager again.

"What is your problem, Seth? I want you to tell me the truth. Are you gay?"

The question was so unexpected Seth dropped down on the couch and laughed.

"Are you drunk on two beers? I'd be mad, but I can't believe you'd ask such a stupid question. Have you seen Jenna? You know, the incredibly hot woman I'm dating?"

"Yes, I saw Jenna. In fact, I saw a lot of Jenna, and so did thirty other horny guys in Eddy's Bar when she bent over a table to hug her mother."

Seth opened his mouth, but nothing came out. He closed it again and put his hands over his eyes. The thought of other men seeing Jenna dressed up the way she had been made him nauseous. He watched Casey take off his jacket and yet somehow keep the glare in place.

"Did you really send Jenna away tonight? *In that dress?*"

"No. I did not send Jenna away," Seth protested. "I got a phone call from Japan I'd been waiting for all evening. Jenna must have left while I was talking. When I finished the call, she was just—*gone.*"

Seth ran a nervous hand through his hair.

"It's okay. I sent flowers and an apology note. Tomorrow I'll call her. This will be okay. It's happened before."

When Casey swore viciously, Seth winced at the amount of anger in it.

"Yeah, I heard all about how it wasn't the first time when Jenna was complaining about it to Alexa and her friends."

Seth could only blink in reply. The information was not really sinking in. Why would Jenna tell her mother that she'd tried to seduce him. He watched as Casey threw up his hands.

"Do you have any idea how much trouble Jenna went through to try and seduce you? Do you know how long it takes a woman to get that dressed up? It takes hours, Seth. Hours."

Seth closed his eyes, mostly to block out Casey's glare. "*Okay, I know.* I messed up—*badly.* I sent flowers. This will be okay."

"I hope so for your sake, but I don't think flowers are going to make up for Jenna sleeping alone tonight when she so obviously had other plans. You better hope she's as much in love with you as you are with her. Otherwise, she's going to be looking for a man who doesn't own a cell phone."

Seth swiped a hand through his hair in frustration again. Why couldn't everyone just wait a little bit longer? He was almost there.

"You know, I'm trying like hell to put my expensive Harvard education to good use by getting my business going. I just need a couple more months, and then I can have a different kind of life."

"I hope you get lucky then, because you sure as hell aren't being very smart about Jenna. There were lots of men in the bar tonight who looked as good in a suit as you do. You're going to have to commit to the woman if you want to keep her. If you don't have time for her, cut the woman loose."

Seth sighed heavily as Casey walked off mumbling about dresses and stupidity, leaving him digging in a side table for the pills he took to settle his stomach. He refused to think tonight was the disaster his cousin seemed to think it was. He was in love with Jenna, had been in love with her since the first time he saw her. There was no choice except to believe their problems could be fixed.

If not easily, he'd just see to it they did anyway. Through his business, Seth had discovered he was very good at making things work out.

***

A couple weeks after his argument with Seth, Casey stood outside the building where he knew Alexa Ranger worked. He had accused his cousin of being dumb about Jenna, but later realized he was being just as dumb about his attraction to her mother. When a woman was on a man's mind as much as Alexa Ranger was on his, it was time to explore it and see if it was worth taking to the next level.

The doorman of the building opened the door and nodded respectfully as he walked into the lobby. Casey could literally feel the man's curiosity and concern about his limp.

"Morning, sir. Let me get that for you," the doorman said with a smile.

"Thanks," Casey said, noting the man's concerned gaze dropping to the cane. "I'm good—just a military injury. Cane beats a chair any day." He delivered the explanation with a shrug, before smiling and walking on.

"Indeed it does, sir," the doorman answered with a respectful nod. "Thank you for your service to our country."

"You're welcome," Casey replied, nodding respectfully in return.

At the elevator, he scanned the building occupants' list looking for Alexa's business. He called the elevator and moments later was standing in the middle of the most chaos he had ever seen. A giant sliding door off the receiving area was opened, revealing what might have been an impressive art gallery, but was instead filled with several nearly naked women standing around in nothing but underwear.

After almost two years with no woman in his life, the sight of so many scantily clad ones had Casey momentarily frozen where he stood. A multitude of pleasing female faces looked up at him briefly. One or two smiled and finger waved, causing Casey to grin, but eventually they went back to their tasks, which seem to include all of them talking at once.

Casey shook his head. There was a time not too long ago when his presence would have earned more than just a brief glance. One of them might have broken away to come speak to him, at least until Susan chased her away. Maybe the cane was slowing him down a bit. Until recently, he hadn't given much thought to what women he met might think about his injury—or him. Now he suddenly found himself wondering how Alexa would react.

"Can I help you?"

Casey turned a little too quickly at hearing the distinctly masculine voice behind him and stumbled sideways into the owner. "Damn. Sorry about that."

"Easy," the man said with a small laugh, making sure he was stable before letting go. "I didn't mean to startle you. Let's not do more damage to that military injury."

Casey was surprised at the accurate guess, but the man merely smiled. "Did the doorman call you or is it tattooed on me somewhere? I thought they removed the label before I left."

"It's the haircut. Plus you carry yourself like a soldier. And judging by the haircut," the man said, his gaze inspecting Casey's head with a serious perusal, "I would guess you served in the Marines."

"And you would be correct," Casey admitted, surprised again.

The man just smiled and shrugged. "I've dated a few."

Dated a few? Of course, Casey thought, instantly grinning. It made all the sense in the world to him that only a gay guy could work sanely around all those scantily clad women every day.

"Forgive me, I'm being rude," the man said, reaching his hand out. "Sydney Banes—Alexa Ranger's assistant. What can I do for you today?"

"Casey Carter," he said in return, shaking automatically.

"So how can I help you Mr. Carter?"

"I'm here to see Alexa." Since he hadn't thought to have a good excuse, the truth came slipping out. "Actually, Alexa is not expecting me. I was in the neighborhood and thought I might surprise her with a visit."

Sydney narrowed his eyes as he noticed the slight flush accompanying the smooth statement. Granted, it had been a couple of years since a man had been a problem around the office, but he still recognized the signs of interest. The hopeful expression and the dreamy look were unmistakable.

Though Sydney had never known Alexa to date a military man, there was always a first time. What interested him most was Case Carter being younger than the stuffed-shirt 50-somethings Alexa usually dated. Maybe she was taking his advice after all. Whatever the case, his gut instinct said to let the wounded hero in to see her. And he rarely acted against his gut.

"I apologize for the chaos, Mr. Carter. We're prepping for a buyer show this weekend. Alexa is hiding from it in her office. Let's walk back and see if she has a few minutes."

Sydney motioned for Carter to follow him down a long hallway, feeling a little guilty when the man limped slowly after him.

196

Alexa stood at the biggest window in her office, staring out into the street while counting her many blessings. She had a business she loved, some really great friends, and a wonderful—even if odd—family. Now if only Jenna could find a way to be happy, her life would pretty much be complete.

But what about you? a voice inside her taunted. *What about sex? Love? You deserve those too.* Sure she did, but then so did everyone.

At fifty, Alexa was old enough to know for a fact that life didn't always work out the way you wanted. She was at least content with most of her life, which was much more than many people could say at her age. She scolded her inner voice for stirring up trouble where there was none.

Sydney called her name as he knocked and opened the door. "Alexa? I brought someone by to see you. He said he wanted it to be a surprise."

Alexa watched Casey Carter come through the door behind Sydney. She noticed the cane and how good he looked at the same time. It took nothing away from the man. The entire package was sexy as hell.

"Casey?" Alexa was almost shocked speechless. "This is definitely a surprise."

Casey walked into the office slowly, looking around in awe at the expensive furniture and the beautiful woman in the middle of it. It was also the office of the person in charge. Oh hell—maybe he should have called first. "Sorry to barge in on a business day. I was just in the neighborhood and wanted to talk to you about something if you have some time."

Alexa motioned with her hand to one of two brightly patterned chairs in front of her desk. "Sure. I can take a few minutes. Sit—please. Sydney, will you tell Angela I'll be a little late? She can start the meeting without me."

Sydney nodded and closed the door with a decisive click as he left.

Casey sat, relieved to rest his leg and hip. He would have to take a taxi back. Walking six blocks had not been a good idea today. In his determination to come see Alexa, he had all but forgotten some days were a lot better than others.

"I don't mean to keep you from working. I just didn't know how else to get in touch with you."

Alexa waved his apology away and walked from the window to sit at her desk.

"I love a surprise now and again." Turning her chair in Casey's direction, she locked her gaze with his and smiled fully. "So. What can I do for you?"

Casey's mind easily drew a picture, even when he could do nothing more than stare. Alexa Ranger was the most beautiful woman he'd ever met. From her curious, but only friendly stare, she also seemed to want to pretend she hadn't felt the instant lust flare between them last month. Today her smile held nothing remotely hinting of their shared moment. No signs of blushing were happening either. Well damn it, Casey thought, chagrined to think he might have made more of it than it had been.

"I like your office," he said, stalling while he considered how to explain coming to see her. "The doorman is very nice."

"Eric? Yes, Eric has been here a long time," Alexa replied dryly, wondering why Casey was chatting about the doorman. She watched him caressing the end of his cane while he searched for what he wanted to say next. She decided she liked his hands. They were big and looked strong.

They are strong. You remember his grip—so stop pretending you're not interested.

Giving in to the voice at last, Alexa let herself imagine how wonderful Casey's hands might feel on her. A harmless fantasy, she assured herself, refusing to feel guiltier as her mind conjured up all kinds of delightful scenarios.

"So do you lease your space?" Casey asked.

While she had been fantasizing about his hands, it seemed Casey had been lusting after her real estate. Her smile threatened to become laughter over it, but she held it back and answered as seriously as she could.

"Actually, my company owns the building. We lease out the first and fourth floors. I was already settled on the second floor when the sale went through. I was too lazy to move."

Casey mentally searched for another safe topic of conversation while he pondered the wisdom of telling Alexa why he'd really stopped by. Despite his attraction to her, she was a lot more intimidating in her office than she had been in Seth's condo. Her rock-steady composure actually made him wonder if he'd imagined her blushing.

"How's Jenna doing since the break-up?" Casey asked. "I think Seth's hoping she'll eventually forgive his stupidity. Granted, he needs to learn how to appreciate a sexy, intelligent woman who's crazy about him."

"Maybe you could give him lessons," Alexa teased, the provocative statement sliding smoothly off her tongue like it had been waiting years to be said to this man.

She held Casey's gaze, pleased with the interest in his eyes, not so pleased with the confused expression on the rest of his face. *Bad girl, Alexa,* she told herself, fighting a grin. *Don't make things worse by flirting.*

"Lessons? What kind of lessons?"

Casey frowned and wondered if daily exposure to Alexa would grant him immunity to her teasing smile and the sexy dare in her gaze. What had she said to him?

When he noticed the corners of Alexa's mouth tilted in a smirk, Casey decided he'd like nothing better than to kiss the amusement right off her beautiful face. Maybe then he'd stop being so intimidated. It also might make her think twice about torturing him in the future.

Alexa gave Casey points for not swearing or yelling at her yet because he looked quite capable of both. She laughed softly when he just kept frowning. "You heard me. Stop playing dumb about it. Do you know how to treat a sexy, intelligent woman well or not?"

Her outright laughter broke whatever spell her smile was casting over his brain. Once free of it, he glared back, embarrassed and turned-on at the same time. He also wished like hell he could pass a little of his personal discomfort back to her. Irritation made his voice rougher than he would have liked as the unvarnished truth just came pouring out.

"Well, I sure as hell wouldn't have sent a woman in a seduction dress away from my door to take a damn phone call, if that's what you're asking."

Alexa was delighted with the genuine disgust in his tone. The next laughter rose from her gut. "Well, I'm really glad to hear you say that. I would have hated for my instincts about you to have been wrong."

She leaned back in her chair and studied Casey's face. He was about as embarrassed as she had ever seen a man be, but still managing to hold his ground with her. Most men fled from her teasing when they got offended. Alexa found she liked Casey's emotional courage. She liked it a lot, actually. So she decided to just tell him the truth.

"Sorry for teasing. I get a little wicked sometimes. But since you asked, let me tell you about my daughter, Casey. Since Jenna was old enough to date, I have always insisted that she keep searching for that one person who could best meet her needs. Sex. Love. Caring. All of it. Do you know what I mean?"

Casey nodded yes. Of course. Wasn't that what everyone wanted from a relationship?

"Then along comes Seth into her life. I think Jenna may be a little in love with him, but his rejections have hurt her pride. Right now, I'm forbidden to speak his name around her." Alexa turned her head, frowning into the space beyond her desk. "Jenna told me she broke up with Seth through a text message. She told me it was poetic justice since the man was so obsessed with his phone."

"I can't argue with the phone obsession part," Casey said quietly, "but Seth does have reasons for being so focused on his work."

"Yes, I'm sure he does. Don't get me wrong. I don't think Seth is a bad guy at all. I probably share that work-obsessed quality with him. Jenna didn't come home from her job even for her birthday last week. She doesn't currently want to be in the same town as Seth. My daughter can be very resistant when she has her mind set against something. She gets that trait from her father."

Casey studied Alexa who had dropped her gaze from his again.

"Everyone is resistant sometimes. I'm sure even you are," he said, mouth quirking as he watched her study her manicured nails as if she had never seen them before.

"No, I am very flexible and forgiving about most things. I roll with the punches life throws and jump back up for more. My experiences have required me to react that way. Jenna is a product of her own life."

Alexa felt the heat come into her eyes to match the anger she felt in the rest of her.

"I will tell you quite frankly that I didn't raise my daughter to be ignored by anyone. Even at Jenna's age, I would have snatched the phone from Seth's hand and thrown the damn thing across the room."

"Really? What would you do now?" Casey asked.

"Now? Same thing probably, but at my age I can't imagine thinking any man was worth that kind of drama. Besides," Alexa said with a dismissing wave of her hand, "the kind of men I like would toss the phone themselves. I don't think younger men work that way."

Casey laughed, appreciating her honesty. He was immensely glad Alexa had stopped flirting to really talk with him.

"Seth was just being stupid about priorities. I'm pretty sure he's learned from the experience."

200

When Alexa smiled at him fully, the corners of her eyes crinkled, causing her laugh lines to take center stage in her amazing face. His body tightened immediately, wiping away any remaining doubts about whether her age bothered him. It for sure didn't stop him from wanting her. Casey figured his reaction made him exactly her kind of guy whether she knew it or not.

"Okay. I've run out of small talk. I didn't really stop by to talk about Seth and Jenna. I came to see you. Have dinner with me tonight," Casey ordered, pleased at the shock Alexa wasn't able to hide. He smiled, letting his wicked thoughts run free at last. "I can't believe you didn't see the invitation coming. I've spent the entire time here trying to ask you out."

Alexa raised her eyebrows. "Ask me out? Why? Don't you think I'm a little too old for you? I certainly do."

But as soon as the words were said, Alexa looked away. She couldn't help herself. After the thoughts she'd been allowing to obsess her lately, the last thing her ego needed was to see confirmation of her aging.

"Too old? What's too old?" Casey asked. "Hell, I'm too old for some things. But I'm definitely not too young for you."

"A smart woman never gets tired of hearing a sincere compliment," Alexa replied with a soft smile. "However, I simply can't imagine dating someone your age. Jenna said you weren't even forty yet."

Casey imagined tracing her smile lines with his tongue, making her laugh just for him, and then he thought of a very pleasurable way of showing her just how sexy she was. He started to tell her what he was thinking, but noticed her gaze was reluctant to hold his. Her vulnerability triggered the urge to comfort her again. It suddenly didn't bother him that the young lingerie models hadn't found him very interesting. He only cared that the older one across the desk from him liked him enough to take a chance.

"So what if I'm thirty-eight and you're fifty? Beautiful women like you are ageless anyway. I'm sure you don't need my reassurance about how attractive you are."

"Who knew you were such a flatterer?" Alexa declared with a laugh, caught off guard enough to start flirting again.

"Look, I appreciate that we're playing nice with each other, but it's taking all my nerve to keep asking out a woman who looks as good as you do. Can you just put me out of my misery and say yes to dinner?"

Alexa fought a growing urge to giggle at Casey pressing his advantage. "And now even more flattery. Just what do you want, Mr. Carter? And when can I give it to you?"

"If you've got a little more time this afternoon, I can make you a list," Casey said with a true smile.

Alexa laughed and searched his teasing gaze, more than a little intrigued by the genuine interest she found there. He probably does want to make me a list, she decided, feeling the urge to giggle again at the knowledge. The man was certainly fun to flirt with. Was this what she had been missing?

Before she could figure it out, Alexa's gaze fell from Casey's face to her watch, making her sigh. She was running much later than she had planned.

"Sorry—I just realized the time. I'm afraid your list will have to wait. Right now, I really need to go to a meeting. I'm glad you came by, Casey Carter. It was a lot of fun talking with you."

Alexa stood and started to walk around the desk.

"Wait—stay. You haven't answered me yet," Casey ordered sharply, not yet moving from the chair.

"What do you mean?"

Alexa frowned. Did Casey Carter just order her to stay? She was torn between laughing in his face and telling him off.

"I'm actually a passable cook," Casey said, grinning at her frown. "Come to dinner tonight and see."

When she looked panicked at his demand, his smile widened. His determination to talk her into it grew larger as she hesitated.

"It's just dinner and you have to eat. What could it hurt? Seth will even be there to chaperone."

Alexa knew she'd been out of the loop for a while, but the gaze holding hers was definitely saying dinner wasn't all he had in mind. Going would be a bad idea, but not going would make more of it than there was. Going might be the easiest way to prove to both of them there was nothing between them worth pursuing other than a friendship.

And maybe he was a passable cook. He was right. She had to eat.

"Okay, I'll come to dinner, but I doubt we need a chaperone." His answering laugh did not reassure her that she was making a wise decision.

Not able to put off standing any longer, Casey stood and stretched his legs, walking a bit stiffly to her door. Alexa followed slowly behind him.

"Great. I'm glad you're coming. See you tonight about seven. Do you like pasta?"

Alexa nodded earning her another wide smile. She walked beside Casey down the hall, his spicy masculine aftershave pleasantly tingling her senses and making her aware of him. When she found herself thinking Casey's scent was a reflection of his personality, it was fairly obvious why she'd given in so easily. She wanted to know more about him even if she didn't think there was any future in it. Casey was the most interesting man she'd met in a long time.

And it was just dinner, she reminded herself. They could visit, talk, and move their attraction into friendship. *You mean friends-with-benefits*, her inner voice corrected.

"No. That would be a very bad idea. I don't think I'll be sleeping with this one," Alexa said aloud, once the main office door had closed behind Casey.

She was glad Sydney wasn't at his desk to hear her to talking to herself.

Visit **www.donnamcdonaldauthor.com** for more info

ABOUT THE AUTHOR

Even as a child, I was an active dreamer. Now I find writing to be the best way to channel those dreams into something creative.

Needing to satisfy both sides of my brain, I have become a cross-genre author of contemporary romances, paranormal romances, and some fantasy. It takes a lot of variety to keep my mind occupied and out of trouble.

One of my greatest blessings as an author is that I have the most amazing readers. My books regularly appear on bestseller lists for humor, romantic comedy, sci-fi romances, space opera, and more.

It is a truth that I crave laughter from my readers which is why I focus most of my writing attention on making that happen as often as possible. My idea of success is catching someone laughing at something I wrote.

Emails and messages are always welcome because I love to hear from anyone who has read my books. Readers can reach me through my website at **www.donnamcdonaldauthor.com**.

Made in the USA
Charleston, SC
09 November 2014